DEAD
TIME

The MURDER NOTEBOOKS

DEAD TIME

ANNE CASSIDY

Walker & Company ✸ New York

First published in Great Britain in May 2012 by Bloomsbury Publishing Plc
Published in the United States of America in May 2012
by Walker Publishing Company, Inc., a division of Bloomsbury Publishing, Inc.
www.bloomsburyteens.com

For information about permission to reproduce
selections from this book, write to
Permissions, Walker BFYR, 175 Fifth Avenue, New York, New York 10010

Library of Congress Cataloging-in-Publication Data
Cassidy, Anne.
The murder notebooks : dead time / Anne Cassidy.
p.   cm.
Summary: Five years after seventeen-year-old Rose's mother and Joshua's
father disappeared, when the step-siblings reconnect in London, Rose
witnesses two murders which she fears are linked to coded notebooks
Joshua has found and his investigation of the disappearance.
ISBN 978-0-8027-2351-2
[1. Missing persons—Fiction. 2. Murder—Fiction. 3. Ciphers—Fiction.
4. Books and reading—Fiction. 5. Stepfamilies—Fiction. 6. London (England)—
Fiction. 7. England—Fiction. 8. Mystery and detective stories.] I. Title.
PZ7.C26857Mur 2012   [Fic]—dc23   2011024962

Typeset by Hewer Text UK, Edinburgh
Printed in the U.S.A. by Quad/Graphics, Fairfield, Pennsylvania
2 4 6 8 10 9 7 5 3 1

To Alice Morey and Josie Morey
My favourite teenagers

DEAD
TIME

ONE

Rose looked at the blood on her arm. She held it under her bedside light and saw pinpricks of red across her skin. She blotted them with a tissue, then watched as a shape emerged; tiny ruby bubbles that looked like jewels and formed a raw outline of gossamer wings. Rose carefully unrolled the sleeve of her shirt and covered the wound, letting the cuff hang. She hoped the blood would dry soon. Tonight, of all nights, she didn't want any trouble with her grandmother.

Her arm was still painful, though.

Think about something else, she told herself sternly, think about meeting Joshua, about getting out of the house without her grandmother knowing where she was really going. Think about keeping her butterfly private, covered up with a sleeve. The man in the tattoo parlour had told her to leave the dressing on for five days but she hadn't been able to wait. She'd wanted to take it off in time to see Joshua. And now she'd made it bleed.

Rose, Rose, she said to herself, *don't be so impatient all the time.*

She could hear Anna, her grandmother, downstairs. She looked at her watch. It was almost seven and she needed to leave soon. She picked up her violin case, took out her violin and placed it on the bed. Then she packed her stuff in; her make-up, a top, a notepad, her laptop and a book. She closed the case, making sure it was fastened tightly. She shook her arm, aware of the sleeve irritating and sticking to the raw skin. She looked at her white shirt. The red was seeping through. It would stop soon, she knew that. It would scab over. Then, in days, she would see it come to life on her arm. A Blue Morpho. Her favourite butterfly.

Her violin was still lying on her bed.

She stepped across to the chest of drawers, opened the bottom drawer and made a space. She carefully placed the violin inside, arranging some clothes on top of it so that it was hidden.

Now she was ready. She had half an hour to get to the Dark Brew, the coffee shop she used in Camden. Just thirty minutes and then she would meet Joshua again for the first time in five years.

She was excited.

She didn't mind the blood on her arm any more.

A little bit of bleeding didn't do anyone any harm.

Now all she had to do was to get past Anna.

*   *   *

'You're wearing black and white again?' her grandmother said.

She was standing by the front door, like a sentry, her eyes travelling up and down Rose, looking closely at her.

'Are you telling me that I can't wear black and white?' Rose said stiffly.

'A little colour wouldn't hurt sometimes,' her grandmother sighed.

'I'm not keen on colours.'

'You look like an old photograph.'

'Is this a new rule? Am I no longer allowed to pick my own clothes?'

'Of course you are. Don't be dramatic. I was just suggesting a bit of colour.'

When Rose didn't answer, her grandmother shrugged, as if in defeat, then opened a large purse and pulled out two twenty-pound notes. Rose couldn't help but stare at her fingernails. Each one carefully manicured and decorated with a line of glitter in the shape of a half-moon.

'How are the violin lessons going?'

'Fine. They're going well,' Rose said, looking down at her boots.

'Because I don't hear much practising.'

'Do you want me to give it up?' Rose shrugged.

'Then what would you do with yourself?'

'There are plenty of things I can do. I could go out with friends.'

'Those awful types from your school? Oh no, dear. I didn't pay for you to go to boarding school for five years so that you could start loitering around with those types of people.'

'I should be off,' Rose said, her fingers tapping impatiently on her violin case. She would not be drawn into another row over Anna's snobbish attitudes.

'At least you've stopped wearing that black make-up on your eyes.'

'You know me,' Rose said, sidestepping Anna and reaching for the front door. 'I always do what you say.'

Rose looked in the mirror of the public toilets. Her eyelids were dark grey and her lashes were thick black. She took a minute to apply some amber lipstick, using a pencil to outline the shape of her lips. When it was done she nodded to herself. She didn't look like Rose Smith any more. Not the Rose Smith that Anna knew.

She left the toilets and headed for Parkway East station. The ticket office was closed and she passed it and walked over the bridge and down the staircase to the platform. She smacked her lips together, tasting the sweetness of the lipstick. She ran her finger along her hardened eyelashes. She was no longer wearing her white shirt. She'd changed it for a black silky top that she had bought online. It was the first time she had worn it.

What would Joshua think of the girl he hadn't seen for five years? What would she think of him? For a second she faltered, pausing on the steps. Was she really doing this? Meeting Joshua against Anna's express instructions? She carried on down, putting a spring in her step. But to see him again, after so long! What could be better? What did it have to do with Anna anyway? She was weary of her organising her life, telling her what to do. In two years' time she would be at university and then she would get a flat on her own. She wouldn't have to live with Anna any more. At twenty-one she would have her mother's money, then she would be truly independent.

The platform was almost empty. Further along was a single figure, a young man. She glanced at him and then looked away. The electronic board showed that she'd just missed a train and it was eleven minutes until the next one was due. She should have been quicker in the toilets.

She could have taken the bus, it was only half a dozen stops, but she liked the train. She liked the way it cut through the landscape, the neat, clean track that sliced its way through the urban brickwork from one place to another. The bus, by contrast, stopped and started and wove in and out of the chaotically untidy roads. This she didn't like. It irritated her. Clean straight lines made her feel calm.

She was aware that the young man further along the platform was moving in her direction. She frowned. She realised then that she knew him. Her shoulders tensed and her fingers tightened on the violin case. It was Ricky Harris, a student from her school. She didn't like him. He was in her form group and seemed to pick on her constantly.

'Hi, posh bird,' he said.

She gave a stiff smile. It was always better to rise above this kind of stupid talk.

'What you up to, posh bird?'

She held up her violin case.

'What you got in that? A machine gun?' he said, laughing out loud at his own joke. 'You look different,' he said. 'You don't look half bad.'

He was standing very close to her, in her personal space. His eyes dropped down to her sparkly top and he stared at her chest. She stepped away from him but he moved with her as though drawn by a magnet. She looked past him at the electronic board and saw that her train had been delayed by three minutes.

'Can't you shove off?' she said. 'I prefer to be on my own.'

'That's not very polite.'

'I'd rather you didn't talk to me.'

'*I'd rather you didn't talk to me!*' he mimicked her voice in a silly way.

'Push off,' she said, stepping sideways.

'Stuck-up cow,' he said, following her, grabbing hold of the sleeve of her jacket just above her raw tattoo. 'Just because you went to a private school you think that you're better than everyone else.'

'I don't!' she said, pulling her arm away.

He'd said this sort of stuff to her in school. There she was able to ignore him, to sink back into the crowd, to watch him get swallowed up by other people and other conversations. Here, on the platform, there was no way to avoid him. She stared across the tracks, letting her eyes blur. She would just blank him, not respond to a single thing he said. Then maybe he would get tired and go away. A beep sounded, distracting him. He pulled his phone out of a pocket and studied it. She strode away to the furthest point of the platform, clutching her violin case as if she was afraid of him taking it. She stopped when she got to the barrier and felt herself calm down. The track stretched off into the silent darkness. On one side were houses and on the other was the local cemetery.

This was how she liked it. On her own.

Away from people like Ricky Harris.

She didn't socialise much in school. There were a couple of girls she liked in her English group, Sara and Maggie. Sara and Maggie had been best friends since nursery but they seemed happy for Rose to tag along for a sandwich with them at lunchtime. Mostly, though, Rose preferred to be alone. The other students had come through *normal* schools and she was the only one who had come from a boarding school. She sounded different to them, she acted differently to them. In the few weeks that she'd been at this school she'd learned to keep herself to herself.

'Hey!'

Ricky Harris called out to her.

'I heard a story about you the other day.'

He was walking towards her. She looked up at the electronic board. It showed that it was still six minutes until her train. Even then she might not get rid of him. He might insist on sitting beside her, talking at her through the whole journey, spoiling the moments when she could relax and think about the evening ahead.

'Someone told me that your mum got murdered.'

She stood very still.

'Is it true?'

She couldn't manage an answer. A blank feeling was holding her to the spot. He was looking at her in a questioning way, his head bent to the side as if in sympathy. She realised she disliked him a hundred times more than she had five minutes before. She stepped round him and walked away towards the bridge, but he followed her. When she got to the middle of the platform she gave up and stopped.

'Well?' he said.

'My mother did not get *murdered*. She disappeared,' she said, turning to him, her voice strong and direct. 'There's no evidence that she is dead. No one knows exactly what happened to her.'

'More than likely dead, though.'

'She just *disappeared* five years ago.'

She gripped the sides of her violin case. How dare he speak to her like this! He didn't know her one bit and yet he thought he had the right to pry into her darkest places.

'I heard she was murdered,' Ricky Harris said, his voice more determined.

'You heard wrong,' she said curtly.

The platform seemed darker. She wished she could hear the sound of the train in the distance. A curl of noise that started small and got bigger as it got closer. She longed to see the lights of the engine tunnelling its way through the darkness towards her.

Instead Ricky's phone began to ring and he looked at her and put one finger in the air to indicate a call as if she hadn't already worked it out. She felt angry. How many people knew about her life? She had thought she was safe at her new school.

Up above, on the bridge, the walkway lights were on. The usual dodgy one was flickering on and off. It looked quaint, like something from a film that was set in the past. During the day there were always people going back and forth across the walkway. Now it was empty. It was almost quarter to eight. It wasn't cold but there was something in the air that suggested autumn. A whiff of burning fires, a hint of sulphur from a match, the damp smell of leaves that had been trodden into a pulp.

Ricky Harris's voice interrupted her thoughts.

'Change of plans. Got to meet someone,' he called.

She tried to keep a straight face. It was a relief that he wasn't coming on the train with her. He began to walk off. After a few moments he shouted, 'Here's your train, posh bird.'

She leant forward and looked up the line. She saw the lights of a train. She allowed herself to move back along the platform and watched him disappear up the stairwell. She felt herself relaxing. He was a hateful character and she'd just have to try harder to avoid him. All that stuff about her mum. How could he ask that? How could he intrude into her deepest, saddest places?

The train was coming nearer so she stepped towards the edge of the platform. It wouldn't be long until she was meeting Joshua. A tingle of pain from her arm made her clasp it gently. What would he think of her butterfly tattoo? What would he think of *her*, Rose Smith, seventeen years old, his stepsister, who he hadn't seen for five years?

'See you later, posh bird!'

Ricky Harris's voice came from above and she looked up to see him walk on to the bridge. There was someone coming from the other end. A man in a hoodie striding out, rushing probably, so as not to miss the train. She glanced down at the track and saw the engine slowing, then her eyes travelled back up to the bridge.

Ricky Harris was talking to the man in the hooded top. She stared, puzzled.

There was a row, loud voices which she couldn't make out because of the sound of the approaching train. She glanced down at the track and then back up at the bridge; once, twice, three times. There was a tussle of some sort; tugging, pushing, pulling.

But it stopped suddenly.

The hooded man turned and walked away, jauntily as if his shoes were on springs. She saw the back of his hood disappear across the bridge. She strained her eyes to see if she could glimpse Ricky Harris's head above the side of the bridge.

Had he been knocked out?

She huffed. Why should she care?

The train pulled up in front of her. A noise like a long sigh emanated from it and inside a man in a black over-coat got up from a seat and walked towards the door. Rose looked up at the bridge again. There was still no sign of movement.

What did it matter?

The carriage doors were about to open. Rose could see the man inside waiting patiently, looking at his mobile. There were only a couple of other people on the train, both reading newspapers.

She stepped back and looked up. Had she somehow *missed* Ricky Harris getting up, stumbling off towards the ticket office, following the other man out of the station?

The doors of the train stayed shut. The man inside was looking puzzled, his finger poised to press the *Open Doors* button again.

She was only a few metres from the stairs. She took a quick decision and walked towards the stairwell. Then she ran up the stairs, her violin case bumping at her back as she went. At the top she stopped to get her breath. When she looked along the walkway she saw Ricky Harris lying face down about halfway across. Above him the dodgy light flickered on and off, stuttering against the night sky.

She heard the sound of the train doors opening down below.

'You all right?' she called.

She turned back, looking down the stairwell. She needed to catch that train

'Are you OK?' she said, louder.

He didn't move. She could hear footsteps on the stairs behind her. More than one person. She hesitated. She had to catch that train. She turned to go but something caught her eye.

A glint of red. It was by Ricky Harris's waist, on the walkway. Rose stared at it. Then she heard the doors of the train shutting below.

It was too late for her to catch it now.

There was blood on the walkway coming from underneath Ricky Harris. It seeped out from beneath his jacket, dark red. She stood perfectly still. The blood glinted under the flickering light like liquid jewels. She didn't move. She *couldn't* move.

TWO

The station was closed. Trains were going straight through without stopping. Rose could feel the floorboards vibrating in the ticket office. The passengers who had come up the stairs behind her had already given their names and addresses and been allowed to go home. Rose was sitting on a chair behind the ticket machines. The door was open and she could see out into the public area. There were a number of police going to and fro, a lot of talking and the sound of radios. On the desk in front of her sat her violin case. She found herself tapping it lightly. Inside the case was her laptop. She had an urge to get it out, to switch it on, so that she could do something with her fingers. Her mobile was right next to her. She'd already sent a text to Joshua to say that she couldn't come. The message was short and didn't explain a thing. **Can't make it. Will call you. Rose.** She hadn't bothered to contact Anna. Anna wouldn't miss her yet.

She felt odd. As if she should be crying. Someone had died metres away from her and yet she felt completely cold about it.

A man in a tracksuit had his back to her. He was fiddling with a kettle and cups. A young policeman stood near to him. He had bicycle clips on and his hair stood up at the front. Up against the wall outside was a police bicycle, a safety helmet hanging from one of the handlebars.

Rose shivered.

'Are you cold?' the young policeman said.

'No.'

'It could be shock. The tea will be ready in a moment,' he said and turning to the man in the tracksuit he added, 'Put two sugars in, will you?'

'I don't take sugar,' Rose said.

'It's good for shock.'

'Who is that?'

Rose pointed at the man in the tracksuit. He turned round at that moment.

'Area Manager. On call,' the man said and pointed to a beeper attached to a belt on his waist. 'I was running nearby when I got the call. There's an official response to an incident like this and I'm part of it.'

He pushed a steaming mug at her and she took it.

'Drink the tea, Rose, and I'll be back soon,' the police-man said.

He left and the Area Manager turned back to a computer and started to tap at the keys. Rose sipped the sweet hot tea. She grimaced at the syrupy taste. The clock on the wall showed that it was 8.35; forty-five minutes since she had seen Ricky Harris on the bridge, his blood spreading on to the walkway.

Four passengers had come up the stairs behind her. One of them, a bald man in overalls, had pushed past them and squatted down next to Ricky Harris. He'd used his two fingers to feel for a pulse but quickly began to shake his head. Then Rose and the others had edged along the bridge past the body. When they came to the blood Rose had looked upwards as though she was on a tightrope. She had taken one narrow step after another and could hear the voice of the man in the dark overcoat behind her calling the police. By the time they got to the other side she thought she could hear sirens but it probably wasn't anything to do with them because no one came for what seemed like a long time. Then everyone, the ambulance and the police and the man from the railway, turned up at once.

Some frantic questions followed. Had anyone seen anything? Rose was the only one to say that she had. The others were allowed to go but her policeman, the one on the bike, took charge and guided her into the ticket office and wrote down everything she said.

She put the half-drunk mug of tea down.

Any contact with the police made her feel uncomfortable. There'd been a lot of police around during those first weeks when her mum and Brendan, her partner, had disappeared. Smart-looking men and women in uniform with long faces and no answers. Rose had often felt distracted during the times when they were giving her and Joshua information. She'd stare at their hats, their earpieces, their flak jackets, their belts that seemed to hold everything; baton, gloves, flashlight, knife. Sometimes there was even a stun gun. The police it seemed were ready for every eventuality.

Except when her mum and Brendan vanished. They were not ready for that.

Her shoulders softened and she felt the old grief sweep across her chest like the brush of a feather. It hurt less now, a distant reminder of those deep dark days when the loss was angry and raw. She crossed her arms so it looked as though she was hugging herself.

Her mum and Brendan. She hadn't seen or spoken to them for over five years. The police thought they were dead. She half believed it herself. She had pictured a hundred different places they might be but always, in the end, she came back to believing that they were gone. Now she'd seen this boy face down dead on the ground. Was that what had happened to her mum? To Brendan? The notion made her rock back and forward. The man in the tracksuit looked round. He seemed startled so she made herself slow down, keep calm. She counted her breaths. She tried to hold herself still and firm. She didn't want her emotions tumbling out like tangled-up fabrics bursting out of an old clothes box. She had to hold them in. She'd *managed* to hold them in for five years.

'You all right, Rose?'

The young policeman's hand was on her shoulder. His hair looked untidy but stiff as if he gelled it.

'Can I go now?' she said, standing up, patting down her clothes, picking up her violin case.

'I've managed to bag a car so I can take you home.'

'I can walk from here,' she said.

He shook his head decisively.

'You've had a shock. I want to see you safely home.'

'I'm all right,' she said. 'I didn't see the actual – you know – *stabbing*. I didn't even know the guy well. I didn't even like him. The truth is I couldn't stand him, you know, so it's not like I'm upset.'

But her voice was rising and had in it a hint of hysteria.

'Come on, someone's died. Anyone would be upset.'

He looked disappointed with her. He expected her to be sad but it wasn't his fault because he didn't know about her life. She had no sorrow to spare.

But she realised there was no point in trying to be huffy with him. She followed him out of the ticket office, past the other police officers. They stepped over

18

the crime-scene tape and pushed their way through some young kids who were watching the drama.

'The car's over here,' he said, peeling away from her across the empty road.

She followed him in silence. As they drove away from the station she spoke, her voice sounding scratchy.

'You can just leave me at the top of my street.'

'No, right to the door, I think,' he said, giving her a sideways smile.

Squeaky voices were spilling out of the radio. The roads were busy and the car had to stop several times at crossings and traffic lights. She noticed that the policeman still had his bicycle clips on. She stared at them.

'My name's Henry Thompson,' he said.

She looked away and stared out of the window. As they got further from the station the streets became darker and emptier, the houses bigger and the roads more leafy.

'Your mum and dad must have a few bob. These are posh houses.'

She didn't answer. She hated the word *posh*. She thought of Ricky Harris and his nasty comments to her. Now he was dead. She concentrated for a moment to see if she felt anything *now* but nothing came. Was she that cold?

'I live with my grandmother.'

'I'll come in if you like and fill her in on what's happened.'

'I can do it myself. I'm not a child,' she said.

'Sorry! You're right. But you've witnessed a terrible thing.'

'I'll tell my grandmother myself. I'm seventeen. I don't need anyone to hold my hand.'

'Are you always this challenging?'

'Yes.'

'Here we are,' he said.

The car pulled up outside a detached house. Rose had the car door open and was out in a second. The front of the house was lit up, as it usually was.

'Thanks for the lift,' she said, moving away from the car.

'I'll contact you tomorrow, about making a statement down at the police station,' he called.

'Mm . . .' she said, turning away, pushing at the gate.

She walked quickly up the path. Looking round she could see that the police car was still there waiting for her to go inside. She huffed, opened the door and felt the familiar feeling of gloom that settled on her whenever she went into Anna's house. She could hear music playing from inside: orchestral, Schubert perhaps. It sounded sombre and yet racy at the same time. It fitted her mood.

She closed the door behind her and stood for a moment in the hallway and looked around. She wondered what the policeman would have thought of this house. It was the kind of place you might see in a magazine. She had certainly never been inside a house like this until she'd come to live here. The hallway was as wide as a room and the parquet floor was glowing with polish and had oriental rugs dotted here and there. A huge hallstand with a large vase of flowers on it stood to one side. The stairs swept upwards in an 'L' shape and were carpeted in royal blue.

Rose took her jacket off. She let it lie over her arm. There were no hooks for her to hang it on. *Take your clothes up to your rooms, dear.* Anna wanted no sign of Rose in the common areas of the house. All her things had to stay in her rooms. Rose's bag never hung over the banister, her iPod never sat on the coffee table, her school things never lay on the kitchen worktop.

The music was coming from the right of the house, her grandmother's drawing room. She pictured Anna sitting in her armchair. Sometimes she had friends in there but often she was alone. She would have her eyes closed while listening to the music with one arm stretched out like a baton conducting an imaginary orchestra.

She wouldn't hear Rose come in. She never did. That's why it was all right for Rose to leave her make-up on. In the evenings Anna liked to be alone. She had made that clear often enough. Not that it was any great loss to Rose. Time spent with Anna was always difficult. One wooden conversation after another, Anna invariably asking her about her plans for university. Rose could almost see her doing mental arithmetic calculations. How soon would she have done her duty with regard to Rose? How soon until Rose could live somewhere by herself so that Anna could resume the life she had when Rose had been at boarding school, or the life she had had before Rose had been forced on to her.

Rose had no interest in spending an evening with Anna but tonight it would have been nice to come back and spend time with *someone*. To sit in the kitchen with a hot drink or a sandwich and talk about what had happened at Parkway East.

She went upstairs to her rooms. The first one was a small study. There was a desk and a swivel chair. On top sat a computer screen and keyboard as well as masses of her school files and papers. On the other side of the room was a large chair opposite a wall of shelves on which sat a television, a CD-player and a number of books and CDs and DVDs. Through a door was her bedroom and en suite. She dropped her coat and put her violin case on the bed, took out her laptop and laid it on the duvet.

She looked around. These were her rooms but they had Anna's name written all over them. She always felt like an intruder. They'd been decorated and furnished by Anna. They were cleaned by Anna's cleaner. They were inspected, from time to time by Anna herself, checking up on her property. It felt like a hotel suite. She suddenly couldn't bear to spend the night there.

She went into the en suite, ran some hot water in the sink and washed off the black make-up and then coated her skin with cream. She changed into her pyjamas, pulled on some slipper socks and shoved her feet back into a pair of lace-up boots. She put her laptop and mobile into a rucksack and pulled a fleece out of her wardrobe and put it on. Then, she closed the study door and went downstairs.

In the kitchen she opened the fridge and took out a drink and some cheese, then grabbed a box of crackers from the cupboard. She put these things in her rucksack. She opened the back door and stepped out into the garden and closed the door quietly behind her. She followed the garden lights for ten, twelve, fourteen steps until she came to the laurel hedge that shielded the outbuilding that had become her studio. It was an old brick structure that had once been used as a garage and had been big enough for two cars. Now it had fallen into a kind of pretty disrepair with Amazonian plants climbing up and over it. When it became clear that Rose was coming home from boarding school for good to go to the local high school, she had set her eye on this building as a special place for her. It could be her art studio, she had said to Anna, hoping against hope that she would agree. Somewhere she could work and it wouldn't matter if she made a mess.

Anna had been pleased. She had even given her a hundred pounds to do it up and allowed her to have a broadband connection. When Rose had finished and asked her to come and look she'd said, *Very nice, dear.*

Rose walked around the laurel hedge and was surprised to see a light coming from the window of the studio. She'd been in there earlier in the day. Had she left the light on? She tutted. The music from the house was still in the back of her head. It sounded like it was reaching some kind of crescendo. Had someone broken in? There was nothing much to steal. Her art books and drawing materials. An old sofa that Anna had allowed her to take from the utility room, pillows and a duvet she'd bought. A brilliant wicker chair that she'd found on a skip and half a dozen giant cushions she'd bought along with some pictures she'd found at a boot sale. There was a small fire and a kettle but it was all old stuff, or second-hand, taken from Anna's kitchen with her permission.

She stepped forward again and placed her fingers on the door. She listened. After the events of the day she felt rattled and edgy. She didn't need this. She just wanted to go into the studio and relax, listen to some music, check her emails, eat and drink and maybe doze off to sleep.

Pushing the door gently, Rose looked inside. It was the small lamp that was on, the one she used to read. It gave off a light yellow glow as thin as mist. She let the door open further.

There, lying on the sofa, was the figure of a boy. He was still, his face visible; his eyes shut, his mouth slightly open.

She'd seen a still boy a couple of hours before at the railway station.

This wasn't like that, though. This boy was asleep.

She felt her chest fire up at the sight of him.

This was a special boy. Her stepbrother, Joshua Jackson, who she hadn't seen for five years.

THREE

Rose closed the door quickly behind her, pulling it shut so that there was no strip of light to be seen. She put her rucksack down on the floor. In seconds she became anxious. If Anna knew Joshua was here, in her home, there would be trouble, a lot of trouble. She would almost certainly lose the freedom she had gained over the last months, the agreement they had made about her leaving boarding school to go to the local high school. She opened her mouth to speak to him, to wake him, to shoo him out.

But then she found herself looking at him, fast asleep on the sofa. The boy that she hadn't seen for five years.

Why not leave him there? Anna was safely settled in her room. There was no reason why she would come out into the garden. None at all. Rose slipped her feet out of her boots and sat in the old wicker chair with her legs doubled up underneath her. She folded her arms and nestled against a cushion and looked at Joshua.

He'd emailed her one day the previous spring. Since then they'd kept in touch. Now, though, he was here in flesh and blood.

He was lying on one side facing her, his chest barely rising and falling. Her eyes travelled along his body. He was still wearing his jacket over a sweatshirt, jeans and plimsolls. On the floor beside him was a huge bunch of keys and a screwdriver. She frowned. Had he brought it along to *fix* something?

Years before, when they lived together, Joshua had made a habit out of bringing old things home and fixing them. She remembered finding old clocks on the kitchen table and a number of pairs of roller skates in the living room. That and a variety of wheels, handlebars and frames from old bikes that people didn't want any more which sat in the garage or the hallway or in Joshua's room much to the annoyance of her mother. *That boy of yours,* her mother would say to Brendan, *he's a magnet for junk!*

The first day they moved in Rose had been shy of the tall eleven-year-old boy who carried in his belongings in cardboard boxes. She'd watched from the top landing as the front door was hooked back and Brendan (who she had met) and Joshua (who she hadn't) walked back and forth to the van bringing their stuff with them, piling it along the hallway so that there was hardly any room to get past.

'You know Brendan?' her mum had said to her a couple of days before.

She'd nodded. Brendan was nice. Her mum hadn't known him for long but Rose liked him better than the previous boyfriend who stood back as she passed him and never allowed anyone to touch his laptop or phone. No one. Ever. Brendan was easy-going and was always forgetting his things; his mobile, his BlackBerry, his wallet, his book.

'He's having some trouble with his landlord so I've said that he and his son can stay here for a few weeks until they get a new place? Is that all right with you?'

Rose had shrugged. Why not?

Her mum gave her a sideways hug, squeezing her shoulders tightly.

'Mum, you're breaking my bones!' she'd said but she was smiling.

When Brendan and Joshua had finally unpacked their stuff into the house at Brewster Road the four of them went to Pizza Hut and celebrated. Rose looked shyly at Joshua, who had his own mobile phone and loads of computer equipment piled up in the corner of the box room. He was so grown-up. Like the boys from the big school. His voice was gravelly and his hands were as big as Brendan's. On the way home from the restaurant he asked her which programmes she liked to watch on television and whether she liked music.

'I play the violin!' she said. 'What do you play?'

He laughed. 'I play PlayStation!' he said.

At first she found it odd him living in her house. He always seemed to be in the toilet when she wanted to go or he was watching some sport on the television when she wanted to watch something else. Or he was making a noise in the box room while she was practising the violin, banging and shifting things around. Once she popped her head in his tiny room and saw him red-faced trying to find a place for all his stuff.

'This room is really the TARDIS,' he said. 'It's bigger than you think.'

'Only in the Time-Space-Continuum,' she said quickly.

He began to laugh. She stood still for ages watching him, her violin almost touching the floor, then she began to laugh as well.

'Why don't you get one of those high-up beds? Then you can put all your stuff underneath it,' she said.

He looked at her.

'You know what, Rosie, that's brilliant,' he said slowly. 'That is one great idea.'

'My name's *Rose*,' she said, miffed.

Brendan and Joshua made the frame for the bed. It took days while large lumps of wood were carried up the stairs and back down again to be sawed up in the back garden. When it was finished Rose looked in amazement at the platform bed reachable by a small stepladder and the desk and computer equipment underneath. Behind the door, hidden from most people's view, was a wheel with some of its spokes warped.

Once the bed was up it was clear that Joshua was staying for good.

It was three happy years.

Rose stared at him asleep on her sofa. She'd told him about her garden studio in her emails. When she had texted saying she couldn't meet, he must have come to her. The thought made her smile. She looked him up and down. He was tall, his legs and plimsolls hanging over the end of the chair. His hair was curly and there was a shadow on his jaw as if he hadn't shaved.

He moved and groaned as he did so. His head turned back so that he seemed to be looking up at the ceiling. She remembered again the other boy she had seen lying down that evening. He had been on his front, his face flat against the cold concrete of the walkway, his blood spreading out from under him. Rose wondered what it would be like to be someone in Ricky Harris's family. To have a policeman come to the front door and announce that their son, their brother (maybe even their stepbrother) was dead. She looked at Joshua and felt the loss keenly. She who had already lost her mother and Brendan. How awful it would be if it had been Joshua lying on that bridge. How dark the world would be then.

The tears finally came. Tears for that stupid idiot Ricky Harris who called her *posh bird* and kept on and on at her in school. Why was she crying for him? A boy who had been nasty to her, who had taken every opportunity to make fun of her. Her form teacher had spoken to him several times and even one of the IT technicians had told him to *lay off*. He had had a girlfriend, she remembered. A thin pale girl with hair extensions. She seemed to walk after him everywhere like a puppy.

Here's your train, posh bird! were the last words he spoke before encountering an argument on a bridge, a fight and a fatal wound.

She pulled a tissue out of her pyjama pocket, half aware that Joshua had moved and was looking around the room.

'Rosie?' he said, sitting up.

She dabbed her eyes.

'What's up?' he said, smiling. 'Am I that big a disappointment?'

She shook her head and he got up and came across to her. He squatted down in front of her and grabbed her hands.

'Hey, sis? What's up?'

'I'm not your *sister*,' she said, the crying getting worse instead of better.

'Stepsister, then.' He was grinning.

'Not even a stepsister. Not really.'

'Well, then, what's up? Why the tears?'

'I saw someone get killed tonight, that's all,' she hiccupped out the words.

'Ah,' he said, standing up, taking her hand, pulling her up and hugging her. 'Is *that* all it is?'

She sat on the sofa next to him and told him all about it.

'I don't know what to say,' he said, when she'd finished.

'Me neither,' she said. 'It's just like being witness to a car accident. It's being there at *that moment*, pure bad luck. Bad luck that Ricky Harris walked across the bridge and got into a row with this guy and one thing led to another . . .'

'Awful.'

'And it's made me think about Mum all over again.'

She meant Mum *and Brendan* but hadn't said it.

'Dad's *never* out of my mind,' he said.

'I didn't mean that! Mum's always in my mind! Of course she is!'

She was instantly irritated and moved away from him further along the old sofa, her shoulders stiffening.

'I know that. I . . .'

'I think about her all the time. What I meant was I started to think about the things that happened over those days. The police . . .'

'Sorry.'

She couldn't speak. Her jaw felt tight.

'Hey!' Joshua said. 'Is this our first argument? I've only been here for ten minutes!'

'I'm just upset,' she said, staring at the wall.

"Course you are. Anyone would be!'

Joshua put his arm around her shoulders and gave her a squeeze.

'Your bones have got right angles,' he said. 'I think I've been injured.'

She turned to him, her face breaking into a smile.

'It's good to see you, Josh. It's been a long time.'

'Have I changed?'

She shook her head.

'You're still as annoying as you were five years ago.'

'What have you done to your arm?' he said, reaching across her front and lifting her wrist. She looked down and saw the scab mark along the edge of her pyjama sleeve.

'Just a scrape,' she said, not wanting to show the tattoo until it was healed. 'How did you get in here? The back gate is locked.'

'I climbed over it.'

'What's that for?' she said, pointing at the screwdriver.

'I had it in my pocket. I must have left it there after fixing something.'

Rose shook her head. She had a sudden memory of Joshua's tools scattered around the house in Brewster Road. A hacksaw by the fruit bowl, a claw hammer by the shoe rack.

The sound of music playing loudly broke into her thoughts.

'What's that?' he said, looking puzzled. 'It sounds like you've got an orchestra playing in your garden!'

Rose could hear it. Anna's music. It was as if she'd turned the volume up. But it wasn't that. Anna had opened the back doors of her drawing room. She was out in the garden. She was coming down to the studio for some reason.

'You have to hide. If she sees you here it will cause a lot of trouble.'

She looked round the tiny space. He met her eyes and gave a hopeless shrug. The studio was a square room. There were no alcoves or cupboards. There was no screen to step behind and the only big thing, the sofa was too heavy to be moved easily.

There was nowhere for Joshua to hide.

'She'll be here in a minute!' Rose said, panicking.

'I'll face up to her! She can't tell you who to see and who not to see!'

'No, you don't get it. She'll make things difficult. Quick.'

Rose grabbed Joshua's arm and pushed him against the wall adjacent to the door. She looked round hurriedly and picked up his jacket, his keys and screwdriver and shoved them at him seconds before the door swung open and Anna was standing there.

'Rose! I've just had a call from the police. What are you doing down here? It's almost midnight. Come back into the house,' Anna said, stepping away from the door, 'It's cold out here and we need to talk.'

'I'll just get my things.'

Without looking at the open door and Joshua's plim-solls sticking out, Rose picked up the water and cheese and her rucksack.

'Just putting my boots on!'

'The police said you were a witness to a murder, Rose. Why on earth didn't you come and tell me?'

Rose moved behind the door to push her feet into her boots. She mouthed *Sorry* at Joshua. He smiled at her as she backed away, carrying her things.

'Hurry up, Rose.'

She pulled the door to and Joshua moved out from behind it. She paused by the light switch. With her back to Anna she grinned back at Joshua. Then she turned the light off and closed the door tightly.

She followed her grandmother up the lawn. All the way to the house she felt Joshua's eyes on her back.

FOUR

School was uncomfortable for the next few days.

'Are you the girl who saw Ricky get killed?'

'Are you Rose someone? Who was there when Harris got stabbed?'

'Did you see the stabbing?'

'Did you see who did it?'

'Are you the kid who used to go boarding school? You saw Harris get it? Is that right?'

Rose didn't like it. People thrusting their faces into her space. She was used to being anonymous, left alone. She liked the sense of wandering through this alien world unnoticed. She had come from a small girls' boarding school in the middle of the countryside into this huge mixed high school, where students walked in battalions and took no prisoners. She liked to sit on a seat in the cafeteria and just watch it all happening around her. Girls and boys eyeing each other up; boys standing in groups talking and shouting and shoving and practising football with an invisible ball; girls sitting round tables whispering or, shrieking, looking at their phones. Then there were the studious types, in twos and threes out of the way, looking at handouts or books, the wires of their iPods mingling with their hair.

There was noise all day long. Rose was used to the hushed tones of the corridors of Mary Linton School for Girls. Only soft shoes were allowed inside the building so the sound of three hundred plus girls walking around was negligible. When lessons were on there was quiet, just the sound of a tuba or violin playing or the tinkling of a piano. In the high school the noise was like a wall; it got lower at certain points but it was always there. Fifteen hundred seventeen- and eighteen-year-olds moving round. Then there was the tannoy and the lesson buzzers and the traffic from the busy road that ran along one side of the building.

Rose had spent the last few weeks being a silent spectator of this. Sometimes she sat with Maggie and Sara in the cafeteria but the rest of the time she was on her own, walking along the edges of the corridors, sitting in the private study area in the library or on one of the benches that were dotted around the outside of the building.

When she was sitting down she liked to have her laptop open and go on to social networking sites. It was easy to contact girls from her old school and find out what was going on. She found it easy to swap small talk with people whom she hardly ever saw. She also liked to go on sites about books or art, movies or music, and she often left comments. Rose, who was shy and stand-offish with real people, found social interaction easy in the virtual world. Then she had her blog, Morpho. It was somewhere for her to write about things that were happening in her life.

But now people were seeking her out. She had to look up from her laptop, log off and close the lid. When they got her attention they eyed her with suspicion.

'How come you were there when Ricky Harris got stabbed?'

'Who are you?'

'What form are you in? Were you *friends* with Ricky Harris?'

She was polite but short and firm.

'I was a witness. I saw him get into an argument with someone on the bridge and that was it. I never saw the actual stabbing. Don't ask me anything else because I don't know.'

Three days after it happened she had the words off pat and the number of people who had only just heard had dwindled to a trickle. Just after lunch when she was sitting thinking about seeing Joshua after class an odd-looking girl charged up to her. She was tall with orange red hair which was cut asymmetrically. She was wearing what looked like a man's jumper over tight-legged jeans. She had glitter lipstick on. Next to Rose, who was wearing her customary black and white clothes, the girl looked like a clown.

'Someone wants to see you,' she said, without making eye contact.

Rose felt weary. She'd said as much as she cared to say about what happened to Ricky Harris.

'I'm busy,' she said curtly.

'You're not busy. You're just sitting here,' the girl said, looking Rose in the eye.

'I'm thinking,' Rose said.

'Is it right what people say about you? That you're a stuck-up cow?'

'I'm just minding my own business!'

'Were you minding your own business on Tuesday night when Ricky got killed?'

Rose opened her mouth to speak but what was the point? Was this garish girl suggesting that in some way she had something to do with what happened to Ricky? It wasn't worth the breath a reply would take. She stood up so that she could walk away but the big girl moved to the side and blocked the way. Rose felt her temper ignite. Was she going to have to be physical with this girl? How would that work? The girl was a head taller than Rose.

Just then a small thin girl emerged from a nearby doorway.

'Leave it, Sherry,' she called out.

Sherry turned and tutted, saying things under her breath. The girl walked forward and Rose knew her immediately. It was Ricky Harris's girlfriend. She had no make-up on and her face looked white, her eyes sunken. Her hair was tied back and she had gold hoops in her ears that seemed to drag the lobes down.

'I just want to have a word,' she said.

'I never saw anything, not really,' Rose said, her voice a little softer.

'I'm Emma and this is my stepsister Sherry.'

'Stepsister?' Rose said, smiling, thinking of Joshua.

'Something funny about it?' Sherry said.

Rose shook her head.

'It's just I have a stepbrother. Well not *in law* as such. My mother wasn't married to his father but we lived together as a family.'

Sherry looked puzzled. Emma smiled.

'You're not that different to us. Bits and bobs of families,' she said, slipping a stick-like arm through Sherry's. 'I just want to talk to you about what happened to Ricky. That's all.'

'All right,' Rose said.

'Not here, though. Come in to my form room. It's quiet there.'

Emma and Rose sat opposite each other as though they were working as a pair in the lesson. The table between them was bare except for a pink mobile phone that Emma had placed there. The rest of the room was empty and Sherry was standing by the closed door to stop anyone barging in.

Rose told the story again the way she had on the first night and then to Joshua and her grandmother and then at the police station the following day when she made her statement. She told it slowly and tried to be less unpleasant about Ricky Harris. She left out the part where Ricky had asked her whether her mother had been murdered. In fact, she'd left that bit out *every time* she told it.

'And he said *Change of plans* and went off up the stairs just as the train was coming in. He'd just got a phone call.'

'Was it from a girl?' Emma said in a kind of whisper.

'I can't say. I walked away. He talked for a short while and then said *Change of plans!* He seemed really happy.'

'Happy?'

'In a good mood. At first he seemed a bit off but then, when the call came, it seemed to lift his mood and he went trotting up the stairs. He even called out to me, *Here's your train, posh bird.* In a jokey way.'

'But you saw him on the bridge?'

Rose nodded.

'And this guy stabbed Ricky?'

Emma's eyes were looking glassy. It seemed like it was an effort to hold them open. Her face was reddening. After a moment she blinked and looked down and Rose saw her use the crook of her finger to wipe away a tear.

'I think he must have. I didn't actually see the . . . attack. I just saw the scuffle and then the guy just did an about-turn and walked away. I mean when he walked away he seemed to be like bouncing along.'

'Bouncing? What's that supposed to mean?' Sherry said.

'I mean the way he was walking, well, sometimes you just know, don't you? When someone's got their back to you, you can just tell?'

'Tell what?' Emma said, using a tissue that had been folded up to blot her eyelids.

'I think he was smiling. That's what it seemed like from behind.'

Sherry swore.

'Did you see his face?' Emma said.

Rose shook her head.

'Just the back of his head.'

'But if you saw him again, the guy on the bridge, you might recognise something about him? You know you said about the way he walked . . .'

'I don't think so.'

'Negative or what!' Sherry said.

'I'm not being . . .'

'Just come with us for five minutes,' Emma pleaded. 'That's all I'm asking. Just for a short walk. To look at someone.'

Emma stood up. Rose was hesitant. She didn't want to be involved in this. She wanted to put it behind her.

'Please,' Emma said.

Rose reluctantly stood up. She followed Sherry and Emma out of the classroom and along the corridor, side-stepping crowds of kids. Some of them knew Emma and were clearly aware of what had happened to her, their voices dropping in a kind of reverence as she passed. They walked towards the cafeteria. Official lunch hour was over but the cafeteria was still serving drinks and snacks and there were a couple of hundred kids in there, some of them on free study periods and others just avoiding their classes. Emma wove through the tables followed by Sherry and then Rose. When she got to the far corner she gestured for Rose and Sherry to sit down. Rose put her stuff down on one chair and sat on the other. The table in front of her was littered with polystyrene cups and curls of cellophane and plastic knives and forks. She sat a bit back from the table and looked round. It was a corner of the cafeteria she never used. It was a place where a lot of the loud kids hung out. It was known as somewhere you could pick up dope and other stuff.

'You'll see him in a minute,' Emma said.

Sherry had a mirror out and was pulling one side of her hair into a hook around her face.

'Who is it you want me to see?' Rose said, feeling the hopelessness of the situation. All she had seen was the back of someone's head inside a hood. What use could she be?

'Lewis Proctor.'

Rose didn't comment. It was not a name she recognised. Why should she? She'd only been at the school for a short while. She hadn't been to the schools these students had come from and neither did she live in the nearby streets or estates.

'Here he is,' Sherry said, without looking away from the mirror.

A tall white boy walked towards their corner of the cafeteria. There were others in the group but Rose had a feeling that this was the boy Emma had brought her to see. He was wearing black jeans and T-shirt, and over the top a hooded sweatshirt, the hood down. His very short dark hair was spiked up on the top. He noticed Emma straight away and came towards them. A few metres away he stopped but didn't speak until his mates were around him.

'Any news on who did your boy?' he said.

Emma didn't answer. She shook her head silently.

A dark-haired girl emerged from the group and put her hand on Lewis Proctor's shoulder. She was tall and thin and one wrist was heavy with silver bangles. Rose looked her up and down. She had silver boots on and her feet were poised as if she was a ballet dancer.

'Bad day. Some people might say Ricky had it coming,' Lewis said.

Lewis Proctor leant down and picked up a plastic knife from a table and mimed stabbing it into his own chest. Sherry swore at him. His friends all started to laugh and he chucked it across the hall. The girl didn't laugh, just turned her back and walked away. Other kids sitting at nearby tables looked on puzzled. Rose felt herself sinking into the seat, her shoulders getting rounder. She wished she could be somewhere else. Emma turned her back on him and he shrugged dramatically and then pretended to wipe away tears. Then he turned and walked off.

Both Sherry and Emma looked straight at Rose. She concentrated on the back of Lewis Proctor, on the way he walked, the shape of his head; how it might look if his hood was up. Was it the same person who had been on the bridge that night?

She couldn't tell. He looked like any of a hundred other boys who paraded round the school.

'I don't know.'

Emma stood up. 'Thanks, anyway.'

'*Lewis Proctor*. Write his name down,' Sherry said to Rose as though she had made a positive identification.

When they were gone Rose opened up her laptop and spent a few moments looking at emails. There were two from Joshua. She was tempted to read them but wanted to do something first. She went on to Facebook and put the name *Lewis Proctor* into search. A few seconds later his page appeared. Photos. Messages. Friends. His smile looked like that of any other teenage boy. One of the pictures showed him with a hood up. She looked hard for a few moments but couldn't see anything familiar.

Later on, when she was on her way out of school heading for Joshua's flat, she thought of the boy in the hood again, the way he had picked up the plastic knife and pretended to stab himself, mocking Emma about her dead boyfriend.

Lewis Proctor. It was a name Rose wasn't going to forget.

FIVE

The flat where Joshua was staying was above a shop in Camden Town, a vegetarian cafe and takeaway called Lettuce and Stuff. Rose knew that it belonged to a friend of his, Darren Skeggs, an older boy who he'd got to know when he first moved to Newcastle five years before.

Darren Skeggs was in the third year of an Art degree. Joshua was a first-year undergraduate in Engineering. Darren had let him share the flat for practically nothing. It was the reason why Joshua could afford to study at Queen Mary College. Joshua had told her this and a lot of other stuff in emails he'd sent when they first got back in touch six months or so before.

Rose got off the tube at Camden Town and looked at her map. The shop Lettuce and Stuff was a few streets away. She headed off, feeling the weight of her bag. After a day at school it would have been good to go home and shower and put her things aside. But going home meant that Anna would want to know where she was going, what she was doing, who she was seeing. Since Tuesday, when Ricky Harris had been stabbed, Anna had been fussing over her. It gave her an uncomfortable feeling. There had been many times, in the past, when Rose had wished that Anna would take more notice of her, offer some support or even affection but it hadn't happened. Since Tuesday night Anna had seemed on the brink of something. She had been talking to her a lot more, standing a bit closer, reaching a hand out as if she were about to pat or touch Rose.

It made Rose feel very uneasy.

She saw the shop on the other side of the road. An odd feeling went through her. She felt inexplicably shy as if *this* was their first meeting. Her memory of seeing him late on Tuesday night had been suffused with the events at the railway station hours before. She had tried to separate them, to box off what had happened at the station and just think about being with Joshua, but she hadn't managed it.

As she waited at the crossing for the lights to change, she wondered what the flat would be like and whether Darren Skeggs would be there. She hoped not. She was keen to spend time with her stepbrother alone. She wanted Joshua to fill in all the gaps in the last five years. The emails he'd sent to her had sketched out his life in Newcastle after their parents went missing. He'd headed them as Chapter One, Chapter Two and so on. She had printed them off and read them over and over, piecing together the important events. She'd also saved them on to a file even though she knew them off by heart.

The lights changed and Rose walked across the road and found herself outside Lettuce and Stuff. The door to the flat was at the side of the shop entrance just as Joshua had described. She looked at her mobile. It was 4.32. She was a little early. She moved forward to ring the bell but suddenly felt tentative, awkward. Shy.

She wasn't ready to go in and see him.

The door to Lettuce and Stuff opened and a couple came out arm in arm, holding takeaway cups of coffee, the man giving the woman a kiss on the forehead.

Rose slipped into the cafe and up to the counter. She waited to be served, then got a peppermint tea and sat down at a table. The tea had been served in a tall glass with a silver handle. She stirred it with a long spoon, the kind that was used for a sundae. She looked around. At the next table was a young girl with a baby in a pushchair. The baby was sound asleep; the girl had headphones on and was nodding to the silent beat. Two young women were sitting at another table talking quietly, one of them giggling at what the other said. The cafe door opened and a bald man came in holding a folded newspaper under one arm and carrying a red holdall with the other.

Rose glanced up at the ceiling. Joshua was one floor above her. When she'd had a few minutes to relax and get herself together she would go out and ring the bell, and when he opened the door she'd say *Hello* or *Hi!* in some breezy way as if she was used to visiting him; as if they had never been apart, as if they hadn't been rudely separated five years before.

She stared out on to Camden High Street. The cars were queuing, cyclists weaving in and around them. Some school boys in purple blazers were walking along in a straight line, causing pedestrians to sidestep them.

She remembered that separation keenly. Her grandmother had eventually taken Rose to live with her and Joshua had gone to his uncle Stuart's in Newcastle. After the split they had gradually faded out of each other's lives.

At first they'd stayed with foster carers, Paul and Alice Townsend. They'd been there since a couple of days after their parents disappeared. For two weeks they'd huddled together in various rooms throughout the house, keeping themselves to themselves. They didn't say much to the others who were there, a surly teenage boy who stomped around the house wearing his coat most of the time and a tiny girl of about seven who sat sucking her thumb, her eyes glued to the television set. They had rooms next door to each other and they spent most of their time in one or the other. Late at night, when Paul or Alice said it was time for lights out, they would separate.

They talked about what had happened non-stop.

From time to time they looked out of the front windows of the house in the hope of a police car pulling up outside. They were eager to see a policeman, any policeman who had some information for them.

Paul and Alice told them as much as they could. No, there was no fresh news. Yes, the police had questioned the people at the restaurant where her mum and Brendan had gone for a meal. Yes, the other shops and pubs and bars had been questioned but no one had seen the couple after they left the restaurant. And yes, Brendan's car, a blue Audi, had been found parked in a side street.

Then one day a female social worker came to the house. She wanted to speak to Rose alone. She told her about the grandmother she never knew she had. She took her to a house in Belsize Park. Rose walked hesitantly through the big front door and was faced with a tall stiff woman with shoulder-length hair, a streak of grey at the front. The woman had held out her hand formally for Rose to shake. She'd noticed the nails then, pale pink, rounded, like shells from a beach. Anna Christie her name was and she was dressed smartly – like someone going to a wedding. Rose noticed her patent high heel shoes clicking on the wooden floor. She followed her further and further into the big house, glancing backwards until she could no longer see the front door. They had tea in the conservatory and her grandmother asked her some questions about her life. She did not mention Rose's mother.

Not once. Nor did she ask any questions about the night her mum and Brendan went out for a meal and never came back.

When Rose returned to the foster home she spent every minute with Joshua. She sensed that she would not be there for long. Joshua had had a phone call from his uncle in Newcastle. He was to go and live with him.

Paul and Alice Townsend hugged them and wished them luck. The little girl waved from her place on the settee, her eyes leaving the television for only seconds, then returning to the screen. The boy was upstairs somewhere and didn't answer when they called *Goodbye.*

We'll keep in touch, Rose had said.

I'll see you soon, Joshua had said, *I'll visit. You can come up to Newcastle.*

But it hadn't happened.

Rose hadn't understood why Joshua couldn't come to live with her and her grandmother. He was her stepbrother. She'd lost her mum and Brendan. Why should she lose Joshua as well? Her grandmother had been brisk when the subject was raised. Her eyes had rolled and she'd made a *tsk*ing sound. It was not how things were done. Joshua had to go and live with his blood relatives. That was the law. She wouldn't be drawn on it. Rose and Joshua had written to each other and there were a number of awkward phone calls when the conversation dried up after a few moments. When Rose went to boarding school these things less happened less often until eventually they lost contact.

Then six months ago, when Rose was looking at her laptop, she got an email message. Joshua had contacted her to say that he was coming to London to study. After that she received long emails from him and sent long replies.

Now she was sitting in a cafe looking at an empty glass of peppermint tea, aware that Joshua was in a flat above her. She looked around. There was only the man with the red holdall left. The others had gone. It was almost five o'clock. Why not go out and ring on the bell? Then she could go up to his flat and see how he was living. She could find out all the stuff she'd wanted to find out on Tuesday night before the events at the station. Why not? Why was she feeling so awkward about it?

She sighed and went to the counter again. She bought a blueberry muffin and a bottle of water. When she sat down the man looked up at her. He gave a polite smile and she felt she ought to respond. For a second he looked familiar so she averted her eyes. The last thing she wanted was some small talk with someone she vaguely knew. She pulled out her laptop and set it up on the table, then waited for it to load up. She tweaked a corner of the muffin and felt it crumble on her tongue.

She looked at her email and smiled, seeing another message from Joshua.

Rosie, looking forward to seeing you later!

She moved it into the folder marked *Josh*. It joined a long list of saved emails and she scrolled up them. She highlighted one and then another, scanning the content, remembering the information from when she'd read it the first time. She took a chunk of her muffin and ate it, chewing it slowly, looking over the paragraphs that Josh had sent. Then she opened one with the title *Flat in Camden*. It was the story of how Joshua had got to know Darren Skeggs. She glanced over it and then closed it down. Then she went on to Facebook and looked up Joshua's page. She scrolled through his friends to see if there was a picture of Darren Skeggs. There wasn't.

When Joshua had started at a local boys' school in Newcastle he'd had to prove himself. He had lived in and around London all his life and when he had gone back to the place where his dad was brought up he stuck out like a sore thumb. *There was blood spilt*, he'd told her in the email. She'd remembered those very words with a chill.

One day he had found Darren Skeggs in the toilets. The boy was in a state, beaten and bruised. Joshua had helped him up and got tissues so that he could wash himself. *If that had been all that had happened I would have just left it. Violence in a boys' school; it's practically mandatory*, he'd said. But Darren's asthma inhaler had been chucked down a filthy toilet. *It made me mad*, he'd said. *It sent me into a rage.* He'd found the boys concerned and dragged one of them back and made him put his hand down and retrieve the inhaler from the fetid water. Some of the boys' mates turned up to help him but Joshua didn't back down. *I took the kid's mobile, expensive it was, and I dropped it into the same crappy toilet.*

Darren Skeggs had been left alone after that.

'Excuse me, you're a student at Camden, aren't you?' a voice said.

She looked up, her reverie broken. The bald man was standing at his table as if he was about to leave. He had a leather jacket on, like a biker's jacket. There was no crash helmet although his bag looked big enough to hold one. It was a bright red colour and there was a chequered flag on it, the kind that is waved in front of a racing car.

'Yes,' she said, pulling the lid of her laptop half closed.

'I thought I recognised you. I work there. I'm a technician.'

'Oh, hi,' she said, giving a stiff smile.

'You are the girl who was involved when that boy got killed?'

She nodded. Did absolutely everyone in the world know about it?

'I remember you,' he said. 'That boy was nasty to you. I had to speak to him about it.'

'Yes,' she said, tapping her fingers on her laptop.

'Anyway. Terrible thing. I'll let you get back to your work.'

The man turned away and went out of the cafe. The door hung open for a second, letting the cold air in. Rose relaxed. Then she felt immediately guilty. Why was she so ill at ease with people? The man had done her a favour – why couldn't she be more pleasant to him?

She thought back to the day in school a couple of weeks before when she'd been in the IT suite working on some graphics for an art project. She'd been deep in thought and felt someone flick the back of her head. She looked round to see Ricky Harris standing behind her with a couple of his mates. She'd turned back to her work, ignoring him and blushed quietly as she heard him talk loudly about her.

'You know what private school girls are like. They give it away to anyone. They'll do anything you ask them to. Right slags.'

Rose felt her temper rise but made herself sit very still.

'You!' a strong male voice called. 'Leave that girl alone. What's your business in here? Have you got a pass? What's your name?'

Rose looked round to see one of the technicians striding across the room, his identity tag flying out. He was a tall bald man. The top button of his shirt was undone and his tie knotted loosely. He had black jeans on and his legs looked thin and long.

'All right, gay boy. Calm down,' Ricky Harris said.

'Get out of here,' the technician said.

'I will. I don't want you to get the wrong idea. I don't want to get touched up. Wait, you sure you've had one of them CRB checks? Sure you're not on the sex offenders' register?'

'I'll be speaking to your form tutor.'

'Speaking to him. I bet you'd like to do more than that!'

They left, laughing. The technician looked flustered. Rose saw his name tag then: *Frank Palmer, IT Technician*. Kids were looking up from their computers and a couple of the other technicians were looking over at him, talking to each other.

'Thanks, you didn't need to say anything . . .' she said.

'You should speak to your form tutor. No one should treat you like that.'

The cafe was empty and Rose began to pack her laptop away. Why hadn't she been nicer to the man when he spoke to her? He had only wanted to pass the time of day. In any case why was she still there, sitting in the cafe? Her muffin was finished, the paper case baggy, its pleats misshapen. Joshua was expecting her.

But she couldn't get Ricky Harris out of her mind. His bullying had got to her. Then, on the walkway above the railway lines, someone had bullied him. Should she feel a tiny bit *pleased* about that? He had turned on to the walkway and taken the last steps he would ever take. He had come face to face with the person who would kill him seconds later. Someone who was past throwing stuff down toilets and tormenting shy classmates. This was a person who meant business, who carried a length of steel that slid in and out of flesh as though it was butter.

The thought made her feel weak for a second.

Ricky Harris had no doubt been grinning to himself because he had ruffled the feathers of the posh girl from school. Perhaps he had had a smile on his face. Was it likely that that smile had offended another young man who had a name to make for himself? A young man like Lewis Proctor? *What you smiling for, Harris?* he might have said before putting his hand into his pocket and pulling out a knife.

She walked to the door of the cafe.

Violence and boys. Why did these two words fit so well together? Joshua said that it had been round every corner in his boys' only school. She pictured packs of snappy dogs eyeing each other, their tails stiff with apprehension. How different from her boarding school. There had been no violence at Mary Linton School for Girls. Nothing physical; no blood, no bruises, no hair pulling. Nothing so common for so many well brought-up girls. There had been other stuff, though; hurt and embarrassment, shame and envy. She thought of Rachel Bliss for the first time in months. Her oldest friend. Her closest friend. Rachel who had a soft smile and a hard heart.

It gave her a momentary jolt.

She'd spent too long thinking about the past.

Joshua was upstairs and she needed to go and see him.

She opened the cafe door and went out into the street. Moments later she was standing by Joshua's front door and ringing his bell.

SIX

There was the sound of heavy footsteps coming down the stairs. Rose expected Joshua to open the door. She worked herself up to a smile to greet him. She heard bolts being pulled back. The door opened abruptly and a young man with heavy black glasses and flat black hair stared at her.

'What?' he said.

'I'm here to see Josh,' she said, as pleasantly as she could.

The young man who she supposed was Darren Skeggs gave a sigh and turned away. He trudged up a narrow stairway shouting Joshua's name. She stepped inside, assuming she was meant to follow. At the top she could see Joshua and hear him saying something. Then he gave her a beaming smile.

'Hi, Rosie. Put the bolts on, would you?' he called.

The door had a metal bolt at the top and a smaller one at the bottom. In the middle was a chain. Puzzled, she fastened them all and went up the stairs. Joshua gave her a hug.

'You've met Skeggsie, my landlord?' Joshua said.

Rose looked again at the young man, her eyes fixed on the heavy black glasses. His clothes were close-fitting and the shirt he had on seemed to be buttoned up to his chin. He was a complete contrast to Joshua, who had fair hair flicking round his ears and was wearing a faded, wrinkled T-shirt with a row of beads around his neck.

Skeggsie nodded stiffly at her. She opened her mouth to say something but he turned away and walked off. She frowned.

'Come on, let me show you the flat,' Joshua said, oblivious to her discomfort. 'Put your bag down. Take your coat off!'

She placed her bag on the hall floor and shrugged off her coat, taking care with her arm which was still tender from the tattoo. She let it hang down by her side.

'Come on!' Joshua called.

He showed her a huge living room, one corner of which was filled with one of the biggest televisions she had ever seen. Opposite was a long low sofa, the kind you might find in a hotel foyer. A coffee table sat in front of it, every centimetre of which was covered by piles of books and DVDs. There was nothing else in the room. The floorboards were polished and the walls were four different colours. It was odd, like a set for a play and yet Rose quite liked it.

'My room's here,' Joshua said.

His bedroom was small but neat. Rose was reminded immediately of the box room he had had when they lived in Brewster Road. Then his bed was high up so that he had space underneath. Now a double bed took up most of the space in the room. A rail sat alongside the opposite wall, crammed with clothes, some of which were on hangers, some just draped over the top. On the ground were trainers and boots piled on top of each other. By the side of the bed was a full-length mirror fixed on to the wall. On the bedside table sat a screwdriver. It was squat, bright yellow, different from the one she had seen him with on Tuesday night. There was a narrow rug on the floor with just enough space to walk along it to the bed and back.

'It's compact,' she said.

'I've got another room, a study.'

The room next door was twice the size and held a desk and a table and a couple of chairs. The walls were covered in posters for bands and movies and there were some big beanbag-type cushions in one corner underneath an old standard lamp with no shade. She looked back to the desk and the table alongside it. There was a computer monitor and a laptop, and a printer and a black box with a light blinking. There was wire snaking in and out, hanging precariously off the table, cascading down to a multi-plug adaptor.

'Wow,' she said, 'you've got a lot of hardware.'

'This is nothing. You should see Skeggsie's room.'

She screwed her face up thinking of the rude young man. Joshua seemed to read her expression.

'Skeggsie's all right. His people skills aren't great but he's a brilliant guy. Put your coat down,' he said, pulling her jacket out of her hand and laying it over the beanbags, 'Here, come and see my websites. Sit here.'

He pulled one of the chairs back and she reluctantly sat down. He'd mentioned these websites to her a couple of weeks before. She wasn't looking forward to seeing them.

'Skeggsie helped me set these up. Without him I couldn't have done it. This is the first.'

He tapped on the keyboard and then, on the screen, a website appeared, **missingones.com**. The background was deep red and underneath the web name was a brief outline of the site. Rose let her eyes run across the words. She was distracted, though, by the photographs which materialised down each side of the page. Her mum and Brendan. She stared at each one until it faded and was instantly replaced by another. Her mother's face, smiling, her glasses slightly crooked, her hair pulled back; Brendan grinning at something off camera; Brendan with a peaked cap; her mum wearing dark glasses, looking sombre.

She looked back to the words, trying to ignore the images.

Each year 275,000 people disappear.
Most of these people return to their families within a day or two.
The number of people missing from their families for more than a year is 16,000–20,000.
Kathy Smith and Brendan Johnson are two such people.
We want them back. We need them. This site is about them and about the circumstances of their disappearance.

Rose felt her throat begin to tighten. She looked away from the screen at Joshua's profile. His eyes were fixed on the images, his jaw and neck tense. The beads, which had looked so casual moments before, seemed tight like a choker. He turned to her before she could look away. Their eyes met.

'I know you don't approve of all this,' he said, holding his hands out, encompassing the technology that sat glowing in front of him, 'You said that in your emails. But I have to go on looking for Kathy and Dad.'

'I understand,' she said softly. 'But the police explained . . .'

'But nothing is *proven*. Nothing is certain. That's why I have to keep looking. And in any case if the police were right, if they were . . .'

He licked his lips before going on.

'If Kathy and Dad were *killed* then I've set up this other website. Look.'

He pulled the laptop towards him and tapped on the keys. Its screen was smaller but in a second a website filled the space. This time the background was black. oldmurders.com. The font was sombre. Rose frowned. This was stark, funereal. There were no photographs, just some text that had been bulleted.

- Many murders go unsolved.
- They sit in police files for lack of resources.
- The murderers are free to get on with their lives.
- This site is about a possible murder.
- Kathy Smith and Brendan Johnson disappeared.
- The police think they were murdered.
- Help us to find out one way or another.

Underneath was a menu: Biographies; Last Known Whereabouts; Witnesses; Maps; Car; Contact us.

'See, these websites can reach two potential communities. People researching crime or murders, other police forces, private investigators. Look, I've tagged all the important words. So, say if anyone was searching for the Tuscan Moon, for any reason, then this website and missingones.com would come up.'

Joshua seemed breathless. Rose gave a smile but it wasn't an encouraging one. He carried on, not giving her a chance to speak.

'I know you don't think I should do all this . . .'

'It's up to you what you do,' she said.

'You have your way of dealing with what happened. This is mine.'

'I don't exactly deal with it. I just accept it.'

'I can't . . .'

'You can't let it go,' she said slowly, almost to herself.

He shrugged.

The sound of footsteps going downstairs made Joshua look around. Then the bolts of the street door shot back. The door opened and closed with a slam.

'Skeggsie's gone out,' Joshua said with a half-smile.

'Without saying anything? Isn't he a bit odd?' she said, moving her chair back, relieved to be turning away from the content of the screens in front of her.

'He is odd. But trust me,' Josh said, standing up, fiddling with the beads around his neck, 'he is the best.'

'What's with the bolts on the door?' she said.

'Ah, the bolts,' he said. 'Come on, I'll make you a coffee and explain. Oh no, wait! It's not coffee. It's *tea*. Tea bag left in for exactly sixty seconds, a touch of milk and no sugar,' he said.

She smiled. He'd remembered what she liked. He, on the other hand, had large mugs of lukewarm, milky coffee. When they had lived in Bethnal Green with her mum and Brendan she would sometimes find them in his room days after he'd made them, a third of the liquid left, the top covered in a chocolate-coloured scuddy skin. It used to turn her stomach but still she carried them downstairs and washed them up before her mum or Brendan noticed.

As they left the room she turned back for a second to see the screens sitting side by side, the monitor big and brassy, the words **missingones.com** dominant. The laptop was smaller, at a slight angle, the word *murder* just visible.

While Joshua was fussing with the drinks Rose thought of the Tuscan Moon. It was her mum and Brendan's favourite restaurant and they went there regularly. Rose and Joshua had been there a few times with them for an early meal. The waiters spoke a lot of Italian and there were pictures of Italian footballers all over the walls. Rose used to have a Margherita pizza and some garlic bread but Joshua liked the lasagne and insisted on having it with chips much to everyone's embarrassment.

The Tuscan Moon was the restaurant her mum and Brendan went to on the night they disappeared.

'Here you are!' Joshua handed her a mug of tea.

They were sitting at a small table in a long narrow kitchen.

'What's with Skeggsie and the bolts?'

Joshua let out a sigh.

'He's had some bad times. You remember I told you how we hooked up? Me and him? Well, he's the kind of kid who seems to attract – I don't know – nasty types.

His dad bought this flat. And during his first year at uni he had a couple of other students share it and they took advantage. He had trouble getting rid of them. During his second year he lived here alone. He was burgled, though, and he's sure, *positive*, that it was some of the kids who had lived here with him. A couple of weeks ago he was in the flat on his own and he was sure he heard someone open the front door. He called out thinking it was me but it wasn't. When he went downstairs the door was wide open. It freaked him out. Hence the bolts.'

'Oh, not good.'

'But it's more than bad luck and it's more than about security. He is a bit obsessive. You know I sometimes hear him have showers three, four times a day. And the bolts thing? He likes it locked every time we come in. When I go out I have to lock two separate Chubb locks. He's a little *insecure*.'

'I didn't warm to him,' Rose said.

'You would if you knew him. Actually, I've got something to show you. Skeggsie has this software he's developed. Well, it's hard to explain. Come and see. Bring your drink.'

She followed Joshua into one of the tidiest rooms she had ever seen. It was as big as the living room and seemed to be divided in half. On one side was a bed and wardrobe and chest of drawers. The bed was made, the doors and drawers were shut and apart from a couple of photos in old-fashioned frames there was nothing on the surfaces. No books, magazines, no personal items, nothing. The other side of the room was full of computers. She gasped at the amount of equipment on view. A long table, like an old dining table, was flat against a wall. There were four monitors, one of them huge, like a widescreen television set. Under the table were four base units. The rest of the space was covered in electronic equipment, things she had never seen before. Amid it all were the spaghetti wires that ran in between the machinery.

'Here, look,' Joshua said, holding up an A4-size photograph.

Rose took it.

'Skeggsie's got this way of getting into programs? He calls it a Trojan Horse Incursion. This is the Network Rail CCTV system. Look, this is a photo of you. Last Tuesday night.'

Rose looked hard at the dark grainy picture. It showed a railway station platform. On it was a girl and a boy standing together. At the bottom was a date and a time. The date she saw was the previous Tuesday and the time was 19.46. With a shock she registered that it really was her and Ricky Harris. They were standing a metre or so apart and as she examined the picture she saw that in fact Ricky Harris was talking on a mobile phone.

It was the night he was stabbed.

'I don't understand,' she said. 'How could Skeggsie get this?'

'He's spent the last three years working on software stuff. He's a genius when it comes to all this.'

'And he hacked into CCTV cameras? When?'

'Late last Tuesday. When I got back from seeing you at your gran's house I asked him if he could get an image.'

'Isn't it illegal?'

'It is but Skeggsie does it in such a way that it can't be traced. He lays all these false trails. He's the world's first true Cyber Escape Man.'

'But why?'

'How do you mean?'

'Why did you get him to do it?'

Joshua looked puzzled.

'I thought it would be interesting.'

'This boy got killed . . .'

His face fell.

'It's bad taste, isn't it? I didn't think. I was just showing you how clever Skeggsie is. I'm sorry, Rosie. You know me. I sometimes jump in without thinking.'

'That was a terrible night for me. Why would you think I wanted to be reminded of it?'

She was angry. She took a last look at the photograph and then tossed it aside.

'I'm sorry,' Josh said.

It was only her second evening with Joshua. The first one had been messed up and now she was feeling annoyed.

'I just thought you might want to look at this. It was stupid.'

She glanced round at the wall of computers and pictured Skeggsie sitting bolt upright in front of them, the screens reflected in the lenses of his big glasses.

'He had no right to steal this image of me!' she said.

'It was my fault. I asked him to. I've mucked up big time, haven't I?'

Joshua looked crestfallen.

'No . . .' she said, feeling foolish. 'No, 'course not . . .'

'I have,' he said.

He reached out and took hold of her arm. She flinched, pain crossing her face.

'What?' he said. 'What have I done now?'

'Nothing. Really.'

He took a step back from her. He was upset. The evening was going wrong. She spoke quickly, holding her arm out to him.

'Look, I've got this tattoo.'

She pulled her sleeve back. The tattoo was still red and raised but the blue outline of the butterfly was clear.

'When did you have that done?' he said, a curious smile on his face.

'A week or so ago. It's still quite sore.'

'A butterfly.'

'A Blue Morpho.'

'But why a butterfly?'

'I like the look of them. I like the blueness of it.'

'*Blueness?*'

'Don't mock me,' she said, letting her sleeve drop.

'I would never do that,' he said. 'Actually, this is amazing. Come on, let's get out of Skeggsie's room. I've got something to show you.'

She followed him out and back to his tiny bedroom. Once inside he walked to the wall mirror. She stood by the door, slightly embarrassed.

'Here,' he said. 'Come closer.'

She stood by him. There was no space to move. He crossed his arms and pulled his T-shirt up over his chest and head and threw it behind him on the bed. She was startled but tried to keep a neutral expression on her face. Then he turned away from her and she saw it.

'Oh!' she said.

On the side of his ribs was a butterfly tattoo, twice the size of the one she had, its blueness sharp and vibrant, its wings wrapping around him.

'We're a team, you and me,' he said.

He was staring into the mirror, looking straight at her. She looked back at him, her eye dropping to the tattoo. After a second she reached across with her hand and touched his skin with her fingertips.

Her sleeve fell back to reveal the edge of a blue wing.

'A team,' he whispered, grinning.

SEVEN

On Saturday morning Anna seemed to hang around Rose a lot of the time. She stood at the corner of her study door and watched as Rose sat at her desk working on her laptop. She asked her questions about the events at the station. The questions were separated by long gaps as if Anna was weighing up every word of her answer. Rose typed on and felt Anna's eyes on her back.

In the end she stopped working and turned to face her. Anna, seemingly disconcerted by Rose's scrutiny, picked up a cushion that had fallen off the big armchair and straightened it.

'I was wondering whether it would be good to give violin a miss this week,' she said.

Rose remembered the violin lessons that were no more. After returning from boarding school she'd gone to a woman in Hampstead, Isabel Popper, to keep up her practice. Once a week she went for an hour playing her pieces, practising her chords, preparing for an exam that she had never intended to take. After the summer, when school began, it was easy to say that she was transferring to another tutor nearer to home. She had continued to go out every Tuesday. A small victory against Anna. The money she was given she kept in a box in her room.

'I don't want to miss my lesson,' Rose said.

Her grandmother nodded and paused for a second before walking out of the room. Behind her she left a heavy flowery scent.

When she was sure she had gone Rose opened up her blog, Morpho. She scrolled down some recent links and pictures and clips she'd uploaded and read over the most recent entry she'd made. It was a week or so before she was to meet Joshua. She smiled when she read the optimism there, the feeling that the evening ahead was a new beginning for her and Joshua. Her optimism had been well founded. She and Joshua had met up and were now a family of sorts again.

But in between she had witnessed a murder.

She made a new heading.

Be Careful What You Wish For.

What happens when someone from your school goes out of their way to pick on you and make you miserable?

She paused and thought inevitably of Rachel Bliss, her old best friend from boarding school. How could someone so close have made her so unhappy? Ricky Harris had been completely different. She had never been close to him. She had disliked him from the moment she set eyes on him until he said, *Here's your train, posh bird!* She continued writing her blog.

It happened to me. I hated this boy, Ricky Harris. I detested him. I avoided him but last week I bumped into him while waiting for a train. I had no choice but to listen to his taunts. Was there a moment when I might have unconsciously wished him dead? That I might have imagined him falling on to the tracks as a train thundered in? Maybe. I may well have wished this but never imagined what was going to happen later.
This boy got stabbed. He is dead. End of story.

It was a harsh but truthful post. Her blog wasn't a diary, just a jumble of her thoughts and feelings with pictures and links to other interesting sites and blogs. At the moment she was the only one who read it, but one day she might invite Joshua to look at it. She closed her laptop and stretched her arms up, flexing her fingers.

Later her grandmother joined her for lunch. They talked about Camden.

'Is there a lot of violence there?' she said. 'Day to day, I mean?'

'No. 'Course not. In the time I've been there I've only seen a bit of horsing around,' she said, thinking ironically of Lewis Proctor pretending to stab himself with a plastic knife.

'But you read such things in the newspaper about these institutions,' her grandmother said, biting daintily into a sandwich.

'No,' Rose said. 'It didn't happen in school. It happened outside, on the station platform. It wasn't to do with *school*. It could have happened anywhere.'

But that wasn't true. Rose thought of Little Radleigh, the station in Norfolk which was near to the Mary Linton School. She and some of the girls had used it to get to Norwich at weekends. It was tiny, with hanging baskets swaying in the breeze and the sound of cows mooing from nearby fields. The sky was vast and they could see the train from miles away. It seemed to take an age to get there and when it did it had a single carriage and looked as though it had been abandoned by a rushing locomotive. The girls from the school were metropolitan. They were used to big cities and expensive cars and air travel. Stepping on to the local Norwich train was quaint. Nothing bad could have happened on that platform, Rose was sure.

'Camden really isn't such a bad place,' Rose said.

Her grandmother didn't answer.

Rose studied her. She was wearing a lemon-coloured jumper with cream trousers. Her hair, shoulder-length, was pulled back into a lemon tie at the back of her neck. She had neat gold studs on and the thick gold chain that she always wore round her neck. Rose looked down and saw brown leather high heels. She wouldn't have been surprised to see a matching handbag sitting on the floor beside her. Anna looked like she was going for a job interview even though it was Saturday and she was simply *at home*.

Rose, on the other hand, was in black jeans and a black and white T-shirt. On her feet were pink slipper socks, the kind with rubber patches that stopped her sliding across Anna's wooden floors. Indoors she *was* prepared to wear colour.

She spent the afternoon working on an essay.

A beep sounded. She had a new message. She expected it to be from Joshua. They had been emailing each other on and off since lunch. He had been telling her about a paper he had to give on Brunel and bridges and she had been telling him about the essay she was planning on Dickens' *Great Expectations*.

She looked at her in-box and was puzzled to see the name Emma Burke. *Emma Burke?* She opened the message.

Hi, Rose. Got your email address from school. I wanted to talk to you about something. Could we meet somewhere? Emma.

It was Ricky Harris's girlfriend.

Her first thought was to send a quick answer to say that she couldn't manage a meeting, that she was busy. Her fingers hung over the keys wondering how exactly to word it. She sat back. She had no wish to be in contact with Emma and her difficult stepsister, Sherry.

She decided not to answer the email. She deleted it from her in-box and sent a message to Joshua instead. *How's the computer whizz, Skeggsie? Does he have a life away from cyberspace?*

She got an almost immediate answer. *Skeggsie is his computer. It does not exist without him. He does not exist without it.*

She answered, *Half boy, half chip. Where does he insert his memory stick?*

The answer came seconds later. *He is the human memory stick.*

As she was trying to think of a reply a new message came. The name Emma Burke was in her in-box. She opened it.

Rose, I need a quick answer. This is important. It's about Lewis Proctor.

Rose hesitated before deleting the message.

Joshua sent another. *Fancy meeting up tomorrow afternoon? We could walk over the Millennium Bridge. Part of my research. 3 p.m. St Paul's underground.*

She answered instantly. *Yes, see you outside the ticket office. I'll be carrying a violin case.*

He came back with *And I'll bring the bassoon.*

She looked at the time. It was 16.03. She felt happy. The work was almost finished. Afterwards she intended to go on Facebook for a while and maybe look at some movie blogs.

She pulled her sleeve back and focused on her tattoo. It looked better today. Was that because it was finally healing? Or was it because she had seen that Joshua had a butterfly tattooed on his side? His was bigger, more powerful-looking, its wings at an angle as if it was in flight. Hers was still and flat and beautiful, as though it was in a display case. How had that happened? That both of them had had this tattoo done independently of the other? While standing looking into his bedroom mirror, her fingers on the side of his chest, he had laughed and said *Great Minds Think Alike, Rosie,* and she had looked at his reflection and felt a rush of emotion.

There was a knock and her door opened slightly.

'There's someone to see you,' her grandmother said with a forced smile.

Rose stepped out of her room and looked over the landing. There, in the hallway, was Emma Burke. She was standing close to the front door. She looked up and saw Rose and gave a little wave.

'Who is she?' her grandmother said.

'She's from school,' Rose said, flustered.

How did she know where to find her?

'Do you want me to bring her up here?'

'No, I'll come down.'

Her grandmother went off into her bedroom and Rose went down the stairs.

'How did you get my address?' she demanded.

Emma was wearing a bright purple top. It was tight and stretchy and showed her shape. She was thin, no spare flesh at all.

'Oh, thanks. Hi, Emma, how are you feeling? How are the arrangements for your boyfriend's funeral going?' Emma said, her face puffed up, her fingers tapping the wooden surface of the hall table.

'How did you find out where I live?'

'A mate of Sherry's works in the administration office at school. She gave us your details yesterday, when we were looking for you.'

'What do you want?'

'I need your help. That's why I've come.'

'I don't want anything to do with your boyfriend. It's not my business that he was killed. I was just unlucky enough to be there,' Rose said, looking straight at her. 'I wish I hadn't known him because he was nasty to me. Truthfully, I'm not shedding any tears.'

Emma stared back at Rose, her face stony, only a quiver on her bottom lip showing any emotion. Her cheekbones looked more prominent or maybe she'd just pulled her hair back in a tighter knot.

Rose shrugged.

Emma blinked and a tear hung at the corner of her eye.

'I don't see how I *can* help you,' Rose said hopelessly, 'I don't *know* you. I'm not your friend.'

'That's why. Everyone else is too involved. I need someone who doesn't care one way or another.'

The words stung. Rose was uncaring. Was she?

'You want a drink?' she said.

'No.'

She walked towards the kitchen. Emma followed. She pulled a chair out and sat down and gestured to Emma to do the same. Seated, Emma seemed to shrink against the big room. Above them pots and pans were hanging from a rail, polished and glossy, bunches of dried herbs drooping down between them. On the table there was a pyramid of lemons which sat in a bowl. They were never used, Rose knew, just replaced one by one when their skins started to harden and their colour lost its early morning sunshine glow. It was a showroom kitchen. There were no breadcrumbs on the side, no smeared knives lying around, no half-used tins of beans in the fridge.

Emma shivered as if she was cold.

'I might as well start at the beginning,' she said. 'Me and Ricky were together for three years. We grew up on the same street on the Chalk Farm Estate.'

Rose knew the Chalk Farm Estate. It was where most of the students from school came from.

'I knew he wasn't an angel and he hung around with some bad types. Maybe that was what I liked about him. He was a bad boy. He had a reputation. Maybe I'm attracted to that kind of person. I know he was horrible sometimes but it was just a front. His mum is a nightmare and his older brother made his life miserable. You have to be hard round our way. That stuff he said to you, it was nothing personal . . .'

Rose huffed. It had felt *personal* to her.

'Anyhow, just before the summer we broke up. I was sure he was seeing someone else but he denied it. I didn't believe him so I finished it.'

She hadn't known this.

'I started to see this kid. It lasted about six weeks. It was great at first. We were all loved up but as time went on I got fed up with him. He was immature.'

Rose frowned. She wondered why Emma was telling her this.

'It was Lewis Proctor.'

Now she understood.

'I don't know know why I chose him. Maybe to get back at Ricky? He and Lewis were sort of rivals, I suppose you could say. Two bad boys on the same estate. They had different groups of friends, They hung around in different parts of Camden even though they lived streets away from each other. For a while it felt really good. We spent a lot of time together. I'm not sure when it started to go bad. It was coming up to school time and I saw Ricky around. He was sweet and nice to me and I kept thinking about old times. Anyway I finished it with Lewis on the weekend before school started again and got back with Ricky.

'You think *Lewis* stabbed Ricky?' Rose said. 'That was why you asked me to look at him?'

Emma shrugged.

'Lewis is capable of it. When he was fourteen he was involved in a stabbing. He said he was just an onlooker but . . .'

'Have the police spoken to him?'

'Yeah. Word is that Bee Bee's given him an alibi.'

'Bee Bee?'

'His new girlfriend. She was there the other day. The one with the silver boots. She'd say anything to help him. She's been desperate for him for months. For years.'

Rose was quiet. It was too much information.

'Why are you telling me all this stuff?'

'I got this, today, through my front door.'

She put an envelope on the table. There was a name on it; EMMA.

'Open it.'

Rose pulled out a piece of paper. There were just a few words written in the middle.

Come and meet me at the cemetery at six. That's if you want to know who killed Ricky. Lew.

A heart had been drawn after the name.

'It's Lewis's handwriting. He was always sending me little notes. After I gave him up he sent me a note every day for a couple of weeks. I had to hide them from Ricky.'

'Why does he want to meet you at the cemetery?'

'We went there a lot.'

'The *cemetery*?'

'It's next to the station. You know it?'

Rose nodded.

'It's this private place. Lewis showed it to me. It's huge and has all these hidden areas to sit where no one bothers you. Not many kids use it because they're freaked out by the graves and stuff. It was perfect for me and Lewis. I didn't want to go anywhere where I might come face to face with Ricky and his mates. We just found a bench or a gravestone or some grass by a tree and sat and talked and drank and smoked. There's this rose garden, a kind of walled-off area. There aren't any graves there and it's quiet . . .'

'Why does he want to meet you?'

'I think he wants me to go back to him. He's been making cow eyes at me for weeks. I think the stuff about Ricky is just a way to get me there. Trouble is, I can't be absolutely sure. He knows a lot of people. There are some bad guys out there who didn't like Ricky and Lewis might have heard something.'

'Will you go?'

'I will if you come with me.'

'Why me?'

'Why not?'

'Because this isn't anything to do with me! Ask Sherry to go with you.'

'Sherry's at her dad's in Brentwood. In any case she hates Lewis. She'd just lose her temper and then he wouldn't say anything. She's too involved. I need someone who won't get Lewis's back up.'

Rose shook her head. 'Why not just go alone?'

'I'm a bit nervous. If it's really *not* about Ricky, and if he doesn't want to get back with me, then this might be about shaming me in some way. In front of Bee Bee, maybe. You saw what he was like in the cafeteria the other day. He likes a bit of drama. I just don't want to be on the receiving end of it. Not now. That's why I need someone with me. I don't know who else to ask. You're a hard person. You don't take any crap from anyone. He doesn't know you and I think he would be careful in front of you.'

'I'm not *hard*.'

'Yeah, you are. I see the way you walk round school. Most people say you're a stuck-up cow but I think you've grown this iron shell.'

'I can't come. I don't *want* to come!'

Emma stood up. She looked as though she was about to say something else but instead she pulled her mobile phone out of her pocket and stared intently at the screen.

'I just don't want to get involved,' Rose said softly. 'I want to put what happened last Tuesday behind me.'

'That's OK. I understand. I just thought I'd ask. I'll go on my own.'

Rose closed her eyes. This just wasn't her problem. Emma walked towards the door and she followed her along the hallway. The house was quiet. There wasn't a sound.

'Nice house,' Emma said.

'It's my grandmother's.'

'Be yours one day.'

She shook her head. 'I don't want anything from my grandmother. I have to live here until I finish high school and then I'm gone.'

Emma opened the front door.

'You're not a very happy person, are you?'

'That something else you noticed about me when I'm walking round school?'

'It is. You should lighten up. People might get to like you.'

'I don't care if people like me.'

'I don't believe that. Everybody cares,' Emma said with a wan smile.

Framed by the big doorway she looked childlike. Her hair extensions hung in strings over her shoulder. The pink of her mobile phone reminded Rose of a mobile phone that one of her dolls had had. Emma gave a wave and then turned away. It was the second time she had come to Rose for help. Rose felt herself softening. She called after her.

'What time does Lewis want to meet you?'

'Six,' Emma said, stepping hopefully back towards her.

Rose looked up at the hall clock. It showed twenty to five.

'I'll come. I'll meet you outside the cemetery at ten to six.'

'Really?'

'Really.'

'Why?'

'Why not?'

'You won't turn up.'

'I will come. When I say I'll do something, then I'll do it.'

'At the cemetery?'

Rose nodded.

'At ten to six?'

'I might be a stuck-up cow but I don't go back on my word,' Rose said.

Emma gave a shaky smile. Then she walked off.

EIGHT

Rose left a note on the kitchen table for her grandmother.

I am going out to meet a friend for a coffee. Will be back in a couple of hours. Rose.

It was 5.35. She had fifteen minutes to get to the cemetery to meet Emma. It was light but there was a greyness in the air, a hint of night. Feeling chilly, she zipped up her jacket and walked briskly along. All the houses in the street were set back and there were ornate garden gates and crisp brick walls that divided them from the pavement. Some houses had lines of short conifers or perfectly boxed hedges. It was quiet, as if there was some kind of soundproofing that kept the city noises at bay. It was a picture-postcard street and she should be grateful that she lived there. Anna had told her often enough.

She turned out on to the High Street. There she was met with light and noise and people. Thudding music came from a stationary car which had its windows open. She walked past it and thought of Emma and Lewis Proctor. She was puzzled by the situation. She, who had never had a boyfriend, found it strange that Emma could just finish with one boy and start up with another. She remembered Lewis Proctor from the cafeteria the previous day. She hadn't liked the look of him. He was an example of so many of the boys who strutted round the school wearing their pristine sports clothes and trainers. She'd seen them in her class looking down at themselves, at the shape of their jeans or the length of their T-shirts or the fit of a jacket. They smelled of scent and cream and spearmint. They were interchangeable and Rose found herself repelled by their self-absorption. She suddenly thought of Joshua and his floppy hair and the beads around his neck. There was something soft about Joshua that made her want to touch him. Lewis Proctor on the other hand seemed hard and angular.

She liked Emma. This stringy girl, who at first seemed like a sad puppy dog wandering round after Ricky Harris, did in fact have hidden depths. She was forthright and persuasive. She had a kind of honesty that Rose liked. It made her think, strangely, of Rachel Bliss, her friend at Mary Linton. Honesty was not something that had troubled Rachel.

'Hi!' a voice called.

She looked round and saw a young man with a familiar face.

'Hi, it's Henry. The policeman from last week.'

She recognised him. The officer with the bicycle who had found a police car and driven her home from the station the previous Tuesday. She smiled and turned to walk on.

'Hang on,' he called.

She stopped and waited until he caught up with her.

'What are you up to?' he said.

He was wearing a sweatshirt and jeans. He looked different, odd.

'I can't stop. I'm just on my way somewhere. To meet a friend.'

'Where's that?' he said.

She hesitated. She didn't want to say *the cemetery*.

'Parkway East.'

'I'm going that way. I'll walk along with you.'

She hesitated. It would be downright rude to refuse so she walked on with Henry the policeman beside her.

'How are you feeling? Since last week?' he said.

'I'm fine,' she said.

'Being at a crime scene can be a terrible shock. It can sometimes hit you later, days or weeks later.'

'I've been OK,' she said truthfully. 'Any developments on the case?'

He laughed. A crowd of boys were walking towards them. They made a gap in the middle so Rose and Henry could walk through.

'What?' she said.

'You sound like someone in a TV cop show.'

He was mocking her. She was instantly cross. She had an inclination to speed up and leave him behind.

'The detectives did find out one interesting fact,' he said, glancing sideways at her. 'It'll be in a press release tomorrow so I'm not giving anything away.'

She slowed a bit, craning to hear him.

'Ricky Harris was killed with his own knife.'

'What?'

'The knife that stabbed Ricky Harris belonged to him,' Henry said.

'I don't understand.'

'There are two possibilities,' Henry said. 'Either the person knew Ricky, knew he carried a knife and knew where that knife was . . .'

Rose couldn't help but to think of Lewis Proctor.

'Or,' Henry went on, 'the killer was a stranger who got into an argument with Ricky and it was Ricky who pulled the knife out. In other words Ricky was the aggressor and the other person took the knife off him . . .'

'So it could have been self-defence?'

'It's a possibility. We have other lines of enquiry.'

'Now who sounds like someone off a cop show?' Rose said.

'Rose,' he said, 'allow me to sound like a policeman. It's what I am.'

Rose made a *tsk* sound and looked at her watch. It was 17.48. 'You know what? I'm going to have to run. I promised to meet someone and I'm going to be late,' she said.

'I can walk faster.'

'No, really. Thanks for your help the other night but I've got to go.'

'Rose!'

She turned and saw him hurrying up to her. She exhaled with exasperation.

'What!' she said, crossly.

'Would you like to come to the Sundown Club?'

'What?'

'This club I run for teenagers. It's in a community centre across the road from your school. It's a place to meet other people your own age. Play music, table tennis, chess.'

'Why would I want to go there?' Rose said, astonished. 'I meet loads of other people of my own age. In school.'

'It's somewhere to go at night . . .'

'I don't need somewhere to go at night.'

'I thought as you lived away from the school. On your own, with your grandmother, you could make friends . . .'

'Do you think I've got no friends? 'Course I've got friends.'

'It's just . . .'

'I can make my own friends, thank you very much! I'm sorry. I just have to run ahead now!'

Without another word she ran off along the High Street.

Up ahead was Parkway East station and beyond that the cemetery. She knew now that it was called St Michael's RC Cemetery. After Emma left she'd looked it up on the internet. It was spread over twenty-three acres and had been open since 1868.

She looked at her phone and saw that it had just gone six. She groaned at her lateness. She came to Parkway East and had to move around a taxi that had stopped to drop someone off. She could see further along the gates of the cemetery but there was no one standing there. Most probably Emma had thought she wasn't coming and had gone on in. She was dismayed. She hadn't wanted Emma to think she had let her down. She quickened her step. When she got up to the gates she stepped back to allow a hearse to come out. The big black car slid slowly out of the wrought-iron gates empty of its passenger.

She stepped into the cemetery.

It was vast. Her eye swept across a panoply of gravestones, crosses and mausoleums. From the train she had only seen the edge of it. Here she was faced with row after row of marble headstones, wrought ironwork and brick-built tombs. There were stone angels, and statues of monks and saints, their heads bent over in prayer. In among the greys and blacks of the stone were brilliant splashes of colour where flowers and wreaths broke up the lines and angles of the graves.

Even at six o'clock on an autumn evening it seemed summery.

The sky was darkening, though, and some groups of people were making their way back towards the gate. She looked at the gatehouse and saw a sign that said *Gates Close 18.30*. Underneath, on the brick wall someone had sprayed some tiny graffiti: *DEAD TIME*.

She wondered where Emma was. She remembered her talking about a walled rose garden and saw a high brick wall over to the right at the end of a meandering path. She started to walk in that direction. A hearse was coming from beyond it, inching forward slowly. She passed some mourners at a graveside. Their pale faces and black clothes made her look away. She wondered why on earth Emma and Lewis had met here. An open space it may be but the idea of people enjoying themselves on top of graves did not appeal to her.

Then she saw Lewis Proctor.

He was emerging from an arch in the brick wall.

Was she too late? It was only five past six. Had Lewis said his piece in such a short time? She walked towards him. His face was blank. She didn't expect him to recognise her but he didn't look as though he would recognise anyone. In fact he looked stunned, his steps faltering.

'Are you all right?' she called, getting closer.

He didn't answer. He dipped his head and passed by her, rushing away. Rose watched him for a moment and then walked under the archway into an oblong garden. In front of her were roses, hundreds, thousands of them;

yellows, pinks and oranges. She looked over the top and through them to see if she could see Emma. There was a path round the outside of the garden with benches spaced along it. She walked along to the first corner and looked along the side wall. The benches were empty and her eyes swept back and forth across the area until they caught a glimpse of purple. It was at the far corner of the rose garden and she walked round the side to get to it.

'Emma,' she called.

Emma's gaudy purple top stood out among the light florals. A smudge of dark colour, it contrasted with the fluttering petals and gentle shades of the roses.

'Sorry, I'm late,' she said. 'I got held up.'

Turning the corner she stopped. Emma was not on a bench but on the ground near an archway, a back exit from the rose garden. She was lying on her chest, her face turned to the side, her arm splayed out. A feeling of dread gripped Rose. For a second she was back on the walkway at Parkway East looking at Ricky Harris's body. Then she had frozen at the sight of him. Now she rushed towards the slumped form. When she got there she squatted down.

'Emma,' she whispered.

The girl was completely still, her purple top tightly stretched over her back. Rose could see her bra strap and her shoulder blades and the chain across her neck. The hoop earring was flat on her motionless face. Rose put her fingers out to touch it. Then she looked hopelessly around. The rose garden seemed darker, later, as if it was a different time of day than moments before.

She heard something.

The silence was heavy and yet she thought there was someone there. A rustle of leaves, a puff of breath, a footstep. She turned slowly around but all she saw were the shadows of the brick wall and the roses, a little darker in colour now, sombre in their bloom. In the distance she heard the sound of a train, passing through, on its way somewhere.

She put her hand on the ground at Emma's side. It felt wet.

The blood was warm and was oozing out on the stone pathway.

Rose stood up, her hand stained. Her mouth fell open and she felt a flash of nausea. She stepped backwards away from the girl; one step, then another, then another. She turned and ran along the pathway, cutting the corner, passing the benches until she was under the arch and out into the cemetery. She paused, dazzled by the light. She saw the hearse still making its way back towards the gate and she ran after it. The driver glanced at her briefly and then away. He had no party left to pick up. She was of no interest to him.

But he slammed his brake on when she started banging on his windscreen, leaving dark smears of blood along his glass.

NINE

The police had been cold and distant. Detective Inspector Schillings had interviewed her, asking her the same questions over and over again. At first she had been too shocked to notice their changed attitude and their businesslike way of dealing with her. The previous Tuesday night there had been sympathy and tea with sugar and concern for her well-being. Henry had driven her home like some kind relative. This time she was put in a room by herself for what seemed like hours. Her grandmother was called to the station and sat beside her while she was interviewed.

Why did the deceased visit you at home?
What reason did Emma Burke give for her visit?
Are you friends with Emma Burke?
What is your relationship with Emma?

She had cried until her eyes were sore. Not with grief but with shock and sadness. She hadn't known Emma, not really, but still there had been a spark there, a tiny link between them. Emma had come to her for help and she, reluctantly, had agreed.

When DI Schillings continued to repeat his questions, she began to feel angry.

Why did you have Emma Burke's blood on your hand?

Is there some reason why the deceased's blood was on your fingers?

How did Emma Burke's blood come to be on the windscreen of a hearse in St Michael's Cemetery?

She'd told him that Lewis Proctor had passed her, that he had been in the rose garden with Emma, but the DI hadn't reacted in the way that she'd thought he would. He'd not given orders for Lewis Proctor to be arrested. He'd simply stared at her, unimpressed with her answers. And suddenly she'd known. DI Schillings thought that *she* had something to do with the murder. When she realised this she felt light-headed.

Her grandmother put a stop to the questions. She stood up and put her coat on, taking a while to wind a silk scarf around her neck.

'I've had enough of this,' she said. 'My granddaughter has had a terrible shock. She needs to recover. If you wish to interview her again, you should make an arrangement with me and I will bring her. You will also need to let me know in advance so that my solicitor can be here. Come on, Rose.'

There was silence on the drive home. Rose was relieved to be out of the station driving away from the policeman and his questions. She looked at Anna's profile. Anna was staring straight ahead, her jawline set, her anger still apparent. Rose was grateful she had come. She was more than grateful.

The streets were busy with people going out. It was just after ten. Sitting at red lights, Rose watched a stream of young people cross the road, talking, laughing, frolicking; on their way out to a pub or club or party.

Rose was tired. She wanted to go to bed. She wanted to close her eyes and put it all out of her head. As soon as they walked into the house she headed for the stairs but her grandmother broke the silence with her words. Her face was stony.

'Spending time at the police station is not something I wish to do.'

'I don't want to do it either . . .' Rose started.

'Last week I had a phone call from the police telling me you were involved in some murder and now this! For goodness' sake. Something could have happened to you!'

'I was not *involved*. I was a witness.'

'Both times it's been to do with this so-called school you go to.'

'Two people have died. That isn't my fault.'

Her grandmother unfastened the buttons of her coat and let it drop from her shoulders. She bundled it over the newel post and turned away. Rose glanced at the coat sitting precariously in a place where coats never sat. The heels of her shoes clipped on the parquet floor. She was angry. She'd seen her like this before. Calm and polite at the police station, she was smouldering underneath. Not that Anna ever lost her temper or flew into a rage. Her annoyance was more like a pot bubbling on the stove, the lid firmly on.

Rose, tired but angry, followed her towards the kitchen.

'I was trying to help the girl, Emma Burke, the girl who came here. That's all I was trying to do.'

Her grandmother dropped the silk scarf on the work surface and leant back against a cupboard. She was still immaculately dressed as usual. No doubt she had changed in order to go out for the evening. She had a camel-coloured jumper over trousers and boots. Round her waist was a plaited leather belt. She had several leather belts hanging from a rail in her dressing room.

Rose stood awkwardly in the middle of the floor.

'I sent you to boarding school, at great expense. I didn't mind. You are Katherine's daughter and my granddaughter and I have a duty to look after you. Last year, when you were upset and said you wanted to leave the school, I offered to send you to another. I found brochures and arranged a couple of visits. You didn't want that. You wanted to return here, to this house.'

Rose listened. Anna's words were on one level as if she was reeling off something she had learned by heart. Her meaning was clear. *To return to this house.* Anna would never say *come home* because this house had never been offered to Rose as a *home.*

'I then suggested a very select private school that I'd heard of up in Hampstead Heath, a short car ride away. You didn't want that. I had grave misgivings about you attending the public school but you insisted and I had to allow you to follow your own particular path. Now I find that all my fears have been confirmed and you have become embroiled in some criminal friendship group.'

'That's not true!' Rose said, a crack in her voice. 'There's no *criminal group.* These people are just other students. I was unlucky enough to be at a station when a boy was killed. Now his girlfriend has been stabbed after she came to see me. Of course I'm involved in some way. I'm not to blame, though.'

'It's the situation I'm angry about. If you had taken my advice you wouldn't be at that school!'

'I wanted to go there because it was the kind of place I went to when . . . When I lived with Mum.'

Her grandmother stared at her, her brows tensing.

'I went to a state school. I mixed with regular kids. I had lots of friends and I was happy. I wanted to be somewhere where it was like that again.'

'But you had friends at Mary Linton?'

Rose nodded.

'I don't understand.'

'I did have friends but I never felt as though I belonged there. I wanted to go back . . . to the way it was, the way I was at school when . . . when I lived with Mum and Brendan and Josh.'

'I don't wish to talk about Brendan Johnson and his son.'

'They were my *family*. When I lost Mum I lost them! I lost everything!'

Her grandmother's lips closed tightly as though she was forcing herself not to speak. Her hands curled up in delicate fists and she seemed to be gripped by some thought that she couldn't or didn't want to say. She looked over to the door and it seemed as if she was on the brink of walking out of the room. Rose was ready for this. Every row she had ever had with Anna always ended when Anna thought that enough had been said.

But strangely she didn't go. Her hands relaxed and her voice softened. Rose was taken aback.

'I understand you long for those days. Going to a particular school isn't going to do that. What you want is your mother and you cannot have her. It doesn't matter what school you go to. She is gone.'

Rose took a step towards the table and leant on it. She felt her anger drain away. It was replaced by a weight of sadness. Her grandmother continued talking.

'I am trying to do what is best for you, Rose. You coming here has been a huge change in my life.'

'I know. And I'm grateful.'

'Do you think I want to see you in a police station? My granddaughter? In trouble?'

Her grandmother stared at her. Her hand was at her neck, fingering the chain that hung there. Rose found herself looking into her eyes, deep and dark. For a second she thought of putting her hand out and touching her, placing her fingers on the sleeve of her jumper. She almost did but her grandmother continued talking, her voice a little sharper.

'That school is not a good place and I'm afraid you will waste the education that I gave you. This is exactly what happened with Katherine. Exactly. She threw away everything I had given her and insisted on going her own way. I just want to stop you making the same mistakes that she made.'

Rose stiffened. How had a conversation about Emma Burke being stabbed become a chance for Anna to criticise her mother?

'I'm not leaving the school. These crimes had nothing to do with me. I was just trying to help someone. I would prefer it if you didn't criticise my mother. You have no right to do that.'

Anna's face hardened.

'I have every right. She was my daughter. I tried to do my best for her and she let me down. She made it quite clear that she didn't approve of my lifestyle and went her own way. And what happened to her? A baby and a string of unsuitable partners. Becoming a police officer. A job that any fool could have done. Everything I did for her wasted.'

Rose crossed her arms angrily. She didn't trust herself to speak.

Her grandmother's voice dropped. 'She stormed out of here and we never spoke again. You haven't seen her for five years – it's been so much longer for me.'

Rose faltered. She stepped towards her grandmother.

'Anna . . .' she started.

'Don't throw away your education,' her grandmother cut across Rose's words. 'You could walk into Oxford in two years' time with your predicted grades. Don't toss it aside like your mother did. That's all I'm asking.'

'I won't talk any more about my mother,' Rose said firmly, turning away, keeping her voice low, trying to stay calm.

'Wait,' her grandmother said.

But Rose was striding along the hallway. She walked quickly up the stairs.

'And don't think I haven't seen that appalling tattoo on your arm. Don't think I haven't noticed it!'

Rose did not stop. She went up to her room and shut the door behind her. There was no lock so she stood firmly against it. She didn't know if Anna would come up but she stayed there anyway, her back to the door, to the house, to her grandmother. Her eyes were hot and dry. She would not cry. She would not.

Much later in bed she kept the lamp on and lay in the quiet of her room. It was quarter to twelve and she didn't think she would get to sleep. She lifted her arm out from under the duvet and looked at the tattoo. The redness and swelling was receding; the blue of the Morpho deepening.

What would Anna have said if she had seen her daughter's tattoo?

Rose thought of the day she had first seen it. It was a tiny butterfly, on the top of her arm, just an outline really, hardly any colour at all. Rose had pointed at it in amazement. It was when Brendan and Joshua were living with them. They'd gone to a football match, and Rose and her mum were getting ready to go out and meet them afterwards. She'd charged into the bathroom while her mum was drying herself. She'd stared at it in wonder. *Oh, this! A moment of madness*, her mum had said jokily, hugging her gingerly.

Rose remembered her mum's hugs, how they had smelled of perfume and hair shampoo and celery and basil and furniture polish and a hundred other scents that clung to her and lived in Rose's memory.

Now Rose was completely alone in the world. She had distant friends and she had Josh but really, when it mattered, she was on her own. Her mother, Katherine Smith, was gone.

She thought of *Smith*, the name her mother had chosen. When Rose had first come to live with her grandmother, she had suggested that Rose change her name back to Christie but Rose hadn't wanted to. *Smith!* Anna had sneered, *what a pointless name. She might as well have called herself Katherine X!* But Rose liked Smith. It was important to her that she kept it.

Those were the days when she tried to distance herself from Anna. She didn't allow herself to think of her as her 'gran'. She was a woman who Rose had to live with. 'Grandmother' implied a familial relationship but she had no relationship with this stiff distant woman. She called her Anna and she thought of her as Anna.

This *Anna* had little to do with Rose and her real *mother*.

She pushed her face into the pillow and tried to picture her mother but it was only a fleeting image. She had a pile of photographs she could look at and often did but when she *thought* about her mother she remembered her mum *doing* things; reading, talking, cooking, driving. The everyday things that happened regularly like cleaning her glasses, using a special spray and cloth to get them just right. And it wasn't just one pair of glasses. She had glasses to go out in, to drive with; she had glasses that she used to wear while working on the computer. She even had a pair of special half-moon glasses for when she was making notes on her work files. Rose watched her reading and writing pages of notes and then signing her name at the bottom, *Katherine Smith*. The K was huge and had a curlicue at the bottom. Rose had tried to copy it but couldn't. She had pages of an exercise book full of ornate Ks and Rs but none of them came close to her mum's handwriting.

When her mother went missing Rose had spent time collecting those pairs of glasses together. She lined them up on her mum's desk. Some of the cases were dented and scuffed. When Rose and Joshua had been taken into foster care she'd left them there for her mother when she returned. But she never had and Rose wasn't quite sure what had happened to them. Years later Anna had told her that she'd employed a firm to clear the house for her. Most of the stuff there was sold but Anna had collected all of Rose's things and brought them home along with family photographs and some possessions of her mother's. Joshua and Brendan's things had been sent to Newcastle.

There had been no glasses.

Rose let her eyes close. There were no tears, just a hollow feeling in her chest. The police had tried to explain. Her mum and Brendan Johnson, both police officers, had been transferred to a unit that worked on old cases. This was where they had met each other. The police inspector who had spoken to her said that in all probability her mother and Brendan Johnson had been killed for their part in one of these investigations. Months after they had gone missing he had visited her. His words had been kind but firm. *I wish I could tell you something different but it is my conviction that Katherine Smith along with Brendan Johnson were both targeted by career criminals. It was a professional job and I doubt very much that any trace of them will ever be found.*

She thought of Emma Burke. In death Emma would leave traces. The investigation would pore over Emma's body, her clothes, the path, the rose garden. They would look for clues; fibres, skin, hair, blood, saliva. Her killer's body would betray him, would tell the police what they wanted to know and they would solve the murder.

But they would never solve her mother's . . .

She shook her head. She would never say or even think the word.

But it sat there in her heart, a splinter that wouldn't budge, that burrowed deeper and gave her a thin sharp pain. *Murder.*

TEN

There was a knock on her door. Rose opened her eyes. Her room was dark because the curtains were drawn. Grey light showed at the edges. She turned to her bedside clock and saw that it was 8.07. She'd slept for almost eight hours.

The knock sounded again. Then the door opened a crack.

'Rose?' her grandmother said.

Rose turned away from the door and stared into the corner of her room.

'Are you awake, Rose?'

Rose made a sound in her throat. She did not turn round to look at Anna. She felt the door open wider and imagined that Anna had stepped into her room. Just inside the door. Anna never came any further into her bedroom while she was in there.

'Rose, some unpleasant things were said last night and I wanted to apologise. I understand that none of what happened was your fault and . . .'

Anna continued to talk but Rose wasn't really listening. Anna always wanted *to apologise* after a row. It was an action she took, a form of words. It was polite and placed Anna back on the right side of the argument but she had never once used the words *I'm sorry*.

'. . . So you'll keep in mind my offer to transfer you to the school in Hampstead Heath but I understand if you wish to stay where you are for the time being.'

The door closed and Rose waited until the outside door to her study closed and then she sat up. That was it. When she went downstairs later Anna would act as though nothing had happened.

But things had been said that couldn't be erased.

She lay there for what seemed like a long time. Eventually she got up and showered. Afterwards she went to her wardrobe and took out some clean black jeans and a white shirt. She pulled out her DMs and looked for some socks. When she was dressed she looked at herself in the mirror. She saw a pale girl with chin-length hair. Her eyes were big and dark and made her look younger than her years. She pulled her hair back and held it behind her ears. She still looked young, not a girl of seventeen.

Her shirt was loose and her jeans were skinny, her boots making her feet look huge. She glanced at her wardrobe. She had a line of hangers with black jeans or trousers and various black or white tops. Anna didn't like the way she dressed but she didn't care. At Mary Linton the talk was always about what you wore, what you looked like, who looked the best, whose clothes were the most expensive. Rose had felt completely at sea among the girls there, never knowing the right way to look. As soon as she got home she got rid of all the colours: the stupid skirts, tunics, leggings, T-shirts, dresses. She took them all to the local charity shop and bought herself some monochrome. She, whose very name suggested a variety of soft pinks, preferred herself in black and white.

In the evening Joshua came. She got a text from him to say that he was in the lane at the back of the gardens. Anna was out visiting a friend so she went down and opened the gate. He gave her a hug.

'Poor Rosie!' he said.

She took him into the studio. Anna wasn't due back until after eleven so she was relaxed. Josh sat on the sofa and she pulled over the big cushion and sat on the floor. The electric heater had been plugged in for a couple of hours so the studio was warm. She'd already told Josh about the events of the previous night in an email.

'If I'd got there earlier . . .' she said. 'If I'd been *with* Emma.'

'Might not have made any difference,' he said. '*You* might have been hurt.'

'The police think I had something to do with it!' she said.

'You're kidding!'

She described the interview she had had and how the detective kept pressing her to answer in a certain way.

'Do they want to see you again?'

She shrugged.

'The one thing I didn't tell them about was this feeling I had when I was in the rose garden. It was as though someone was there. I looked round but couldn't see anyone but I had this certainty that there was someone.'

'A *feeling?* What kind of feeling was it?' Joshua said, looking at her with interest.

'I don't know. I can't say.' Rose was cross with herself for not being able to be more specific.

'Could someone have been hiding?'

'I don't know the place well enough. I was in there for two, three minutes, five at the very most. I was focused on Emma.'

She stopped speaking because the memory was making her feel tearful. Joshua must have noticed because he put his hand out and grabbed hers.

'I'm sorry about our trip across the Millennium Bridge,' she said, pulling herself together, and trying to change the subject.

'No problem. We can go another day. Are you going to school tomorrow?'

'Not for a few days. I can't really face people. First Ricky Harris, now this. It's as if I've got some kind of curse . . .'

Joshua looked thoughtful. After a moment he spoke.

'Do you believe in any of that stuff? Supernatural phenomena?'

'No,' she shook her head. 'Do you?'

'Not sure.'

She felt odd for a moment, as if there was more that Joshua wanted to say. Instead he was fiddling with the beads round his neck. She changed the subject.

'Let's go and see the bridge on Wednesday.'

'OK. Come round to the flat and have lunch and then we'll go. I'll tell you all about different grades of suspension bridges. It'll be massively interesting.'

'As long as I can tell you about T. S. Eliot's poetry. There's a bit in one where he walks across London Bridge.'

Joshua put his hands up. 'That's an unfair swap.'

'OK. I'll tell you about a novel I'm studying and you tell me about the bridges.'

'OK. A *novel* I don't mind. Wednesday. My flat at midday.'

He left soon after, squeezing her hand as he went out of the gate. She watched him walk down the lane as he did a backwards wave. She stood there until he turned a corner and then went back into the garden feeling brighter, happier.

On Monday she waited for a call from the police to go in and see them again but none came. Just after lunch she opened the front door to find Henry Thompson standing there in his uniform, his cycling helmet in his hand, his bike leaning against the edge of the porch. Rose looked down to see the bike clips on his trousers.

Her grandmother came out into the hall. Henry spoke formally.

'Officer Henry Thompson, Mrs Christie. I've come with some information for you and your granddaughter about the events of Saturday evening.'

Her grandmother ushered him into the house and insisted that he come into the drawing room. Rose followed him. He spoke in a low voice to her as he walked.

'Rose, I wish I'd been at work on Saturday night but as you know I was off-duty. When I got a call from the detectives yesterday I couldn't believe it. I did, of course, tell them I'd seen you just before . . .'

'Take a seat,' her grandmother said.

He sat in one of her high-winged chairs looking a little awkward. He put his bike helmet on the carpet, then lifted it up again. He had a bottle of water in his hand and drank from it.

'Would you like me to get a glass for that?' her grandmother said, frowning at him. 'Or some tea? Green tea? Earl Grey?'

'No, thank you. I'll get straight to the point.'

Her grandmother sat down and Rose perched on the edge of the sofa. She picked up a satin cushion that had appliqué flowers. Her fingers played with the petals while Henry spoke.

'I'm here to apologise to you and Rose for the vigorous way in which she was interviewed on Saturday night. We are very sorry for any upset that it might have caused. A murder investigation is a top priority and sometimes people are treated insensitively. Rose must have been shocked and upset, particularly after what she'd been through a few days before. It was not our intention to suggest that Rose was responsible. We are merely trying to find out as much as we can as quickly as we can.'

'It seemed to me that you assumed that Rose was guilty,' her grandmother said.

Henry shook his head but she went on.

'The whole unpleasant affair is in the hands of my solicitor.'

'Mrs Christie. You are entitled to lodge a complaint but I would ask you to think about one thing. Your grand-daughter here was upset and possibly traumatised – but she is now here with you. There is a family on the Chalk Farm Estate whose daughter will never come home to them again.'

He stood up.

Her grandmother nodded stiffly at him and Rose looked at him with admiration. There weren't many people who could silence Anna. She got up and followed him out of the room.

When Henry left she stepped out of the house behind him and suddenly felt awkward. She remembered him asking her to go to a club he ran for teenagers. She couldn't remember the name of it but she hoped he wouldn't ask her again.

'What happened to Emma?' she said, getting to the point. 'You have to tell me. What have the police found out? What's been going on?'

'Confidential,' he said, looking away from her, strapping on his helmet, taking his time with the fastening.

'Please. I was there. I'm trying to make some sense of it.'

He looked at her for a few moments and then lifted his bike away from the wall.

'Walk along with me,' he said. 'Whatever I say to you is between us. Agreed?'

''Course,' she said, and got into step with him as he walked along the pavement, leading his bike by the handlebars.

'The detectives are looking through the CCTV footage.'

The mention of CCTV cameras made Rose feel uncomfortable as she remembered Skeggsie hacking into them the previous week.

'There are three cameras in the cemetery; one at the gatehouse, one in the centre and one at a small tradesmen's entrance on the east side. The CCTV camera at the entrance showed Emma Burke going past just after 5.40.'

Rose's jaw tightened. Twenty to six. That was ten minutes earlier than they said they'd meet. Why had Emma gone into the cemetery early?

'At six Lewis Proctor went in. At six minutes past you went in. At 6.15 Lewis Proctor ran out. There are cameras along Cuttings Lane but they show no movement from 5.40 when Emma Burke went into the cemetery until after the police arrive.'

'Cuttings Lane?'

'It's a footpath that goes between the cemetery and the railway line. It leads to the footbridge into the Chalk Farm Estate.'

Rose didn't know it.

'There have been robberies along Cuttings Lane so CCTV has been installed. There's also a camera on the footbridge which oddly showed a person running across it at 6.20.'

'Why oddly?'

'Because there was no sign of that person along Cuttings Lane. My guess is that they came out of the cemetery. The perimeter is huge and is mostly hedges and fencing with a little brickwork in places. It's entirely possible that someone could enter and exit some other way than either gate. We know that some young people trespass in the cemetery. It doesn't mean that the person on the footbridge has anything to do with the murder but we still have to look into it,' he said.

They were at the corner of the main road.

'Do you think the same person who killed Emma also killed Ricky?'

'We don't know.'

'What about Lewis Proctor? What does he say?'

'He's not been home since this happened.'

'You think it was him?' Rose said, her voice low.

'We don't know. We're still looking for the weapon. It could have been thrown anywhere in the cemetery or kept by the killer.'

They were standing on the corner. Neither of them spoke. Eventually Henry broke the quiet.

'About the other night? When I mentioned the Sundown Club?'

Rose stiffened.

'I probably didn't describe it very well. We meet once a week, on a Wednesday night. There's music and table football. And sometimes we have speakers.'

Rose looked at Henry in consternation. Did she really seem like the sort of girl who would want to hang around with a load of misfit teenagers playing table games?

'I know that this isn't a very good time. What with all this stuff going on. I just wanted you to keep it in mind. Some of the kids who come say that it's a cool place to be . . .'

'Henry,' she said, interrupting him.

'I could do with some help, you see. Someone to help me run it, decide on activities and so on. I think you would be great.'

'Henry, stop . . .'

'Yes?'

When would adults realise that as soon as they pronounced something as *cool* it ceased to be so?

'I will never want to go to your club. It will *never* be the right time.'

He was quiet for a minute, his eyes looking further up the road.

'Point taken,' he said. 'Thanks for being straight about it.'

She'd hurt his feelings. Henry was all grown up, at least he had a proper grown-up job, but underneath the uniform and the bicycle clips he seemed young. He got on to his bike and pushed himself off from the pavement with a foot. She wanted to be able to say something nice to him but he rode off without another word. She felt guilty. She watched him join the traffic on the High Street, then she walked back up the road towards her grandmother's house.

The police were still looking for the knife.

She imagined a line of policemen walking across the cemetery, stepping gingerly across graves, gently side-stepping headstones, walking round mausoleums. She pictured a row of faces, stern, concentrated. Only the stone angels' faces would remain unperturbed, peaceful, their eyes staring blindly around. Silent witnesses to what had happened.

ELEVEN

Rose knocked on the door of the Camden Flat. She glanced towards Lettuce and Stuff and saw that it was busy, the queue almost to the street door. She felt hungry and wondered what Josh had for them to eat. Footsteps sounded from inside the flat and she waited impatiently for Josh to open the door. Lunch and a walk across the Millennium Bridge. She'd looked forward to it. It suggested a kind of normality. An afternoon out with her stepbrother. It was a million miles away from Parkway East Station and St Michael's Cemetery.

The sound of the bolts being pulled back interrupted her thoughts. She started to smile as the door opened but frowned instead. It was Skeggsie.

'Yes?' he said.

'Josh told me to come round,' she said, giving a momentary fake smile.

'He's not here. He had to go out.'

'Where?'

'I don't know.'

'Didn't he say anything?'

Skeggsie shook his head. Rose noticed then that he was holding the door in front of his body as if to shield himself. She sighed and looked round.

'Can I come in and wait?'

Skeggsie seemed to think about it for a moment.

'I suppose so.'

He held the door back and she walked in and went up the stairs. She heard him lock the door and rolled her eyes. She stood at the top of the stairs as her mobile beeped. It was a text from Joshua. **A last-minute tutorial came up. Be back in 15 mins or so. Sorry.**

Skeggsie got to the top of the stairs. He was a little breathless.

'He sent me a text. He'll be here soon,' she said.

Skeggsie blew through his teeth.

'You want a drink?' he said. 'A tea or coffee?'

'OK.'

'It's all in the kitchen. Help yourself,' he said, hooking his thumb towards the kitchen and walking off back into his room.

Rose stood in the hallway for a moment. Her foot tapped on the floor. Would it have killed him to make her a drink? She walked towards the sitting room. She sat down on the sofa and picked up the remote from the top of a pile of books on the coffee table. She clicked it on and watched a programme for a while. Then she turned it off. There was music playing, a band she liked. It was coming from Skeggsie's room. She got up and walked aimlessly into the hallway. She had a peek in Joshua's bedroom and saw the duvet half on, half off the bed. There were clothes strewn around and a plate on the bedside table with a piece of toast on it. He had obviously got up and left in a rush. She glanced into Joshua's study and saw his chair turned away from the computer. She walked over and looked at the desk. There were pens and Post-its, paper clips and highlighters. She sat down in his chair and immediately saw a strip of photographs attached to his console.

It was Brendan and Josh in a photo booth. Josh was younger than she'd ever known him, perhaps nine or ten and Brendan had more hair than she remembered. His face was thinner too.

'What you doing in here?'

She swivelled round.

'Waiting for Josh.'

'I don't think he'd like it if you were in here.'

'Don't be silly. He won't mind.'

'It's his private stuff.'

'I'm his stepsister. He won't mind.'

Skeggsie huffed when she said *stepsister*. She was immediately irked.

'What?' she said.

But Skeggsie had turned and walked out of the room. She pushed the chair back and followed him.

'What?' she called after him.

He went into his room and closed the door. Now she was angry. What was wrong with him? She pushed open the door and stepped inside. Loud music was playing but Skeggsie turned it off and looked round at her.

'Have you got a problem with me?' she said.

'No,' he said, avoiding eye contact.

'You have. Something is bothering you about me. What is it? Have I offended you?'

He turned back to his computer and she suddenly thought of something.

'Is it that CCTV photograph you got hold of? Did Josh tell you how angry I was? You had no right at all to get a picture of me. I never asked you to. In any case it's illegal. I could report you to the police. Apart from all that, it's downright intrusive to poke your nose into someone's life just because you can't pull yourself away from your computer . . .'

'It's not the photo,' Skeggsie said.

'You can't just go grabbing pictures of people on the street or railway platform, whatever . . .'

'That's not it. It's not the photo.'

She stopped.

'But there is something about me that offends you?'

'I'm worried about Josh.'

'In what way?'

'I don't have to explain myself to you. You lost touch with him for years and now you're suddenly around. You say you're his stepsister but that's not true. What do you want from him?'

'What's it got to do with you?'

'He's my friend. I look out for him.'

'I am his stepsister.'

'I don't think so. Your mum and his dad were never married.'

She didn't answer. That was true but it didn't make a jot of difference.

'And you never contacted him for years and now you're around here every day . . .'

'I'm not around every day . . .'

'You're emailing, texting. You want to push yourself into Josh's life suddenly. Where were you all those years when he was in Newcastle?'

She was aghast. This complete stranger was talking to her as if he had some right to judge her, as if he had the *right* to chastise her.

'What's it to you?' she said, her voice raised. 'Who are you? Some kid who Josh saved from being bullied. You couldn't look after yourself so he had to do it for you!'

Skeggsie's face hardened.

She'd said too much. She'd gone too far. *Rose, Rose,* she thought, *think before you speak.* Joshua had told her these things in confidence and now she'd blurted them out. In any case she knew about being unhappy at school. Those days in Mary Linton, when Rachel Bliss had been her best friend, were some of the most miserable days she'd known since the disappearance of her mother and Brendan. How could she use Skeggsie's school experiences as a weapon in an argument?

'Get out of my room,' Skeggsie said, turning away from her.

'Look, I'm sorry. I shouldn't have said that but you've been funny with me from the first time you set eyes on me.'

'Can you leave my room, please?'

Rose slumped. She made a half-turn as if to go but then walked back in and pulled up the spare chair and sat down beside Skeggsie.

'I am really sorry. Josh never said that to me. Those were my words and I don't really think that about you. I just think you're really irritating and rude and you've obviously taken a dislike to me and that's your choice and I don't give a toss but . . .'

'Is this meant to be an apology?' Skeggsie said.

There was a glint of something in his eye. A hint of a smile at the corner of his lips. Whether it was genuine pleasure or some sarcastic ploy Rose wasn't sure. She stared at him for a second.

'I suppose it was pretty clever to break into the Network Rail site and steal an image.'

'More than one image.'

'*Two* images.'

'And the cemetery,' Skeggsie said.

She frowned. *The cemetery? Did he not know when to stop?*

'Is there anything else you don't like about me?' Rose said, moving back to the main subject. 'We might as well get it out of the way now.'

'I don't dislike you. I don't know you,' he said. 'It's just that I don't want to see Josh get hurt. When I first met him at school he was suffering badly. His dad gone. You gone. He talked about it a lot. He helped me, yeah, that's true. I ended up with a lot less bruises because of him but I helped him as well.'

There was a loud knocking from downstairs.

'Josh,' Rose said.

'I'll get it.'

Skeggsie got up and walked out of the room. Rose was unsure of how they had left it. She wondered if he would tell Joshua the unkind thing she had said. She stood up to go and then noticed something odd in the corner of Skeggsie's room. It was a giant glass bottle and it was full of asthma inhalers. Blue and purple and red L-shaped plastic inhalers that had been pushed through the neck of the bottle and dropped into a higgledy-piggledy mess at the bottom.

'Hi, Rose.'

She heard Josh's voice from the top of the stairs.

'Hi,' she called.

He came into Skeggsie's room and found her looking at the glass bottle.

'Skeggie's installation. It's a work of art. We have a flat full of those inhalers. Sorry I'm late.'

Skeggsie was at the door.

'What you two been up to? Getting to know each other?'

'Yeah,' Rose said. 'I think we know each other a bit better now.'

'Um . . .' Skeggsie said.

'I picked up some salad and bread and cold chicken. Shall we eat? How about you, Skeggsie?'

'I could eat something,' he said.

'Rose?'

'I'm hungry.'

'Let's eat. The three of us,' Josh said.

After lunch Rose said, 'I'd like to see the CCTV photographs.'

Joshua frowned. 'I thought . . .'

'From the cemetery,' Rose said, focusing on Skeggsie. 'Can you bring them in here?'

'They're better on the screen.'

'How come?'

'You can enlarge them. You can see more.'

Rose let Skeggsie go first and followed him into his room again, glancing sideways at the bottle of asthma inhalers in the corner. Skeggsie sat down and Joshua pulled out the other chair for Rose. Skeggsie did some fiddling with his keyboard and mouse as one application opened on top of another on his screen. His eyes were glued to it and a second later there was a picture of the entrance of St Michael's Cemetery. The brick building and wrought-iron posts were visible. She saw her profile going through the gate. The face was hazy but she knew it was her. Skeggsie clicked and a couple of other people went through after her.

'Did you get the boy going in earlier?' she said, thinking of Lewis Proctor.

Skeggsie shook his head.

'This system was more difficult to get into and move around on. It was a kind of smash and grab. Get into the Mosaic, get what I could, then scarper.'

'Mosaic?'

'It's how these CCTV systems are set up. Hundreds of cameras everywhere. The whole system makes up a mosaic of images. You get in, find the cameras you want, steal what you can and get out. You have to be careful in case they catch you. The cemetery security is run by a private company and their firewalls are more sophisticated.'

'Than the railway?' Rose said, surprised.

'Yes, much tighter. I got in and out for a second before it closed me down. I couldn't hang around. So I kept going back in every couple of hours and I got various images from the midpoint camera. They're all from the time period after the crime. I just copied what I could and scooted out of there.'

Rose had a picture in her head of Skeggsie actually breaking in somewhere and stealing photographs and running away as quickly as he could. Instead he had been sitting at his computer stealing things with the tips of his fingers.

The photographs came up on his computer. They were low shots as if the midpoint camera was perched on one of the mausoleums. There were a number of them.

'They span a period of fifteen, twenty minutes, after the attack.'

It was still light and the shapes of people could be clearly seen. She flicked through them but just saw blurry faces. The one or two faces that were clear looked pale and sad. People were dressed in muted colours and in the earlier ones they looked preoccupied, but in the later ones they had puzzled expressions and were looking into the distance. They must have been staring at Rose running towards the hearse, shouting out, distressed. It was normal for the cemetery to be a place of emotion but the dramatic scene that Rose had provided five days before was unusual.

'What about Cuttings Lane? It runs between the cemetery and the railway.'

Skeggsie shook his head. 'Tried that. It's part of some police and local authority public safety initiative and is run by the police authority. Can't get into that. No way.'

'And the camera on the bridge?'

'What bridge?'

'The footbridge that leads to Chalk Farm Estate.'

'I didn't know about that.'

'Go on Google Maps and see.'

Skeggsie tapped furiously. A map came up and Rose pointed to the footbridge.

'That'll be under Network Rail.'

'A policeman I know said someone was running across it about 6.20.'

Skeggsie looked as though he was thinking hard.

'Five days ago. I *should* be able to access Network Rail's archives but it might take me a while. You're going out, aren't you? I should have it by the time you get back.'

'We'll be back about five,' Joshua said.

'I should have some stuff by then.'

Rose picked up her coat. She stood still, hesitating as though she had something to say. What had just happened? Had she just asked Skeggsie to access CCTV footage for her? When she'd been so angry about it a few days earlier? Did she really want this?

Skeggsie looked round at her. He used his index finger to push his glasses up on his nose. She noticed then that the cuffs of his shirt were buttoned up just like his collar.

'All right?' he said.

She nodded.

'Let's make a move,' Joshua said.

She followed him downstairs and stood while he unbolted the door. Once outside, amid the people on the pavement of Camden High Street, she paused to put her coat on.

'Listen,' Joshua said, leaning towards the front door.

She frowned, then heard the sound of the bolts being shot. Skeggsie had locked the door.

Joshua gave a half-shrug and they walked off to the station.

TWELVE

Rose and Josh were standing at the middle point of the Millennium Bridge. Josh was talking about the bridge.

'Built for the millennium celebrations. Designed by Sir Norman Foster, famous architect. Trouble was it had to be closed as soon as it was opened. It wobbled. Caused a scandal in the engineering world.'

On the north side of the River Thames was the dome of St Paul's. Its curve lay soft against the scudding clouds.

'That was designed by Sir Christopher Wren. It was built between 1675 and 1710 after its predecessor was destroyed in the Great Fire of London,' Joshua said. 'And the Tate Modern Art Gallery.'

Rose looked to the south side of the Thames. There was a giant oblong brick structure with a chimney thrusting up, piercing the sky. It looked ugly and yet solid, powerful.

'Originally built as a power station between 1947 and 1963. It was designed by Sir Giles Gilbert Scott. In 1997 it was taken over by the Tate and redesigned by Swiss architects. There was a kind of competition . . . Er . . . Lecture over,' he said, looking sheepish.

They both stared at the river towards the Houses of Parliament and the London Eye. The water below was mud-coloured and Rose's eye stayed with a tourist boat as it went under the bridge and disappeared from sight. She hugged herself, her arms feeling awkward without a bag. Joshua had told her to leave it at the flat so that she didn't have to lug it around with her.

'I wonder if Skeggsie has got hold of any pictures,' Rose said, going back to what they'd been doing hours before in the flat in Camden.

'I thought you weren't interested! You nearly bit my head off the other day when I told you about it.'

'I know but this is different. I liked Emma. Well, a little bit. I mean I think I could have liked her a bit more.'

'That's something coming from you!'

'How do you mean?'

'You don't make friends easily, do you?'

He gave her a sideways look and she felt herself on the edge of a blush. She remembered something that Emma Burke had said to her. *You should lighten up. People might get to like you.* She winced at the thought of Emma, who was gone. Not just for a while but for ever. She hadn't been close to her, hadn't known her at all, but now she would never have the chance to.

Did she care if people liked her? She thought of the awkwardness with Skeggsie. That had been his fault. He had been the rude, offish one. But was that what people at school thought of her? In Mary Linton? That she was offish and rude? She had never exactly been overwhelmed with friends. There was Rachel, of course, but she didn't want to think about her. *Joshua* had been her best friend for three years. Now she hoped he would be again. She remembered then something that Skeggsie had said.

'Hey!' she said. 'Skeggsie said that you and I are not really stepbrother and sister!'

'Legally speaking, we're not,' Joshua said.

'But I always think of us as that. Not *brother and sister.* I didn't meet you until I was nine. But I do think of you as my stepbrother.'

'Maybe it would be *common-law stepbrother.*'

'That's a mouthful.'

'But most likely the best description.'

She frowned. It wasn't the answer she had wanted. She'd wanted him to say, *I think of you as my stepsister.*

'But we are related.'

'No, we're not. Not by blood and not by law.'

'So what are we then?'

'Maybe we're just a different *kind* of family.'

'But a family. We are a *family* of sorts.'

'I guess so.'

His answer almost satisfied Rose. To be part of Joshua's family was important to her. She wished he sounded more convinced of it.

'OK, if we are a *family* then there's something I do have to talk to you about,' he said, pursing his lips.

She knew what was coming and she felt instantly on edge. He began to walk along the bridge towards Tate Modern and she followed a little behind. When he got to the other side he stopped and waited for her.

'You know my website OLDMURDERS.COM?'

She nodded. She'd known what this was going to be about.

'I got an email from a woman who worked in the Tuscan Moon. She was there on the night Dad and Kathy had that last meal. She was the waitress. I got it a couple of days ago and didn't know whether to tell you or not.'

'She saw Mum and Brendan?'

'Yes.'

'Why has she got in touch with you? Why didn't she come forward at the time? Did she see something? What did she . . .'

Joshua put his hand up to stop Rose talking.

'She's Russian. She lives near Moscow. She worked in London for a couple of years in her early twenties and then went back home. She says she was researching her London stuff, you know, looking for old friends, places she'd been to and people she'd met and she put *Tuscan*

Moon into Google and came across my website. She read my stuff and remembered that night five years ago.'

Rose didn't say anything. Her face was screwed up, trying to work out how to respond to this. She knew about Joshua's drive to find out what had happened. He'd explained it in his emails and she'd seen the websites herself. She'd also seen how committed he was to it. It wasn't just some project that he was following, some puzzle to be worked out. This was his dad and he wanted to find him.

Why didn't she feel the same? Why wasn't she searching for her mum in the same way?

'Say something,' Joshua said.

'I just think you're going to end up getting hurt again. Haven't we both been hurt enough?'

A great lump had formed in her throat. Why wasn't she bustling about, trying to get to the bottom of it? Why had she accepted the police's explanation that their parents had *almost certainly* been the targets of some underworld gang, some assassination plot. When the the officer had explained this to her, sitting on the sofa in Anna's drawing room, she had nodded and taken in every detail as solid, true facts. She, who was only twelve years old, had drunk in his words and quenched a thirst that had been there since the night her mum and Brendan had gone for a meal in the Tuscan Moon and never returned. Joshua, fourteen years old, sitting in his uncle's front room in

Newcastle, had heard the same story and hadn't been nearly as accepting.

'This woman was *there*, Rose. She saw them after we did.'

'I don't think this is anything to do with me,' Rose said. 'I know you have to go on searching but I think that the police were right when they said . . .'

'They didn't have one bit of evidence . . .'

'Mum and Brendan were working on old criminal cases. They could have uncovered something dangerous. That theory made sense.'

'But that was it. It was just a theory! Why didn't the police follow it up? Why did they drop it? They knew which cold cases Dad and Kathy were working on. They knew all the individuals. Why didn't they track down every lead? They knew everything. Yet they weren't able to show us one bit of solid evidence.'

Rose stared at Joshua. He was looking out at the river. He had become angry. His neck was tense, the veins standing out. His shoulders were square. His head was full of websites and facts and hypotheses. It was as if she wasn't there. She reached out a hand to touch the top of his arm.

'It's only going to upset us,' she said, her voice croaking, her eyes misting.

Joshua looked back at her.

'Oh, Rosie,' he said.

He put his arms around her and pulled her close. His hand patted her back and she hugged him tentatively. *He* was her family now. She didn't want him digging into the past but she knew he wouldn't be happy until he had exhausted the search.

She let go of him and wiped her eyes with the heel of her hand.

'Forward the email to me,' she said, 'and I'll read it. I'll tell you what I think. I'll be honest, though.'

'I wouldn't expect you to be anything else,' he said, smiling.

They went back to the flat. They both stood on the street while Skeggsie came down the stairs and unbolted the door. They followed him upstairs and she headed for the living room to retrieve the bag that she had left there earlier. Then she went into Skeggsie's room to see if he'd managed to get any CCTV images from the footbridge at the end of Cuttings Lane. Joshua was standing in front of the biggest screen. Skeggsie looked round when Rose entered and gave a curt nod.

'Any luck?' she said.

'Skeggsie's got some images.'

Skeggsie looked pleased with himself. He'd most probably been sitting all afternoon using his computer to tunnel away into the Network Rail CCTV footage. Why was he doing it? What was in it for him? Was he just helping her out or just taking pleasure using his own programs to unlock a puzzle. What was it with boys? Why did they have to take things apart to try and understand them? She remembered then the bits of bikes that Joshua kept in his room. He dismantled them until they were just oily joints.

'Look,' Skeggsie said.

On the monitor was a photo.

'The CCTV camera is high up here at the edge of the footbridge. So here we see a person on the far side of the bridge, coming from the cemetery end.'

It was as if Rose was on the first floor of a building looking down. The person in the photo seemed very small, a long way away. It was twilight. There was just enough light to make out the footbridge and the rails beyond. It was wider than the station footbridge and the sides were higher, tightly packed railings with sharp, spear-like ends.

'It is possible to zoom in.'

The image became bigger, cutting out the surrounds and just showing the person.

'Here's the next one,' Skeggsie said.

The person was moving towards the camera, their feet taking giant strides, or perhaps they were running. Now she could see a bit more clearly. The figure was in black and had a hood on. He or she had long thin black legs.

'And here . . .'

The third image came up. This was the closest the figure would get to the camera. The clothes were clear and it might have been possible to get a glimpse of the person's face, albeit a blurry one. It might have shown whether they were male or female, old or young. But whoever it was had turned their head to the side away from the camera.

'Clever. This guy knows that the camera will pick the picture up,' Skeggsie said.

The next picture came up and showed the footbridge empty.

'He's gone.'

'Go back one,' Rose said.

The previous picture came up: the hooded figure seemingly looking to the right, one hand holding the edge of the hood to cover the profile of the face.

'This guy has clocked the camera and knows how to keep his face hidden.'

'What's that?' Joshua said, pointing to the screen.

'What?'

Joshua picked up a pen and pointed to the arm that was hanging down. Rose leant closer but it was hard to see what Joshua was talking about.

'Hang on,' Skeggsie said.

He tapped on the keys and fiddled with the mouse and the picture enlarged so that only a part of it could be seen on the screen. Now it just looked like blocks of blurred colour.

'When you zoom in a lot you lose the sharpness of it,' Skeggsie said apologetically.

'There,' Joshua said. 'What's that? On the wrist?'

The area Joshua was pointing at was the right-hand wrist. The sleeve was showing but there was something on the wrist, above the top of the hand.

'The guy's got gloves on,' Skeggsie said.

'But what's that?' Joshua kept on.

He was pointing at a block of colour above the hand. It had a slight sheen to it. The rest of the image was matt but this section looked as though the light had caught it.

'It's metal. The footbridge light is glinting in it.'

'Is it a knife?' Rose said, puzzled at the chunky oblong mass. 'It's an odd shape. Can we see it more clearly?'

Skeggsie turned back to the screen and continued to move up and down the image as if he was searching for clues amid the pixels, but couldn't improve the image any further.

'How do the police ever find criminals from these pictures?' she said, shrugging her shoulders. 'Anyway, I should be going.'

Joshua followed her down the stairs.

'Still OK if I send you the email from the Russian woman?' he said, unbolting the door.

She nodded without looking round and headed out on to the street.

On the bus she thought of the CCTV image. Now that she wasn't looking at the screen she embellished the figure. Dressed in black with a hood up, she pictured the head turning dramatically away from the camera, one hand up to the face, the other hanging down, one step after another. Maybe the hand that was hanging down swung back and forward, the beam of the footbridge lights catching on something metallic.

Not a knife, though. Not the right shape. And it was above the hand, not *in* it.

She suddenly knew what it was.

Bangles. Silver bangles.

The person on the footbridge was *not* male.

She got her phone out and sent a text to Josh.

Ask Skeggsie to magnify the feet of the person on the bridge. What does it show?

She hugged her rucksack and watched people out of the bus window, walking along the pavement, looking tired, on their way home from work. Among them was a boy on skates. He wove through them turning this way and that. His face was bright, happy and he was mouthing the words of a song.

A female, wearing bracelets, twenty or thirty silver bands that moved up and down the arm, that looked solid when together but split apart like single hairs.

A beep sounded and she looked at her phone.

Seems to have light-coloured boots on? Why?

She smiled to herself.

Bee Bee had silver bangles and silver boots. Rose had seen them that day in the cafeteria when Lewis Proctor was showing off, pretending to stab himself in front of Emma. Bee Bee was Lewis's girlfriend. Bee Bee had been *desperate* for Lewis for months, Emma had said.

Desperate enough to kill his ex-girlfriend?

THIRTEEN

The email from Joshua was there when she got home but Rose didn't open it until late at night. She waited until she heard Anna's bedroom door close. The house was quiet and she padded downstairs for a hot drink. She took it back up to her room and got into bed with her laptop. She spent some time going on Facebook and visiting some blogs she liked. She wrote some things on her own blog Morpho about her day out and about on the wobbly bridge that no longer wobbled. She looked at some emails from school; reminders of work that had to be in, social events, the memorial service for Ricky Harris.

Ricky Harris. She'd almost forgotten him. The unhappiness she had felt over Emma's death had overshadowed what happened to Ricky and now it was as if his death had been a story she had read somewhere in a newspaper. The email was short.

The school will hold a non-denominational memorial service for Ricky Harris on Friday morning. All those who would like to pay their respects are welcome. 10 a.m. George Bernard Shaw Studio.

Would there be another next week for Emma Burke?

Her mind went back to the CCTV images that Skeggsie had found. The figure on the bridge, the silver bangles on her arm, the silver boots. Was Rose reading too much into a hazy picture that was almost impossible to fathom? In any case the police had the same pictures and it was up to them to find out what had happened to Emma Burke.

Rose was feeling unsettled when she finally opened Joshua's email. There was a brief message from him. *Rosie, thanks for a good day. Here's the email I mentioned.* Underneath was a long email from a woman called Valeriya Malashenko. Rose read it. It was clearly the second email that had been sent.

Dear Joshua Johnson, thanks for your quick reply. I do remember that night when I was working in the Tuscan Moon five years ago. I should explain first why I did not go to British police in the days after it happened. Firstly I was an illegal. I am from town outside Moscow. There were no jobs so another girl and I were smuggled into Britain by a cousin who had visa to study at Canterbury. We visited him on holiday and did not go home. I spent two years in London. I did many jobs. I worked for cash. Not very much for London peoples but a lot for me. That was my first reason for not going to the British police. The second reason I will say later. I remember the night your people came into the Tuscan Moon. 4th November. There were lots of fireworks going off and I had just screamed at some boys out in the alley behind the restaurant for throwing poppers or bangers I think you call them. Your peoples came in and sat at their usual table. I remember them you see they came into restaurant a lot. They always gave me tip in hand. Five pound note. They did it quietly so that boss could not see (he take tips). This night they seemed unhappy. They did not talk much and I took their plates away with lot of food not eaten. You will wonder why I remember this. It is because of what happened after, the police and the glasses case. Of this I will tell you later. They finished their meal and left. I was out front of shop smoking (alley at the back is dangerous, too dark, too many fireworks). They did not say goodbye which was unusual. They walk away from the shop and then something odd happens. The lady she stopped. She stood still on the pavement and the man he walked on. Then he came back to her and they had some kind of argument. I didn't like to look too much so I dropped my cigarette and went back into restaurant. A minute later I looked out again and saw the man with his hand up and black taxi pulled over. They got in and that was the last I saw of them. The next day the police came to restaurant and I hid upstairs. I am illegal and afraid to be sent back to Moscow.

Rose paused. The email was long. One block of text that seemed to go on and on. She glanced back at the bit that referred directly to her mum and Brendan. They seemed unhappy at their meal. Had they been unhappy when they left the house? She didn't think so. At the time she hadn't thought so but she and Joshua had been involved in a discussion about a programme that Rose liked when Sandy, a girl from down the street, came to sit with them. Sandy was seventeen and babysat regularly. Rose had adored her. She loved her look, her clothes, her squeaky voice, her long nails, her colourful jewellery. Joshua always became a bit strange when she arrived. He usually retreated to his room and played computer games and Rose had Sandy to herself to talk about anything and everything. That particular night was no exception. Rose had been keen for her mum and Brendan to go out so that she and Sandy could sit alone in the living room and talk about books and bands and clothes. There'd been a call from the hallway – *Bye!* Had she even answered that call? Had she just said a half-hearted *Yeah, bye* and continued to be mesmerised by Sandy and her sparkly jeans and her fringe that hung in strips.

Had she even noticed her mum and Brendan leaving?

She looked back to the email.

I work in restaurant for a while but whenever police came I kept out of the way. My boss did not care. I left soon after but I watched the story in newspaper. I felt very guilty about not speaking up because of glasses case. I will tell you about glasses case. When I saw your peoples get into the black taxi I went to clear their table for next customer. I found glasses case on one of the chairs. I picked it up and took it to counter and left it there in case they came back. I forgot about it for a couple of days remember I was worried about British police. When the police stopped coming I found the glasses case and remembered that it had come from their table. It was blue leather case. I opened it and inside were some lady glasses.

Rose held her breath. Her mum's glasses left behind in the restaurant. The blue leather case. She remembered it. It often sat by the front door with some reading glasses in it so that her mum wouldn't forget to take a pair out with her. Her eyes followed the words on the email, her hands gripping the sides of the laptop.

There were other things in glasses case. There was a business card for a hotel and ten British fifty pound notes. I kept the case for many weeks. I hoped they would come back in. I did not want to give it to Boss because he would take the money. The card had the name of a hotel in Twickenham. I remember place because I have friend who lived in Twickenham (my cousin's old girlfriend) The name of hotel was something like Star. I remember this. I have to confess something. I am shamed to say that after three weeks I took the money and got rid of the glasses case. I knew that the man and lady were miss-ing. I took the money and I never felt good about it. This is why I have sent you email. To clear my conscience. I am honest girl but living in London was not always very good. Please ask me any questions you need and I will tell you anything else I can remember. I owe this to your peoples. Valeriya

Rose lay back on her pillow. The laptop slid to the side. Why did they have ten fifty-pound notes in the glasses case? Why were they so unhappy during the meal? What was the row they had on the street outside? Why did they get into a taxi when their own car was parked round the corner?

She closed her eyes. She'd known this email would open up old wounds. And what was the point? They would never find them. Five years without a word. Five years without being able to see or touch or talk to her mum. Five years without smelling her mum's perfume or laughing at her poor jokes.

She lay like that for a long time. Then she sat up and caught sight of the email, still displayed on the screen of her laptop. She shut it down and placed it on the floor beside her bed. The hot drink she had made was still there untouched. She turned the light off and lay in the dark.

Five years of emptiness.

Except for the sightings.

Three times in the first year after the disappearance she thought she saw her mother. At the time she'd been *positive*. She would have sworn to it and almost went to the Head of House to tell her but then stopped at the last minute, afraid that she would say that the sighting was a product of her overactive imagination. As time went by she even began to believe that herself. But in that moment the joy she felt at seeing her mother was tangible; her hair, the shape of her shoulders, the funny way she stood; that joy was *real*.

Had she imagined it?

All three sightings were during her first year at Mary Linton. The first time she'd been standing at the side annexe when the leaving bell was ringing. She watched parents moving out of the school building after dropping their children off for the beginning of term. In among the coats and scarves and boots she glimpsed her mother's profile. Her head was down and she was deep in the middle of the chattering crowd, some people turning back to wave, others rattling car keys, others hugging themselves against the cold. Rose had taken a few shaky steps forward but lost of sight of her and even though she stepped this way and that she couldn't see her. When the crowd melted away there was no one left. Her mother had gone.

The second time was just weeks later when she had woken up in the middle of the night. The other girls in her dorm room had been sound asleep and she'd been restless, unable to settle. She got up and tiptoed to the window, holding her breath in case she woke anyone. It was bitterly cold, with a light dusting of snow across the school car park beneath her dorm. Her eye swept across the emptiness to light on a figure standing in the corner under the trees. With a shock she saw her mother's face. Rose stood perfectly still for a long time, tears blurring her vision. She reached round for a tissue and blew her nose as quietly as she could and when she looked back there was no one there. The car park was empty, wisps of snow ebbing and flowing across the ground.

Then there was the night of her thirteenth birthday, 18 September. She had been back in school for three weeks and hadn't settled well into her second year at Mary Linton. In previous days she'd been unwell, feverish. The Head of House had said she should sleep in the sick bay. She woke very early in the morning. It was dark but she could see the luminous numerals from the clock. 5.12. She lay and watched them for a while and felt her eyelids grow heavy and it was then that she heard what sounded like someone breathing. She made no move because she thought it would be the matron checking up on her but after a few seconds she sensed that this sound, this breathing, was different, lighter, hardly audible. She turned to look and saw, across the room, her mother, standing by the door. She was buttoning her coat. Rose remembered her mother's fingers fiddling with the top button and just as Rose was about to say something, her mother went out of the door and closed it gently behind her. It seemed as though Rose got up and went after her mother but the next thing she remembered was the matron waking her up. Light flooded the room and she looked at the clock to see the faint outline of the time – 8.03.

Three sightings and no more.

Except that sometimes she felt as though she was being watched. She had never told anyone about this but every now and again she would feel as though someone was following her or watching her. Recently, since changing schools and living at Anna's, she'd noticed it more keenly. She'd been walking along the street or dawdling in a shop or having coffee in the Dark Brew and a kind of prickling feeling would start in her shoulders and she'd glance around sure, positive, that someone was watching at her. Waiting in line to enrol at Camden she'd felt it and looked around to see if she could pick someone out of the crowd who was showing an interest in her (she knew, in her heart, when she used the word *someone*, she meant her mother) but the hall was jam-packed with new students and parents, teachers and staff. In the days afterwards she'd walked to and from the station and felt as if someone was looking at her but when she turned around the streets yawned back at her emptily, deserted, the lines of hedges and walls hiding nothing but flowers and shrubs. She'd tried to snap herself out of it but the feeling, the anxiousness stayed with her.

A psychologist would say that these manifestations were a projection of Rose's desires. She wanted to think that she had sighted her mother and she wanted to think that her mother was watching her, keeping an eye on her like some guardian angel. Rose wasn't stupid. But these memories and feelings were all she had left. Joshua had his websites and his plans and she had unreliable sightings and a vague feeling that her mother was watching over her. It was a tenuous thread and she wanted to hold on to it even though the sensible side of her brain told her that it was just grief and loss playing tricks with her.

Now she sat up in bed and turned the light on.

There would be no sleep for a while.

She picked up her laptop and puffed her pillows up behind her. She opened it up and began to read the email from Valeriya Malashenko once again.

FOURTEEN

The George Bernard Shaw Studio was in a new block of the school. At just before ten on Friday Rose found herself outside the main door with a number of other students and staff. A few minutes later the doors opened into the auditorium. People filed in and she followed. It was the first time she had been in the studio since the beginning of term when there had been a welcome session from the principal for all new students.

The seats were tiered and she sat in a row by herself, halfway up. There were about thirty students there, some who she knew, partially filling up the first three rows or so. Dotted in among them were members of staff; her form tutor and others that she recognised.

There was classical music playing and a table had been set up centre stage with vases of flowers and in the middle was a large picture frame showing a photograph of Ricky Harris.

Rose sat back in her seat as far as possible. She wasn't sure why she had come. She certainly had no feelings for

Ricky Harris, not even in a general *it's a shame when people die* way. But Ricky's death was inexorably linked with Emma Burke's. How could it not be? They were boyfriend and girlfriend and she had been near to each of them when they died. When Rose thought of Ricky's death, Emma came into her head and vice versa.

People were shuffling in their seats and whispering to each other. Maggie and Sara appeared at the studio door and headed towards her. These girls from her English group had been looking after her one way or another over the last couple of days. They had made sure that they were with her during breaks and lunch-time and before and after school. It meant that other kids didn't get the chance to quiz her or say things. Sitting between Sara and Maggie meant that she could relax and just ignore the pointing and the looks from curious students.

She'd told them what had happened on Saturday, how Emma had come to see her and how she'd said she would go and meet her at the cemetery. The two girls had been uncharacteristically silent, giving the tiniest nods. They, who never seemed short of conversation, couldn't find much to say about a dead girl.

'Hi,' they both mouthed, coming up to her row.

'Hey,' Sara said in a loud whisper. 'I got this for you.'

She handed over a strawberry lip salve.

'Only I noticed your lips were dry. Probably the stress.'

Rose took the tiny pot and felt suddenly emotional. It was a kind act. Solid in their own friendship for many years, they had enough warmth and generosity left over to look after a loner like Rose. She unscrewed the lid and put her finger into the pink greasy ointment. Then she spread it over her lips and felt them soften.

'Nice flowers,' Sara said.

'Not like Emma Burke's, though. We went to see them yesterday after school. We, like, looked for you but you must have gone home. In any case we didn't know whether you'd want to go back to St Michael's. Not after . . .'

'Flowers?' Rose said.

'Oh my God! You should see them. All along the path in the rose garden. You know where . . .'

Rose knew only too well.

'The police were going to clear them away but Emma's family hit the roof. Now they're just lying there. It's, like, really beautiful.'

'They're taking them away on Saturday night at six. A week after she . . .'

There was a gap in the conversation. Maggie quickly filled it.

'You know you said that Emma Burke had a note from Lewis Proctor asking her to meet him?'

Rose nodded.

'It turns out that Lewis had a note from Emma telling him to meet her! This girl in my Key Skills group is a friend of Bee Bee Marshall? Bee Bee told her! Bee Bee found it in his coat.'

'And,' Maggie continued, 'Lewis Proctor has been arrested. Police found him at his uncle's house in Southend.'

'And this girl says that Bee Bee is going to withdraw the alibi she gave him for when, like, Ricky Harris was killed,' Sara carried on, breathless. 'She says why should she lie for Lewis if he was, like, going to see Emma on the quiet!'

They carried on for a few moments going over the details. Rose listened but didn't respond. She was taken aback. *Lewis also had a note.* Maggie and Sara seemed to sense the fact that she had stopped listening. They began to chat quietly to each other. The murmur of their voices receded as she took in the new information.

Lewis Proctor's alibi was gone. He hadn't been with Bee Bee on the night that Ricky was stabbed. Perhaps he *had* been at the station.

Rose had thought and thought about it over the last couple of days. It kept her mind from going back to the email from the Russian girl and Joshua's attempt to find out what happened to their parents. Lewis Proctor had been Emma's boyfriend over the summer and then she finished with him and went back to Ricky Harris. Ricky and Lewis had been rivals; two bad boys from the same estate. Maybe, when Emma first started seeing Lewis, after finishing her long-term relationship with Ricky, Lewis had been euphoric. He had delighted in getting a girl who he liked and getting one over on his rival. Maybe he strutted around, thrilled with his acquisition of Ricky's old girlfriend. They had been all loved up, Emma had said. It was an odd phrase. *Loved up*. The very words gave Rose a shiver. She, who had never been kissed by a boy, had only an intellectual notion of what it might be like. She'd read books and heard girls from Mary Linton talk about their experiences with boys and she'd smiled in an embarrassed way. She had experienced strong feelings for someone, of course, but that was different. Entirely different and a lifetime ago.

So possibly Lewis Proctor had lorded it over Ricky, had spent the summer telling his mates, showing Emma off. All the while Bee Bee, who had wanted Lewis for months, for years, had been watching from the wings, waiting to see what happened.

Then Emma cooled off and dropped Lewis. Had Lewis felt furious enough to kill Ricky? Or had it been a spur of the moment action? Ricky Harris had been with Rose on the platform of Parkway East. He'd got a phone call from someone. He'd been pleased. *Change of plans, posh bird!* he'd said and gone off. Had Lewis been coming on to the bridge at the same moment? Had these two lads not been able to pass each other without some words being said? Perhaps Lewis had disrespected Ricky in some way, made reference to his girlfriend. Maybe Ricky pulled out his knife, intending to shame Lewis into backing down but Lewis had had enough, his girlfriend going back to Ricky after he had been so sure that she was his? Possibly Lewis had simply taken Ricky's knife from him and in a moment of rage stabbed him in the chest and left him to die.

And Lewis definitely was at the cemetery on the evening when Emma was stabbed. He had got a note asking him to go there. Bee Bee had found it in his pocket. Had *she* followed him to try and catch him meeting Emma? Was that why she was running across the footbridge minutes after Emma had been killed?

Could Bee Bee have *stabbed* Emma?

Some new people had come into the studio. Rose recognised Sherry, Emma's stepsister. Her orangey hair had been pulled back off her face with a black band. She was pale and wearing a black shirt over leggings and boots. Another girl was linking her arm. They both came up the stairs of the auditorium and sat across the aisle from Rose. A couple of Rose's teachers came in and one of the secretaries from the office. The principal burst through the door then with a sheaf of notes in her hand. After her came a male member of staff, his name tag tucked into the pocket of his shirt. Rose recognised him. It was the technician who had stuck up for her that day when Ricky had been nasty. She remembered that Ricky had called the technician gay and had tried to embarrass and insult him.

How odd that he should come to this. How odd that he should feel any need to pay respects to a boy who had been vile to him.

Was he gay? Rose looked him up and down. He was wearing black trousers and a white shirt and tie. He looked like many of the male teachers. They wore so-called *smart* clothes but looked uncomfortable, as if they were wearing a uniform they didn't particularly like. When she'd seen him in the cafe the previous week he'd been wearing a biker's jacket. He looked different out of his work clothes, less stiff, more friendly. But had he looked *gay*? He hadn't looked any different to any other man. Was there a gay look? Some gay people did seem to go out of their way to dress and act in a certain way but most gay people were probably just like everyone else. Trying to look the best they could with what they had been born with.

Why would he come to Ricky Harris's memorial?

Maybe he was a church man, a Christian. Possibly he was here to forgive.

She looked back to the principal, who had started to speak. Her voice was low and respectful. *A young man who had had some challenges in his life. A young man who had strayed. A young man who had started school in a positive way. A young man whose life had been cruelly shortened.*

Rose felt her mobile vibrate and she looked at the screen. She had a text message from Joshua.

Can you meet me at the Dark Brew after class? Say five? It's important.

Normally a message from Joshua would lift her spirits but this time she felt apprehensive. It wasn't just a social meeting. This was something to do with the email from the Russian girl. She sighed as she sent a reply.

See you there.

There was music playing. It was not a band she recognised. No doubt it had been one that Ricky Harris had liked. The mood had lifted a little and the principal had sat down in a chair and looked as though her mind was already elsewhere. Some kids in the front rows were shifting in their seats. It would be over soon.

'You all right?' Maggie said.

She nodded. Maggie and Sara were looking at her with concern. They both had short dark hair and pale faces and looked like sisters. They weren't related, Rose knew that, but perhaps their closeness over the years meant that they had dressed alike and had similar haircuts and styles. They liked the same bands and movies and read book after book about vampires. They seemed to know what each other was thinking and sometimes finished each other's sentences. They were studying the same subjects, probably had the same plans for university.

Rose was grateful to them in a way she couldn't express.

Friendship was a difficult thing. At Mary Linton it had seemed easy but in the end she had been bruised. Really, if she was honest, the only person she wanted to be friends with was Joshua. That was why she would go to the Dark Brew and talk about the email from the Russian girl.

She glanced around the studio as people started to stand up, picking up their bags and walking towards the door. Was anyone from Ricky's family here? How many of the people who were here were actually friends of Ricky's? How many cared about him one way or another? She looked around, across the aisle at Sherry. The girl with her was on her feet but Sherry was still sitting staring at the front. Rose focused on her. Sherry's shoulders were shaking and there were tears coming down her face. It puzzled her but then she remembered that she had come to the memorial not because of Ricky but because of Emma. Perhaps Sherry too couldn't think of Ricky Harris's death without thinking about her stepsister, Emma, and how she was gone.

Sherry looked round unexpectedly and Rose found herself meeting her stony gaze. The girl's face flickered with recognition. Rose gave what she hoped was a sympathetic smile but Sherry stood up and began to walk along her row towards Rose. The girl with her followed.

'You!' she said, loud enough for people down the front to hear. 'You should have been there to stop my sister getting hurt. Where were you? How come you were late?'

'I got held up,' Rose said, looking round, embarrassed.

'Something held you up,' she said derisively. 'My sister came and asked for your help and you couldn't make it! Why was that? Was my sister too common to be seen with?'

'No!' Rose said. 'I did go. I got delayed.'

Sherry's face was right in front of her. Rose found herself getting annoyed. She squared her shoulders at the girl and stared at her. She spoke clearly and firmly.

'I tried to get there. I had no idea anything bad was going to happen!'

In any case, she wanted to say, *your sister went into the cemetery ten minutes before she planned to meet me!*

'Bitch,' Sherry said. 'I told Emma you were just a stuck-up bitch but she had a soft heart. She felt *sorry* for you. And look what's happened to her.'

'Leave her alone,' Maggie said.

Rose felt herself shaking. She couldn't trust herself to speak. She felt Maggie's hand on her arm and looked round to see Sara standing straight behind her. She pulled herself away and walked down the stairs towards the exit. Some of the kids who were dawdling looked at her and whispered between themselves. They all knew her. She was the girl who had been at not one murder but two.

She ignored them but felt the weight of their scrutiny as she left the studio and headed off towards her next class.

FIFTEEN

The Dark Brew was a cafe in Kentish Town that Rose went to a lot. It was in a parade of six shops amid some imposing-looking houses. A bell tinkled as she entered and she saw Joshua already there, sitting at a table with his laptop open. Even though it was just after five and still light, the inside of the cafe was darkish. There were six tables, each with a low light hanging above it. The front windows were small and dimpled, making the place seem like someone's living room.

'Hi,' Rose said, feeling like she should speak in a whisper.

The cafe felt church-like. There was no radio playing and people usually seemed to be reading a book or gazing at a laptop or speaking in whispers. The sombre atmosphere suited Rose's mood.

'You want something?' she said, pointing to the counter.

Joshua shook his head. She bought a hot chocolate and sat down across from him, the light making a small tent around them. Joshua was tapping at the keys and when he looked at her there was a glint of excitement in his eye.

'I got another email from Valeriya Malashenko.'

Rose had thought it would be about the Russian waitress.

'She's remembered the name of the B and B in Twickenham. It's the *Northern Star*. Here, I've got its web page.'

He turned his laptop round so that she could see the screen. There was a photograph of the outside of a building, something like a large house, and then address details and smaller photos of the rooms. She tried to look interested but really she didn't know what to say about it.

'I'm going to go, tomorrow. Skeggsie's coming with me. I'd love it if you came as well.'

'Why is Skeggsie going?' she said.

'He's interested *and* he's got a car.'

'A car?'

'A Mini. He says he'll drive me there. Come with us. Let's see what we can find out.'

She tried to keep a positive expression on her face but it was difficult.

'I don't think I've got time . . .'

Joshua closed the laptop. He looked disappointed.

'Rosie, this is a breakthrough. The first thing in five years. We should follow it up.'

She went to speak but stopped. She was tired. The day had not got any better after the memorial and Sherry Baxter's words had been ringing in her ears all afternoon.

'This is no time to be half-hearted,' he said and pulled his laptop back towards himself, mumbling something and tapping on the keys.

She drank her chocolate even though it was too hot. It was six days since Emma Burke had been stabbed. She'd been thinking about nothing else all afternoon. She'd tried to recreate the evening in her head, her discovery of poor Emma's body, but she hadn't been able to. She realised that she had no memory of what the rose garden looked like. On top of everything else this had upset her. It was as if she'd carelessly wiped it out of her mind, as if she'd deleted the whole sorry mess from her thoughts and didn't care what had happened there. She wished now that she'd revisited the rose garden in the days since.

She remembered what Sherry Baxter had said about her stepsister. *She had a soft heart. She felt* sorry *for you.* The words had hit their mark because Rose knew they were true. Emma had felt sorry for her. And she had asked her for help.

Now she couldn't even picture the rose garden. The station, the walkway where Ricky died was clearly in her mind, she'd been across it half a dozen times since then. But the cemetery was fading, the rose garden a vague image in her head, never the same twice, just the flapping blossoms and in the background the jarring colour of Emma's purple top.

'You're miles away,' Joshua said.

'Sorry.'

'I know you're sceptical about the email but won't you at least give it a chance?'

'You go,' Rose said. 'You can tell me what you find out.'

'Thanks! Thanks very much for your support,' he said, annoyed.

Rose felt grazed by his words. He was so excited about the Russian waitress that he had forgotten about her feelings.

'Support! Do you remember what I've been through the last ten days?'

A couple of people looked over at them. She lowered her voice.

'I'm worn out. Don't accuse me of being half-hearted.'

'This is our *family*.'

'Our family is gone!'

'It might not be. And even if it is I want to find out what happened.'

'Josh, if they were alive we would know.'

'If they were dead there would be some evidence. A trail left by someone.'

'This is grasping at straws. This woman, this Russian person, her memories might be mixed up. She was in a strange country doing a hard job. She didn't speak very good English. She might have an entirely different couple in her head. Not Mum and Brendan at all. Mr and Mrs Frank Bloggs, white, thirty-five to forty, brown hair, bald head; two ordinary-looking people who also used the Tuscan Moon.'

Did she believe this? What about the thoughts she'd had about the glasses case? Hadn't she almost convinced herself that it had been her mum's glasses?

'In any case what can we find out from this B and B? Is it likely that they will have any information? That the same people will work there? It was five years ago. What do you hope to achieve?'

He didn't answer her. His eyes flicked to the side and for a second she thought she saw the glint of a tear.

'I just want to go there. If Dad and Kathy were there, then I want to walk in the front door. I want to go up to reception. I want to *be* where they were.'

He was upset. She remembered Skeggsie's words a few days before: *When I first met him in school he was suffering badly. His dad gone, you gone . . .* It gave her a great gush of emotion in her chest.

'Just don't get your hopes up,' she said, reaching across the table, touching his hand.

'Will you come? It's important.'

'All right, all right, I'll come.'

'Thanks, Rosie.' Josh grinned at her.

'As long as you come and do something with me. Now, tonight.'

'What?'

'I want to go and pay my respects to someone.'

Joshua looked puzzled. Rose stood up and gathered her things together.

'First I have to get hold of some flowers.'

SIXTEEN

Rose stood in front of St Michael's Cemetery holding a bunch of deep pink carnations. The gates were locked. A sign on them said *Closing Time 18.00.*

'Last week it was 6.30,' Rose said. 'I'm sure it was. I read it. And I didn't get here until gone six!'

'It's the autumn,' Joshua said. 'A lot of places graduate their closing times. It's getting darker earlier. Parks do it. Hey, we can come back over the weekend.'

But Rose didn't want to do that. She had the flowers. She wanted to lay them on the exact spot where she'd found Emma. Tomorrow she might feel differently.

'I want to do it now.'

'Short of climbing over the gate . . .' Joshua said, his hands out in a gesture of hopelessness.

'There are other ways in. My policeman friend told me. Round the back. Off the lane that runs between the railway and the cemetery. Come on.'

'You can't . . .'

Rose walked off. She headed back towards the station. She quickened her pace until she saw the sign for *Cuttings Lane*. Above it was another sign, smaller, less obvious: *Public Footpath to Chalk Farm Estate*.

Joshua caught up with her.

'There's a way into the cemetery along this lane . . .'

'You can't just break in!'

She didn't listen. She walked on. The lane was narrow at first but widened out in parts and the lighting was on so it was bright. On one side was high hedging and sections of brick wall which skirted the cemetery. On the other was a tall wire fence which ran along the side of the railway. From behind she heard a rushing sound and looked round to see two boys on bikes heading towards them. They both stood back and let the bikes pass.

A few metres later the hedge looked brown and sparse. Going close up to it she could see something through the foliage. Something white behind the privet.

'Look,' she said.

There was a small gap. It was narrow where the hedge had thinned out. Looking hard she could see something beyond. A white marble headstone. Rose took her rucksack off, placed the flowers inside her jacket and stepped into the gap in the hedge.

'What you doing?' Joshua said.

'I'm going in to lay my flowers.'

It was a tight fit but she was able to push herself through without damaging the blooms and then she pulled her bag behind her. On the other side she found herself standing in a grassy area of graves. The cemetery stretched away from her, rows and rows of headstones. Up the middle was a winding lane where the hearses drove. Over to the left was the walled garden.

'Rosie!' Joshua's loud whisper came through the hedge.

'Come in. We can walk around the edge and get to the rose garden without passing the CCTV camera.'

There was no answer. Just a grumbling sound.

She looked around at the nearby graves. Most of them were old but one was recent. There was no headstone, just a small simple cross with the name *Gerald Rossiter 1970–2012*. The earth in front of it was newly turned and there were wreaths and bunches of flowers in various stages of decay. He must have been buried there in the last few weeks.

'Josh,' she called.

There was a rustling noise and moments later Joshua appeared through the hedge, brushing his clothes and looking disgruntled.

'Come on,' she said. 'We'll be ten minutes, no more. I promise.'

The cemetery was darker than Cuttings Lane. There were round lights on the main pathway and they glowed like tiny moons. The rest of the graveyard was grey or dark blue with only the white of the headstones or statues standing out.

Rose sidestepped the grave in front of her and then headed for the path that went round the periphery of the cemetery. She looked round to see that Joshua was still standing in the same place.

'Are you coming?'

'I'm not that comfortable here . . . Being in the middle of a load of dead people isn't my idea of a good time.'

'Are you religious?' she said.

Did Joshua believe in *God*?

'No. I just think there are unexplained things and I'm not that comfortable walking past places where people's spirits are.'

'You mean ghosts?' she said, incredulous.

'No, not ghosts either. But I think there may be some force that we don't understand . . .'

'Come on. Enough talk,' said Rose impatiently.

Joshua nodded but his expression was one of distaste.

She got to the path and glanced back to see him walking gingerly along. She waited for him and together they made their way around the edge towards the rose garden. They walked quietly, Rose holding the flowers in front of her like some forlorn bride, Joshua a step behind, his shoulders rounded. The footpath took them away from the main entrance to the rose garden and towards the corner arch where Rose had found Emma. They passed older parts of the graveyard where the headstones were at angles and their inscriptions had long since been eroded. It seemed like a forgotten corner. Just ahead they were coming to the side arch of the rose garden. It didn't look as though it had been used much either. A large bush was blocking the way in.

She pulled back the branches and stepped into the rose garden. It seemed to be in complete darkness. She could make out the shapes of the bushes and the pathway and the other walls but that was all. A couple of metres in front of her was the place where she had found Emma. She gasped when she saw the flowers. They were laid across the path and stretched halfway along the side of the walled garden. It was like a carpet that had been put down. The colours were leached by the darkness so that it looked as though the floral tribute was in black and white. Her own flowers looked a deep purple. She lay them down on the edge.

The garden was quiet as though the walls soundproofed it. Last week she thought she had heard sounds; someone breathing, moving stealthily about. She'd been in shock and hadn't been able to look round properly. Had it been Bee Bee? Hiding somewhere, waiting for the chance to dash out of the arch and escape through the cemetery and across the bridge?

Joshua appeared, looking distinctly uneasy.

'This is where she was killed,' Rose said, her voice sounding strangely loud.

'Can we go now?' he said.

'We've only just got here.'

'Rosie, you've done what you wanted. Let's go.'

Rose didn't like the tone of his voice.

'You don't think this is important?'

He didn't answer.

'You're so full up with this stuff about the website and the Russian waitress that you've got no feelings left for this!'

'I just think that's more important to *us*. I thought you would see that.'

'I was *involved*.'

'As a witness.'

'No, more than that. I stumbled into something and now it's not just about Emma or Ricky Harris, it's about me too. I'm part of it.'

'Just an unlucky coincidence.'

'You mean like Valeriya Marashenko?'

He frowned.

'What if she had made more of an effort five years ago?'

'How do you mean?'

'If she had contacted the police. If she had told them the things she told you. What if she had got more involved? Then we might know something about what happened to Mum and Brendan. But she didn't want to. She had her own life to think about so she kept Mum's glasses and she spent the money and she pushed it to the back of her mind.'

'All right . . .'

'I was here,' Rose said. 'I saw her dead there on the ground.'

She took Joshua's arm and pulled him to the exact spot.

'I am involved. I knew her. Her death touched me.'

'OK.'

'If only Valeriya . . .'

'Stop! You're right and I'm wrong,' Joshua said, looking sheepish.

She was about to answer him but stopped abruptly because a haze of light was coming from the archway.

'What's that?'

The light was dim, faint.

'It's torchlight,' Joshua said.

It was weak and distant but it meant that someone was coming.

'Quick.'

She grabbed hold of Joshua's arm and took a left turn and went down the other path away from the flowers. Glancing back she saw the light getting stronger. She peered into the darkness for somewhere to hide. The brick wall was not straight, she realised, and there was a recess behind a bench. She pulled Joshua towards it and they both stood huddled against the wall as a strong beam of light punctured the darkness. Rose peeked out.

Sherry Baxter was standing holding the torch, staring at the flowers that lay on the path. The circle of light from the torch lit up the far wall. She was very still, statue-like.

'Who is it?' Joshua whispered.

'Emma's stepsister,' she said into Joshua's ear.

There was a sound. Rose held her breath trying to hear what it was. She looked out and saw that Sherry was crying with low, tiny hiccupping sobs that gradually got louder.

Rose was tense, sandwiched up against Joshua. She looked up at him, his face only inches away. She put her finger on her lips. She absolutely did not want to see Sherry. Not after the memorial service that morning. Especially not when she was so upset and grieving for her sister. Not here, when she clearly wanted privacy, wanted to be away from prying eyes.

After a few moments the sound stopped and Sherry bent over to a bag that she'd brought. She pulled something out. Rose couldn't see what it was but Sherry disappeared for a moment behind the rose bushes, further along towards the bulk of the flowers.

'We should go now!' Joshua said. 'Slip out the exit while she's there.'

'She'll see us. I just don't want to face her. Let's wait.'

The torch went off. The rose garden was dark again. Rose looked out. Was Sherry leaving? There was no movement and she was surprised to see tiny flickering lights through the rose bushes. Her eyes darted here and there and saw a number of them, ten, maybe; tiny lights sparking against the darkness.

Sherry had lit candles.

Rose closed her eyes. Was Sherry religious? Was she praying?

She heard Sherry walk back along the path towards the corner arch. Was she leaving? There was the sound of a plastic bag being crumpled and then she went under the brick arch.

Rose relaxed, the tension draining out of her.

A beep sounded, loud and insistent.

It was from Joshua's phone.

'Who's that? Who's there? Is someone there?' Sherry's voice called out.

The phone beeped again.

Rose groaned silently. She heard Sherry's footsteps coming back through the arch.

'Who is there!' she demanded.

In a moment Sherry would walk down the path and find her there. After this morning's performance she would be outraged to find Rose and doubly annoyed to know that Rose had been hiding, watching her grieving for her stepsister, lighting candles.

'We'll have to pretend we're boyfriend and girlfriend,' she whispered in Joshua's ear.

'What?'

She reached up and put her arms around his neck.

'Quick, hold me.'

'What?'

Sherry was walking slowly down the pathway.

'Please!' she said, pulling her hood up so that it covered her head.

Joshua's arms went round Rose in a half-hearted way.

'Tighter!'

He squeezed her ribs and she could feel his mouth on her hair.

'Who's there?' Sherry said, her voice less strident, more uncertain.

The torch went on. Rose sensed the circle of light lying on the path ahead of Sherry. She felt panicky. If Sherry saw her she might mention it to the police and how would that look to Inspector Schillings, who had interviewed her in such a suspicious and harsh way?

The footsteps got closer and the circle of light seemed to rise up and sweep across the wall. It was only a matter of seconds before Sherry would be alongside them.

She pushed her face into Joshua's chest just as the light beam found them. Rose glimpsed it on the wall behind. She closed her eyes tightly, feeling the warmth of Joshua. She wouldn't look around. She would feign embarrassment and keep her face away. It was Joshua who Sherry would see, not her. Tensing, she could feel the throb of Joshua's heartbeat.

'What you doing?'

Rose heard Sherry's voice from behind.

She felt Joshua's head turn away. He was looking at Sherry.

'We're just looking for a bit of privacy, mate, that's all,' Joshua said.

'My sister's flowers are here. You shouldn't be doing this!' Sherry said.

'Sorry. Didn't realise that. We're just spending a bit of time on our own. We're not disrespecting anyone.'

'You won't touch them? You won't mess them up?'

'No. We're stopping for a while. We'll keep an eye on them.'

'Yeah, well . . .'

Sherry turned. Rose could feel her moving away.

'Make sure you don't touch anything,' Sherry called.

Rose peeked round. She was walking away, towards the arch. In seconds she was gone. They both dropped their arms. Rose stepped back away from Joshua. She felt instantly cold, a little disorientated. She patted herself down and caught Joshua's eye. She looked away, a feeling of embarrassment flooding through her. They stood like that until the light from the torch disappeared.

'What was *that* all about?' Joshua demanded, after a minute.

'I'm sorry. I didn't want to face that girl. It was just a bit of play-acting.'

'Come on,' Joshua said, a hint of annoyance in his voice. 'Let's go. This place is giving me the creeps.'

SEVENTEEN

Rose sat in the back of the Mini as Skeggsie drove towards Twickenham. The space was tiny, particularly as Joshua had moved his seat back as far as it would go so that his legs would fit in the front. Rose was behind Skeggsie and she'd unlaced her boots and put her feet up on the seat. Her socks were vivid yellow. There was music playing, a band she liked. Every now and again the satnav gave an instruction. Neither Skeggsie nor Joshua said much so she rested her head against the seat and drifted off into her own thoughts.

Now bear left. Then two hundred yards later turn right.

She had a lot to think about.

Now turn right.

Someone had written notes to Emma and Lewis asking them to be at the cemetery at six. Could it have been Bee Bee? She pictured Bee Bee in the cafeteria that day when Lewis Proctor had pretended to stab himself with a plastic knife. She'd been standing stiffly like someone in a production, as if she was taking part in a play, her silver boots and her jewellery giving her a glittery theatrical look. Emma said she was mad about Lewis, had been for years.

Could she be responsible for Emma's death?

At the roundabout bear left. Then take a sharp right turn.

Perhaps it had nothing to do with her or Lewis. Maybe it was something completely different, unconnected. Possibly Ricky Harris had been involved in something illegal and Emma had known about it. Perhaps, once Ricky was killed, Emma was just next on the list. The killer – whoever it was – had followed Emma to the cemetery and picked a moment when she was on her own, not knowing that she was due to meet anyone. Maybe that person had slipped in and out of the rose garden without anyone seeing them.

She thought back to the rose garden the night before and felt a squirming sensation. Joshua and her pretending to be boyfriend and girlfriend. Holding each other in a clumsy clinch. She'd forced him into it, trying to keep Sherry Baxter from coming face to face with her. It had been awkward afterwards, Joshua walking three or four paces ahead, clearly irritated. But by the time they got out of the cemetery and were walking along Cuttings Lane he seemed to have forgotten it.

It was just a bit of play-acting. It was the kind of thing that children did.

So why did she have this odd feeling about it?

In quarter of a mile keep right towards the A402.

She forced her mind back to the really important thing. The murders. Everything she knew about them was second-hand, gossip, bits of CCTV footage. The police would have a fuller picture with scene of crime evidence, CCTV, witness statements and information about what Ricky Harris and his mates were up to. They may well know exactly what was going on and have a suspect in mind. She, who had been at each scene of crime, who had been closer than almost anyone else to these deaths, had only a fragmentary picture of what had happened.

Continue forward on the A316.

She took out the pot of lip salve that Sara had given her and rubbed some across her lips.

At the roundabout go straight on.

Would she ever know what had happened on that platform or in the cemetery or would she have to wait to read it in the newspapers?

She sighed, focusing on Joshua's profile. He was talking to Skeggsie, his face animated for a moment then concentrated while he was listening to Skeggsie's reply. The music made it hard for her to hear what they were talking about but it didn't matter. She was happier in her little world in the back seat of the car, staring at the patterns on her yellow socks.

In a quarter of a mile keep right for the A316.

'Are we nearly there yet?' she called.

Joshua looked round.

'Don't start that,' he said. 'I had enough of that when . . .'

He didn't finish his sentence but she knew what he meant.

In a flash she had an image of the four of them sitting in the car on a long journey. Brendan driving, her mum in the passenger seat, she and Joshua in the back. Joshua with his nose in a book as the road whipped past them. *How much further!* her body seemed to say, her legs and arms folded up, her bottom numb. When the door of the car opened she pictured herself springing out of it like a jack-in-the-box. *Not long now, Petal,* Brendan would call.

Petal. It was the name that Brendan called her. Not *Rose* but Petal. *You're too small to be a rose. You're just a petal to me,* he said. *Mum, tell him!* she would say but her mum just shrugged her shoulders, laughing. But, actually, she liked the word *Petal.* Her shyness towards Brendan lasted for ages but when he coined this name for her she felt better. *Hey, Petal, lass,* he said, putting on a strong northern accent, *Get us a cup of tea, strong mind, and some Hobnobs.*

Her eyes glassed over and she turned to look out of the side window in case Joshua looked round or Skeggsie noticed her in the rear-view mirror. This was what happened when she allowed herself to think about the past. A memory came from nowhere. It surfaced like some deep-water current stirring up her thoughts. Sometimes she wished that she could forget it all, every bit and start again, as though she had no past, no emotional attachments, but it wasn't possible.

'Don't look so sad, Rosie, we'll be there soon,' Joshua said. 'You should put your boots on. Those socks are unsettling me.'

'What's wrong with them?' Rose said, smiling in spite of herself.

She dragged her boots up on to the seat as Joshua gave her an eye-rolling look.

You have reached the destination. It is situated on the left-hand side.

The car slowed down.

'Park over there, look it's Pay and Display.'

She laced her boots up while Skeggsie reversed into a space, going back and forth three or four times until the car finally came to a stop. The doors opened and Skeggsie and Joshua got out. Then Skeggsie fiddled with the driver's seat so that it folded forward and Rose squeezed out. Skeggsie held his hand out to help her but she didn't take hold of it.

On the pavement she flexed her legs and arms and saw that Joshua was standing stock-still, staring at a building across the road. She stopped moving about and went over to him.

There it was. Amid a terrace of big Edwardian houses was one with a neon sign, *Northern Star*. It was four storeys high and had hanging baskets outside.

'There it is,' Joshua said. 'The B and B that Dad and Kathy had a card for.'

'You think they stayed there?' Skeggsie said.

Joshua said nothing but walked across the road towards the *Northern Star*.

Rose took a deep breath and followed him.

EIGHTEEN

The door to the B and B was closed but not locked and Joshua went in first, followed by Skeggsie and then Rose. Joshua stopped as soon as he was in a wide hallway. The walls were lined with photographs of rugby teams. Some were in black and white but most were in colour. On the stairs was a large ginger cat with a squashed-looking face. It stared at them without moving a hair. From above Rose could hear the sound of feet running across a floor, like those of a child.

Joshua seemed stranded in the middle of the hall-way. Skeggsie was looking at the rugby teams, reading the captions below each photograph. Rose saw a sign for *Reception* up ahead and she edged round Joshua and went up to a shelf that jutted out from the wall and held a signing-in book and a bell. The wall behind it was covered with posters about the area. She put her finger on the bell. The ginger cat tensed and then turned and disappeared up the stairs. Moments later a young woman emerged from a door. She was smiling, holding her hands out in front of her, moving her fingers as if fanning the air.

'Sorry, just put a fresh coat of varnish on. Trust me to choose this minute to do it. I'm Amanda. Can I help you? We don't have any rooms, I'm afraid. We're fully booked up tonight and tomorrow night.'

'Actually, we don't want a room.'

The woman had long blonde hair that she kept flicking back off her face. Her lips were painted pale pink in a perfect Cupid's bow. She blew gently along her nails as she looked questioningly at Rose.

'What can I do for you, then?'

Joshua walked forward and Rose watched as Amanda's eyes travelled up and down his body.

'We're here to find out about some people who might have stayed here. Five years ago. It's a long shot that anyone might remember but . . .'

Amanda adopted a puzzled look.

'You're not the police?'

'No.'

'Our records are private and confidential.'

'I know. I understand that. I just want to find out if a couple of people stayed here on Sunday, 4 November, five years ago.'

Sunday, 4 November. The day before Guy Fawkes night. The day that her mum and Brendan disappeared. It was a date that Rose roundly ignored. The beginning of

November every year meant that she avoided newspapers or registering dates on her laptop. The days would pass, the banging of fireworks and the smell of sulphur in the air would distract her. She usually made sure that she had plenty to do so that the anniversary slipped by unnoticed. This year that might be more difficult.

'You know what?'

Rose heard Joshua's tone change.

'You remind me of someone.'

Amanda's eyebrows went up. Skeggsie walked over and Rose looked curiously at Joshua.

'That girl off the telly? The one on the talent show? With the long blonde hair. Really nice-looking girl. Good singer.'

'No!' Amanda said, smiling.

'No, you're right,' Joshua said. 'The hair's not quite the same. Your hair is more natural-looking.'

Rose looked at the girl with consternation. Surely she didn't believe this nonsense. But Amanda was beaming, her newly painted nails flicking at the ends of her hair.

'Don't be silly,' she said.

'No, really,' Joshua said, nodding his head imperceptibly.

'We should go,' Skeggsie said gruffly. 'She's not allowed to give out any information about your parents.'

'Wait a minute – your *parents*?'

'Yeah. Didn't I say? Me and Rosie, we lost touch with our parents five years ago but we think they came here and I guess we're just trying to find out if anyone remembers them.'

'This is your sister?' Amanda said, her eyes resting on Rose.

'Yeah,' Joshua said without a second's hesitation.

Rose was surprised at how easily Joshua told the lie. He seemed like a different person. And he'd got annoyed with her when she was play-acting! She crossed her arms tightly, determined not to say a word.

'What's happened to your parents?'

'We're not sure. We just want to know if they came here.'

'Well, we do have books. Our books go back for years. Mrs Harrison, the owner, she keeps a record of everything.'

'But,' Skeggsie said, 'they might have signed in with a false name.'

'We usually ask to see their passports. We get a lot of foreign tourists and Mrs Harrison has a rule. See the passport, take the number. It's something to do with the police, I think.'

'So you might actually have those records,' Joshua said, his voice a little in awe, not pretending any more.

'Probably but Mrs Harrison keeps them locked up. She has them in a filing cabinet somewhere. She might not . . . well, she's a real stickler for following rules and regulations.'

'Is she here? Can I speak to her?'

'She's on holiday. Florida. She's due back sometime next week. Not exactly sure when.'

'Listen, Amanda. What about if I gave you my mobile number? Maybe you could give me a call when she returns.'

Amanda looked a bit flustered. Her neck was reddening under Joshua's scrutiny.

'I'd be really grateful.'

'Oh, go on, then. Wait, I'll get my phone.'

Amanda walked off down the hallway. She pushed open a door and Rose could hear music and canned laughter coming from a TV programme.

'What are you doing?' she said to Joshua in a loud whisper.

'I'm just being nice to this girl, Rosie. She might help us.'

'Hotel records are confidential. The owner could be stroppy,' Skeggsie said.

'But you're chatting her up!'

'She's nice.'

'She's not, she's . . .'

Rose didn't know what she wanted to say. There was nothing wrong with Amanda but she hadn't thought that this fluffy girl with the blushes and the shiny nails would have been his type.

The door opened and Amanda emerged. She brought a strong floral smell with her as though she'd just sprayed herself from top to bottom with perfume.

'Here, let me,' Joshua said, holding his hand out for her mobile.

He took it and fed his number into it. All the time Amanda was beaming.

'You the manager here?' Skeggsie said.

'No, just the dogsbody,' Amanda said.

Her eyes seemed to settle on Rose's face as Joshua keyed his number into her phone.

'You look upset,' she said. 'Don't worry, your big brother will look after you, I bet.'

Rose didn't trust herself to speak. She gave a plastic smile and then turned and walked towards the front door, standing aside momentarily to allow a couple of people coming in to pass by her.

On the street outside the B and B she stood against the wall, feeling disgruntled. She had never believed that this trip was worth making, so why should she be irked about what had happened? They had found nothing out, but now Joshua was fawning over this girl and she was basking in his gaze. Even dull Skeggsie was joining in.

There was a bus stop in front of the B and B. Beyond that was the row of cars where the Mini was parked. Sauntering along was a traffic warden. Rose looked away. They had paid at the Pay and Display so they wouldn't get a ticket. A bus pulled up in front of her and its doors opened to let off a number of people. Rose looked round at the B and B. Through the glass doors she could see Joshua and Skeggsie still talking to Amanda. She sighed. This was too much. Driving all the way over here on some kind of fool's errand only to have Joshua smitten by some Barbie-type girl.

Don't worry, your big brother will look after you.

Rose felt herself stiffening.

Was she *jealous*?

She heard shouting and looked along the road to where the traffic warden was standing, writing a ticket. A fat man was remonstrating, speaking in a loud voice, pointing across the traffic. Rose looked and saw a chemist's shop on the other side of the road. The man was obviously making the case that he'd been picking up medication. The traffic warden, an older man with round shoulders and ebony skin, was writing the ticket, giving no sign that he was even listening. She glanced again at the fat man, then at the chemist's shop and something caught her eye. A flash of red and a chequered flag went past. Another bus pulled up in front of her and blocked her view, but she waited for a moment and saw a man emerging from behind it on the opposite pavement carrying a bright red holdall with a chequered flag on it. It only took a second to recognise him. He was bald and wearing a leather biker's jacket. It was the technician from her school, the one who had had the row with Ricky Harris. How odd that she should see him in this part of London. How odd that she should see him at all.

He stopped and her eyes stayed on him even though she could hear Joshua and Skeggsie coming out of the B and B behind her. He went up two stairs to the front door of a house across the road. He put his holdall on the ground while he searched through his pockets. Rose remembered his name then – Frank Palmer. She'd seen it on his name tag a number of times. He pulled a key out of his trouser pocket, opened the door and went inside.

'What are you looking at?' Josh said, coming up to her.

'Technician from my school. He must live here.'

'Long way to commute,' Skeggsie said.

She shrugged. 'Got everything you wanted in there?'

'Yeah. She'll ring me when her boss gets back. Then we can look at those records.'

'Actually, it looked as though you got more than you wanted,' she said, moving off towards the car.

'How do you mean?' Joshua said, catching up with her.

'She means the blonde.'

Joshua made a dismissive gesture with his hand and walked ahead. She caught Skeggsie's eye and he stepped towards her and spoke in a low voice.

'Shouldn't bother you, though? You're his stepsister, right?'

He walked on and her eyes bored into his back.

In the car she didn't take her boots off, she just put them up on the seat. When no one said anything she leant back and closed her eyes and listened to the music. The satnav continued to dictate the direction, the voice sounding like that of a station announcer. She heard Skeggsie and Joshua mumbling from time to time but mostly she just closed her thoughts off and listened to the music.

She wasn't *jealous* of Joshua.

She just hadn't pictured him with a girl like Amanda.

When they were almost home the technician came into her head. It was a long journey to the school from Twickenham; tube and bus rides, she thought. She remembered him at the memorial and wondered if he would go to Emma's. Did he even know Emma? She blew through her teeth. The Ricky and Emma situation was never far from her thoughts these days.

They were back in Camden, the familiar streets busy with people heading for the market or the canal or the shops. They carried on past the stalls, inching through the traffic passing through Chalk Farm and heading to Belsize Park. The music had stopped and there was a heavy silence in the car, Even the satnav had stopped, turned off by Skeggsie as soon as they got north of the river.

'You can let me out at the top of my road,' Rose said, moving her boots off the seat and pulling her bag off the floor.

'Sure?' Joshua said. 'Skeggsie doesn't mind taking you all the way.'

'No, really. The end of the road is fine.'

When the car pulled over Joshua got out and stood on the pavement. He held his hand out so that she could climb out of the back seat more easily. When she was upright she brushed her wrinkled shirt down.

'Thanks for coming, Rose,' he said.

She suddenly felt awkward with him.

'That's all right.'

'We didn't get very far but maybe next week . . .'

She felt as though she wanted to touch him or give him a hug but held back.

'I'll call you tomorrow,' she said, stepping away from him.

'I'll email you,' he said, getting back into the passenger seat.

'Bye, Skeggsie,' she said, in a sing-song voice.

A mumbled reply came from the car and she stood until they drove off. She turned off the High Street and up her road. She felt ill at ease. The trip had been uncomfortable and now she didn't feel natural with Joshua. Was it because she was miffed about the way he had acted in the B and B? Or was it because they had only been together for a couple of weeks and it took longer than that for their familial relationship to re-establish itself? Or because of the play-acting she had forced him to do the previous evening?

She didn't know and it made her feel downhearted. All the joy she had felt in the previous weeks, seeing him again and being with him, seemed suddenly fragile, as if Joshua wasn't her stepbrother but some boy from school who she could easily fall out with and never see again.

That couldn't happen. She wouldn't let it.

NINETEEN

The cafeteria was empty even for a Monday morning. Rose chose a table in a corner not used by many of the kids she knew. She bought a hot chocolate, a croissant and a yoghurt. She'd not had any breakfast because of the row she had just had with Anna. It was early, still twenty minutes to go until classes started. *Her* first class wasn't until ten but still she'd rather be here than sitting in the house in Belsize Park. She pulled the croissant apart and put a piece of it in her mouth. She chewed methodically even though she had no appetite. Her throat felt dry and she suddenly didn't know if she would be able to swallow the chunk of croissant. She took a gulp of the hot chocolate and looked down at the table, feeling her eyes blur at the memory of Anna's words.

Her grandmother had been leaning against the work surface when Rose came down for breakfast. Rose went across to the kettle and was puzzled at her presence. Rose usually had the kitchen to herself. Anna didn't get up early and then spent the day either doing voluntary arts work or saw friends or went to plays or concerts or sometimes did sports activities. Once a week she worked for three hours in the Oxfam charity shop in Highgate.

So Rose was surprised to see her.

'Do you have an early meeting?' she said.

'I saw a friend last night who said she'd seen you getting out of a car with two young men in it. On Saturday evening.'

Rose poured boiling water on her tea bag. She didn't answer.

'You told me you were spending Saturday afternoon researching in the local library. And then you said you were going to meet a couple of girlfriends for a coffee. That was what you said and now I find that you were lying.'

'I'm sorry. I didn't tell you what I was doing because I knew you'd be upset.'

'You lied to me?'

'Yes.'

'Like the friend you were meeting for coffee on the night you went to St Michael's Cemetery?'

'Yes. I'm sorry.'

'On top of this I find that you no longer go to violin lessons. You told Miss Popper that you'd found another tutor. And I have been giving you forty pounds a week for these lessons which you have been stealing from me!'

'I . . .'

'You are a thief and a liar. I am very disappointed in you. I'm not quite sure what I have done to deserve this.' Her grandmother looked upset, twisting her hands.

'I didn't take your money. I mean I still have your money. It's upstairs. It was never about the money. It was about going out without you prying into what I was doing. I just wanted some freedom!'

'And I just wanted to know that you were safe. We may live in a privileged way here, in this house, in this street, but we are not far from rough areas. I have a duty to care for you!'

'Yes,' Rose felt her voice rising up, 'but not to guard me. I am seventeen. I need some freedom. I don't want to have to tell you every time I go out to the shop for a packet of sweets.'

Anna's face was calm. She'd obviously thought about this all the previous evening. How typical that she didn't come straight up to Rose's room when she came in. Having it out there and then on the landing would have involved too much passion, too much spirit. Anna liked everything just so. Especially her arguments.

'Who were these boys?' she said briskly, turning away from Rose for a moment to tidy some jars that were already tidy on the work surface. 'Were they from your school? The same types that have been involved in all this violence?'

Rose slumped. She couldn't win. If she told the truth Anna would be upset. If she told a lie she would be scathing with her sarcasm.

'I'm sorry I took the money. It's all upstairs, every penny. I lied to keep the peace because I knew you wouldn't want me mixing with people from school.'

'Lies are never good . . .'

'And I lied also because I've been seeing my stepbrother Joshua Johnson and I knew you wouldn't be happy with that.'

Her grandmother's face tensed.

'I was with Joshua and his flatmate on Saturday. We went out to find out . . .'

'You've seen Brendan Johnson's son?'

'Yes, he contacted me earlier this year by email . . .'

'You've seen him after I expressly told you not to?'

'But that was months ago . . . When I asked if he could come down to London for a weekend . . .'

'I said you were not to see him. I remember, here in this room, you said you'd heard he was coming to London to go to university and I told you then that I didn't want you to make contact with him.'

'No, you said you didn't want him in this house. That's what you said. I remember.'

'You knew what I meant. How could you see that boy against my wishes?'

'Because I have a right to see people. You cannot tell me who I can and cannot see! He's my stepbrother. We were family.'

'How dare you . . .' her grandmother said, her face reddening.

Rose watched with astonishment as Anna started to cry.

'I . . .'

Her grandmother was standing rigid, tears slipping down her face. She opened a drawer of the cabinet and pulled out a box of tissues. She plucked three in succession out of the box and buried her nose in them. Rose couldn't say a word. In five years Anna had never surprised her in the way she was surprising her now. Rose stuttered as she spoke.

'I . . . I have to make my own relationships. I understand if you don't want any contact with Josh . . . Joshua. Well, I don't really understand that at all but that's your choice, but I have to be able to make my choices. Don't I?'

'So you choose to befriend the son of the person who most likely murdered your mother? You choose to do that?'

Rose gasped. She grabbed the edge of the table.

'What are you talking about?'

'Brendan Johnson! That man! Your mother lives with him and then they both disappear. Do you not think that's strange? That two grown-up people should vanish? Much more likely that he killed her and then ran away.'

'No,' Rose said loudly. 'NO! The police said . . .'

'The police had no evidence. Nothing to go on. They didn't have a clue what had happened to Katherine. Just because this Brendan Johnson was a policeman they chose to believe that something had happened to both of them. What if he had been a bricklayer or an insurance man? Don't you think the police would have been more suspicious then? Would they have accepted the theory of their disappearance? I don't think so.'

'They said that mum and Brendan were working on sensitive enquiries. You know that! That most likely some of the people they were investigating wanted them dead. You were here when the inspector said that!'

Anna was staring at her and Rose realised then that she hadn't been present during that talk with the inspector. He had seen her on her own in Anna's drawing room. Had Anna already spoken to him?

'He killed Katherine. That's my opinion. Now he's living somewhere with a new identity. I wouldn't be surprised if that boy, that son of his, knows where he is.'

'No, NO. That's where you're wrong. Josh is heartbroken about his dad. He is doing everything he can to find him. He has websites and . . .'

'Websites!' she said dismissively. 'The man is long gone. I still speak to the police, you know. Is there any news about my daughter's disappearance? I say. No news at the moment, they'll say. It's still an ongoing investigation and we will contact you as soon as any new evidence emerges. It's like a script. One of them, a policeman, kills his girlfriend, runs away and they hush it up.'

'No, no, no,' Rose cried.

She turned and walked out of the kitchen, her hands in fists. She went straight up to her room and got her stuff ready for school.

It was a lie, a lie, *a lie.*

She shoved everything into her bag and while she was doing it, she remembered the money. She went to her bottom drawer and got out her violin case. She placed it on her bed and opened it. Underneath the violin was a flat black cardboard box, the kind that had once held a necklace. The money was inside, the notes flat. One hundred and sixty pounds. She pulled it out, picked up her coat and bag and walked quickly out of her room and down the stairs.

When she got into the kitchen her grandmother was sitting at the table and there was a fresh bunch of tissues in her hand. She held the money up to her, a fistful of twenty-pound notes. Then she threw it in the direction of the table. It fluttered down on to the floor.

'My mum was not murdered by Brendan,' she said in a broken voice and left the house.

In her heart she wished she never had to go back.

Now she sipped her hot chocolate. The plate with the croissant had been pushed to the side. There was still the yoghurt to eat. That would be easy to swallow. She took her laptop out of her bag and put it on the table in front of her. She went on to Facebook and then on to some other websites she liked. She opened up her blog Morpho. She hadn't written on it for days.

She'd had too many other things on her mind.

Anna was still in her head. Anna, who never showed her feelings, who had never talked about her own daughter in any positive way. Katherine was only ever mentioned in a row or as an example of how things can go wrong. Katherine wasted her chances. Rose was evidence of this. Katherine rowed with her mother and left home. She changed her name (to *Smith* of all names). She went to the wrong university, got pregnant and lived all over the place. She joined the police (of all professions, *the police*) and then got involved with some penniless officer who moved in and offloaded his own son on to her.

Rose thought of her standing rigid in the kitchen saying those vile things about Brendan and she wanted to hate her. But then she remembered the tears. Had Anna been crying in rage or in sadness?

She thought for a while then wrote a title for her blog.

What Anna Doesn't Know
We were a family. My mum, Brendan, Joshua and me. Brendan cared for us. He decorated my mum's

study and did it again when she said she didn't like the way the colour looked. He ironed her blouses when she was late for work and he made pancake batter if we felt like it. We were happy and he had plans that we would all move to a cottage in Norfolk and he would go for long walks with a dog that we would get from a rescue centre.

I wanted to tell Anna about these things but there's never been a right time. She knows nothing of this life we had, this life that was planned, the dog that never got to live with us.

Rose picked up the yoghurt and began to eat it while looking at her emails. She was aware of the noise in the cafeteria and glanced up from time to time to see the number of people increasing. Then the bell went and there was a general exit for the first period. She tapped out an email to Joshua.

Can I come round after school? Had a row with Anna.

A reply came almost immediately.

Come whenever you want. Skeggsie's cooking.

The words made her smile.

'Hi!'

Someone had sat opposite her. She looked up from her laptop and saw Lewis Proctor's face inches away. She frowned. None of his friends were near but three or four tables away she could see Bee Bee Marshall sitting with some other girls, her back to Rose.

'All right if I sit here a minute?' he said.

She'd only come face to face with Lewis twice. The first time he was pretending to stab himself with a plastic knife and the second time was when he was running away from the rose garden after Emma had been killed.

'I wanted to have a word,' he said.

She closed her laptop down and stared at him.

'I don't know you. You're not in any of my classes and I ain't seen you around anywhere but still, people say, you're the girl to talk to.'

'You have seen me,' Rose said. 'You saw me going into the rose garden when you were running out.'

'That's exactly the stuff I want to talk about.'

'Maybe you'd be better speaking to the police?'

'I've been talking to the police non-stop! I've been telling them the truth and they just keep on and on. Look, I gets this note from Emma. It's in her handwriting, right? It says she wants to meet me in the rose garden at six. So I go. I gets there and she's lying on the ground. At first I'm thinking she's fainted or something. I get down on my knees and put my hands under her to help her up and there's all this blood. I just ran.'

'She came to see me and told me that she'd got a note from you. She said she knew it was from you because it was your handwriting and it had a heart drawn on it.'

'I never sent her a note.'

'Was the note you got definitely from Emma?'

'It was her handwriting. It had these smiley faces on it that she used to put when she sent me notes before. When we were together. I'm thinking, Ricky's dead, maybe she's thinking about getting back together. 'Course, I ain't got the note any more. Bee Bee found it and went ballistic.'

'Emma thought you might have killed Ricky.'

'She might have thought that. That's not my problem. I'm not here to talk about Ricky. I just want you to be clear that I never touched Emma. I wouldn't. Someone else done it and here's the thing . . .'

'What?'

'Someone nicked my knife a week or so ago. I had it in my sports bag. I was training and when I got changed it had gone. I wouldn't be surprised if my knife turns up in that cemetery with Emma's blood on it. Someone's trying to fit me up.'

'And what about the night that Ricky was killed?'

Lewis took a deep breath.

'Listen, I don't care what people think about that night. As it happened Bee Bee did give me an alibi and then she changed her mind, but I don't care. Me and Bee Bee? It's just a casual thing. When I got Emma's note, well, I just had to go along.'

She looked over at Bee Bee, who had given up talking to the people around her and was sitting looking at Rose and Lewis.

'I told the police I was with Bee Bee that night. I lied but so what? I didn't kill Emma. I would never have done anything to hurt Emma. You were at the cemetery? You saw what state I was in. Anyway, they ain't arrested me yet.'

'What about Bee Bee? Did they speak to her?'

'Why should they?'

'Because she took the note? Because she had a reason to go to the cemetery?'

'Nah, Bee Bee didn't go to the cemetery. She was babysitting her little brother. He's only six months old.'

Rose thought of the CCTV photos of Bee Bee running across the bridge. She looked around the cafeteria. Glumly she noted three or four other girls with silver boots on. Maybe if she looked closely they'd be wearing bangles as well.

'Why are you telling me all this?'

'Emma told me you were a nice person. You remember that day in here when I was ribbing Emma about Ricky getting stabbed?'

Rose nodded.

'I saw her afterwards. I made it up with her. She told me you were a witness at the station. Emma was a good person. One of the nicest people I knew. Ricky Harris was nothing, a waste of space.'

'You had a reason to kill him.'

He shook his head. 'Loads of people had a reason to kill

Ricky. In any case I heard it was self-defence. I heard it was Ricky who pulled the knife.'

'How could you know that?'

'Word gets round. I should go. I just wanted you to know about me and Emma. I would never have hurt her. Never.'

He pushed his chair back from the table and stood up.

'You going to her memorial? It's Wednesday.'

Rose nodded and Lewis walked off. Bee Bee rose from her seat and walked towards him.

'All right, babe,' she called.

She placed her hand on his chest and Rose's eyes focused on the bangles glinting under the bright lights. She'd thought they were all silver but now she saw that there were a number of gold bangles in among them. Some also had small stones in them, red and green and yellow. They moved up and down her arm gently, separating out and coming back together like a single bracelet.

Rose watched them walk away. Many kids turned their heads and watched. Then they looked back at her. Rose Smith, the girl who wanted to be anonymous and had somehow managed to become the centre of everyone's interest.

TWENTY

Skeggsie had cooked a vegetarian pasta dish that was hot and tasty and she ate more than she thought she would. Joshua didn't say a lot and it suited her mood. She kept looking at him from time to time and remembering Anna's vile comments about Brendan. What would he say if he knew? Maybe he would hate *her* just because she was related to Anna and somehow tainted with Anna's theory.

'It's like a morgue in here,' Skeggsie said.

'Sorry. Just had a bad day.'

'Ditto,' Joshua said.

He ate a little and then went off to his room while Rose and Skeggsie finished the food.

'I suppose you want me to wash up?' she said.

'I'll do it. You can help,' Skeggsie said. 'I know where everything goes.'

The kitchen was carefully organised and as Rose dried each dish Skeggsie gave her instructions as to where it went.

'What's really up with Josh?' she said, placing the knives and forks in the drawer.

'He's anxious. He's waiting for this girl to get in touch. From the B and B in Twickenham.'

'Um.'

'You're not enthusiastic about this search of his, are you?'

'I've got other stuff on my mind,' she said.

'The stuff at the cemetery?'

She nodded. It was true in a way. The killing was at the back of her thoughts no matter how hard she tried to push it away.

'I'm still trying to puzzle it out. I mean, I know it's not really anything to do with me. It's up to the police to do that but . . .'

'The police aren't the answer to everything. They don't always follow each case up with the same gusto.'

'Gusto,' she said, smiling, 'Where d'you get a word like that?'

'I am a third-year arts undergraduate. I am well read. I have a good vocabulary.'

'Sorry . . .' She smiled again.

'It's like Joshua said about your mum and his dad's case – the police had all sorts of trails to follow up but they didn't. It's extraordinary that two people can just vanish.'

Rose frowned. Anna had said that very thing that morning.

'This boy who was stabbed . . .' she said, wanting to change the subject. 'It happened almost two weeks ago and no one's been charged. Now I didn't care much for him but the girl, Emma, she was stabbed over a week ago and there's no news about that either!'

'That doesn't surprise me. Working-class teenagers stabbed. It's not an unusual headline. The police go through the motions but if there were no witnesses and no clues, chances are they'll never find out who did it.'

'Surely the police *have* to find out . . .'

Skeggsie shook his head. 'If it had been the son of an MP or the daughter of a member of the royal family you can be sure that the police would have put masses of manpower on it and the forensic lab would have held up their backlog to process the case material. The Chief Constable would have visited the scene of crime, he'd have had his officers report to him daily. They would have found the murderer. Believe me.'

'How come you know so much about the police?'

'My dad was a policeman. He's retired now.'

This was something she hadn't known. The information puzzled her.

'How come you were bullied at school when your dad was a policeman?'

'Maybe that's *why* I was bullied.'

'*Did* you tell him?'

'No, I couldn't. I knew he would be angry. With me. For not sorting it out myself.'

Skeggsie's voice had become stiff.

'It's weird. The three of us. You, me and Josh. We're all the children of police officers.'

'Yes. I don't see much of my dad, though. That's my choice. Unlike you and Josh.'

There was an awkward silence which she filled by telling him about her conversation with Lewis Proctor that morning. She also talked about Bee Bee and her silver boots.

'Basically, I'm wondering if I was right about the person on the footbridge? I thought it was Bee Bee but . . .'

'Want to look at those images from the cemetery again? Maybe a closer look will show us something we missed last time.'

'OK.'

They passed Joshua's room and she heard some music playing softly. She didn't go in or knock. It seemed like he wanted to be on his own. While Skeggsie was sorting out his files and opening his programs, she told him what Lewis Proctor had said about the theft of his knife. Skeggsie looked interested.

'If that's true then it means that someone has been forward planning. Either Lewis told the story to friends so that he could claim to have had it stolen or someone really did steal it so that the blame could be put on Lewis. But you said that the knife hasn't been found yet?'

'Not as far as I know. It's a while since I spoke to my policeman friend but whatever happens at the police station usually seems to find its way to the school.'

Rose was thinking about the alibi that Lewis had for when Ricky was killed, which Bee Bee had now withdrawn. Everyone at school knew about that. If the knife that killed Emma had been found – whoever's knife it was – word would have filtered through school, she was sure.

The pictures were on the screen. Skeggsie had saved them to one folder. They were tiny, twelve in all, some from the bridge, but most from the cemetery itself taken by the mid-point camera. He opened his side drawer and pulled out some prints.

'I printed these off last week. Have a close look at them. If you see anything then we can enlarge it on the screen.'

She looked through the A4 prints. She'd seen them the previous week, pictures of mourners around a hearse. Most people dressed in dark colours which made their skin tones look creamy and white.

'Look at them in real time order. See the time is at the bottom of each print.'

The prints, six of them, were timed minutes apart. 17.59, 18.04, 18.08, 18.10, 18.13, 18.17. Rose looked at each of them in order. She focused on the figures and the faces. All looked to be mourners and only in the last two did she see facial expressions other than sadness. These were people who had watched her run out of the rose garden and straight into the hearse, shouting and crying and trying to get attention.

'I don't see anything new,' she said.

'I printed this one off as well.'

He handed her an image from the footbridge camera. The time read 18.21.

She looked at the figure, the silver boots, the bangles. In the image Bee Bee was pulling her hood across her face to avoid recognition. If it was Bee Bee. Now she wasn't even sure of that.

'Have a look on screen. We'll zoom in on parts of the images. Maybe before I do that you should say what you think we're looking for?'

'Well, someone running away from the rose garden. Maybe this person,' she said, pointing to the image of the person on the footbridge, 'moving through the cemetery towards the back. Heading for the cut-through into Cuttings Lane, making an escape.'

'OK. So maybe we shouldn't look at the figures in the middle of the photographs but at the background of the photos. If she was going across the bridge at 18.20 then she could be in the background of any of these.'

Rose nodded.

'I've got this program? It enlarges images almost down to the pixels. It's handy when analysing brushstrokes of painters.'

'Let's see,' Rose said.

The background in the first three pictures was clear, just the rows of headstones, statues and mausoleums. It was as if she had a telescope in her hand and was looking behind the mourners; the angels emerged from the blurred background, the ornate brickwork on the mausoleums, even small details of the leaves and trees became sharper.

'How do you do this?'

'It's complicated.'

'What, complicated because I'm a *girl*?' Rose said sharply.

'No. Because you don't know enough about computers. I spend a lot of time doing this stuff.'

'You should go out more.'

'Shall we look at the next one?'

The fourth picture came on the screen. 18.10. Skeggsie zoomed in on the top of the photo and Rose saw something straight away.

'Look at that.'

'Where?'

'Behind that headstone.'

Skeggsie zoomed in again and it showed a shoulder sticking out from behind a large white marble headstone.

'She's hiding there.'

The next picture showed 18.13. Three minutes later. When Skeggsie zoomed in there was no sign of her.

'Zoom in further back towards the boundary of the graveyard.'

Seconds later Skeggsie had an image. This time it showed a hooded figure kneeling by a grave. Rose felt instantly disappointed. It was just another mourner.

'Were we wrong?'

'Let's look at the last one. Here it is. 18.17. Four minutes later.'

This time Skeggsie zoomed right in on the hedge area. The picture wasn't as clear, being so far away from the main focus of the image. It was clear enough, though, to see the figure standing in front of the hedge area. The place where Rose thought the cut-through was.

'There's your girl. She's going out the back of the cemetery at the same moment that you're running out of the rose garden calling out for help.'

Rose looked at it with satisfaction. Moments later this person, possibly Bee Bee, was running across the railway footbridge towards the Chalk Farm Estate.

'Wait. Why was she on her knees in front of a grave?'

Skeggsie looked as though he was concentrating. He clicked back on to the previous photo and they both looked at the blurred kneeling figure.

'She looks like she's praying,' Rose said.

'Or maybe she was getting rid of the knife?' Skeggsie said.

'But the police searched the cemetery for the knife.

If she had chucked it there they would have found it. Wouldn't they?'

'Yeah, if she'd chucked it there. But maybe she didn't chuck it. Maybe she buried it. She must have been there for a couple of minutes.'

'Buried it?' Rose said in wonder.

'It is a cemetery, after all. A place of burial.'

'You are right. You are right!'

Rose stood up, away from the computer. She was excited. In her head she remembered the newly dug grave that was near to the hedge cut-through. She'd stood and looked at it, the earth still in a mound, soft and easy to penetrate.

'She buried the knife. That's why the police haven't found it.'

'It's not like they can start digging up every grave. Even if they wanted to. And let's face it, a couple of teenagers from a rough estate in London getting stabbed and killed, why should they trouble themselves? It's not such an unusual thing. My dad used to say that these crimes are often solved by people boasting to others about what they've done. So maybe the police are waiting for a few weeks until the killer gets too confident. Why should they dig up a whole graveyard when they can find the same stuff out if they just wait?'

'You are so right!'

Rose was buzzing. She had to walk up and down. There

was a noise from the other room and after a moment Joshua appeared at the door.

'Skeggsie has found the knife!' she said.

'It's just a theory.'

'No, it's right. I feel it in my bones.'

'What knife?'

Joshua looked sleepy and his hair was sticking up oddly.

'I'm going to St Michael's. Now.'

'What knife?'

'The knife that killed Emma.'

'Don't get your hopes up, it might be nothing . . .' Skeggsie said.

But Rose had already walked out into the hall and grabbed her coat off the hook. Joshua followed her out, looking perplexed.

'Come with me,' she said.

'You're going to the cemetery *now*? No. I'm not going back to that place.'

'I'll go on my own.'

'Just ring the police if you think you've found something.'

'I want to find this myself.'

'Rosie, you can't just go off . . . The police deal with these things!'

'What? Like my mum and Brendan disappearing? Like the way they dealt with that? You're not happy to leave that. Then I'm not happy to leave this.'

'There's a difference!' Joshua said, raising his voice. 'Five years have passed . . .'

'No difference. I'm going now.'

She picked up her rucksack and headed down the hall.

'Wait! Hang on. Wait!'

She looked round to see Skeggsie standing there. He was holding some rubber gloves and a plastic bag.

'I'll come with you.'

She looked at Joshua, who shrugged his shoulders and turned off into his room. Skeggsie unhooked his coat and walked towards her.

TWENTY-ONE

It was raining when Skeggsie parked his car along from Parkway East station. There was a yellow line but it was after 7.30 so it didn't matter. Rose left her rucksack in the car and just took the bag and gloves that Skeggsie had brought. Skeggsie took a torch from the boot of the car and put it in his inside coat pocket. Passing the station she glanced at the train arrivals board and saw that it was 19.48. She pulled her hood up and so did Skeggsie. They turned down Cuttings Lane and walked along to the place where the hedge was thin and brown.

Skeggsie had hardly said a word the whole drive and she'd been wrapped up in her thoughts. Finding the knife *herself* was important for reasons she couldn't quite explain. If Skeggsie was right and the police weren't treating this case as a priority, then she didn't want to waste her time telling them. In any case any tip she gave them would be viewed as suspect because of the way in which she and Skeggsie had got their information. Skeggsie had hacked into CCTV footage. It was a criminal thing to do and although they had been doing it for good reasons the police wouldn't see it like that. They had their own CCTV footage, of the bridge and the cemetery. It was up to them to search it thoroughly.

She'd also been thinking of Joshua. They seemed to have had a row almost every time they'd met and this upset her. The first few times Joshua had made a joke of it, made light of Rose's outbursts. Tonight he had just walked away into his room. Was it possible that she and Joshua might fall out completely? It was unthinkable.

Now, standing at the tatty, frayed hedge in Cuttings Lane, she paused. The rain had stopped and a stiff breeze was blowing. She held on to the edge of her hood.

'I really appreciate you coming,' she said.

''S OK.'

'I mean, I know you don't go out a lot.'

'I do go out!' he said, looking affronted.

'I know, but Joshua told me that you're not that comfortable among people . . . That you prefer to stay at home.'

'Are you trying to say that I'm odd?'

'No. Well, truthfully, you aren't like anyone else I know.'

'You aren't like anyone else I know. As soon as you start talking you manage to insult a person.'

'I didn't insult you. I was just being truthful. That's what friends are for, right?'

'Yes. And if you *were* a friend of mine you *could* be truthful with me,' Skeggsie said.

She stared at him. How had *this* conversation ended up as a row? Was it her? Was *she* the difficult one?

'Come on, let's do this,' he said, pulling the torch out of his pocket.

She went to speak but didn't. Then she looked up and down the lane to make sure no one was around. Her eye paused on one of the CCTV cameras. It seemed to be angled at the centre path of the lane. She looked to the other side and saw another. It may well pick up on them both going into the cemetery. They both had their hoods up though and in any case they weren't about to commit any crime so there should be no need for anyone to check the footage.

'Come on!'

She stepped into the gap in the hedge and slid through to the other side. She stood very still and waited until Skeggsie had done the same. She looked round. The cemetery was stiller than she remembered, the lights on the path glowing, the rest of it pitch-dark. It was twilight when she and Joshua had come the previous Friday but now it was night time proper. Seconds later Skeggsie was beside her.

'This place is big,' Skeggsie said.

'Twenty-three acres,' Rose said.

'Where's the grave?'

'Over here.'

She walked on a few steps. The newer grave she'd noticed had been close to the edge of the lane. She stood by it and tried to remember the CCTV photo that they had looked at earlier. Was this the grave that they had seen the person kneeling by? She looked at the cross with the name inscribed on it. *Gerald Rossiter 1970–2012*. The man had been forty-two years old when he died. The same age as her mother when she disappeared.

'No headstone on this grave,' she said.

'They don't put headstones until later. The ground has to settle. Then six months, a year later, a headstone is laid.'

'How come you know so much about absolutely everything?' she said.

'It's what happened when my mum died.'

Rose was thrown.

'Your mum's dead?'

Skeggsie nodded. 'Ten years ago.'

She didn't speak. She'd stumbled on this new information after calling him an *odd* person. *I'm sorry* was hopelessly inadequate. Her face must have looked pained because Skeggsie attempted a reassuring smile.

'I don't know what to say.'

'Forget about it. It was a long time ago. I'm all right about it.'

'You've had such a bad time.'

'No more than you or Josh.'

'You know that I really was sorry about that time when I said . . . when I was unkind about you being bullied . . .'

'Forget it.'

'The thing is I had a bad time at school. Nothing like you. I was never physically hurt but I had this friend who just walked all over me. Her name was Rachel Bliss and I thought we were close but she wasn't what she seemed and she treated me badly.'

'Now *I* don't know what to say,' Skeggsie said, pulling at his collar.

'Schooldays are the best days of your life, they say!' she said.

'Come on, let's get started with this search.'

Skeggsie turned the torch on and pointed it at the ground. The grave was surrounded by wreaths and flowers that had faded and dried, some with ribbons that were fluttering in the breeze.

'This has been here for a couple of weeks at least,' he said.

'How do we go about this?' she said, looking round at the silent, empty graveyard.

'I'll hold the torch and you put the gloves on. Then just feel gently around. If it is here I don't suppose it was buried deep. There'd be no need. Just enough earth to cover it up.'

Rose put the gloves on. The torch threw a circle of light on to the mound. She knelt down. The ground was wet. The knees of her jeans would end up damp. She found herself looking at the cross and the name, Gerald Rossiter. *Sorry*, she mouthed silently and holding her palms downwards she began to pat the mound of earth starting with the top right-hand corner, the place where Bee Bee would have knelt if they were right about the photo.

The earth was soft and had a kind of mulchy smell. The wind blew her hood back and she used her knuckles to try and pull it back into place. She looked up at Skeggsie from time to time and saw that he was concentrating, moving the torch very slowly so that she could cover every section.

A noise broke the silence and made her turn quickly. Skeggsie turned the torch off. It came from outside in Cuttings Lane. It was the high tinny sound of an MP3 player. Someone who had earphones in but still had the music as loud as possible. She waited for it to pass but it didn't. It was as if the person was standing still at that very part of the lane. Then the hedge started to rustle and she realised that whoever it was was coming into the cemetery.

'Quick,' she said, moving swiftly past the mound of earth to the next grave, which had a substantial black marble headstone.

She knelt on the damp earth next to Skeggsie. Looking out from behind the headstone, she saw two people, a boy and a girl. They looked young, still at school. The boy had his arm around the girl's neck and he was talking quietly to her and she was giggling.

'Who is it?' Skeggsie whispered.

She put her finger to her lips and waited a second before looking again. This time they were standing very still, sandwiched together in a deep kiss. The boy and girl continued for what seemed like minutes and she was holding her breath, watching the boy's hand slip inside the girl's coat.

'Don't!' the girl said. 'Not here. Someone might see.'

'What? Round here? Like the undead?'

'Don't say that. You'll make me scared and then I won't *do* anything. In any case it's raining. Let's go up to the archway.'

'You know someone got offed there?'

Rose heard an exclamatory sound as they moved off round the periphery of the graveyard. They were heading for the far corner of the rose garden, going the same way that she and Joshua had gone a few days before.

'I'm wet,' Skeggsie whispered.

Rose looked across at the cemetery lights. There was a halo of light around each one and in it she could see the rain spearing down.

'Come on, let's do this quick.'

Rose got back to where she had been and Skeggsie knelt down beside her. He turned the torch on and held it close to the ground. She moved a couple of the decaying wreaths and began to feel across the place where they had been laid. Somewhere, underneath, she hoped she would feel the handle or the blade of a knife. Maybe the knife that had been stolen from Lewis Proctor or maybe a different knife entirely. She paused. There would be blood on the blade, Emma's blood. The thought made her feel a little nauseous.

'Come on!' Skeggsie said.

She kept going, the earth like clay in her fingers. It was only moments later when she felt something hard underneath.

'Here!' she whispered.

Using her cupped hands she scraped away the soil. Underneath the top layer it seemed dry and almost dusty. Could it be the knife? Could they be that lucky? So quickly?

'Hold the torch, here,' she said.

Something was wrapped in tissue or kitchen roll. She picked it up and felt instantly disappointed. It wasn't the shape of a knife. It was small and rectangular.

'What is it?'

She peeled the paper back. Inside there was a mobile phone.

A lurid pink mobile phone.

She knew instantly that it had belonged to Emma.

*   *   *

Back in the car they sat with the heater running. The rain was heavier, hitting the windscreen, running down in glistening droplets. Rose's jeans were wet at the knees and her coat was clammy. Skeggsie had put the rubber gloves on and was handling the mobile. He had plugged it into the car phone charger. He flipped the top off and Rose could see the charging symbol light up on the tiny screen.

'It still works,' she said, amazed.

'Being buried was the best thing. If it had got wet . . .'

'It's definitely Emma's phone. Why would someone hide it? What's the point of that?'

'Maybe there's something on this phone that the killer doesn't want anyone to see. Text message, call history or photos.'

'It's just a supermarket phone. It probably doesn't even do photos,' she said, dismissively.

'We can look at call history, now that it's plugged in. Here, you put the gloves on and do it. My fingers are too big.'

Rose put on the gloves and took the phone. She used the cursor to look at recent calls. The reading on the last call was 29-09 17:00, and it was to *Sherry*. At five on the afternoon that she died Emma had called her stepsister. Sherry had been in Brentwood with her dad, Rose remembered. She must have told Sherry during that call that she was meeting Rose to go and see Lewis. She remembered Sherry's scathing words to her, the previous week at Ricky's memorial: *You should have been there to stop my sister getting hurt. How come you were late?* But it wouldn't have mattered if she had been on time because Emma went into the cemetery at 5.40, ten minutes earlier than she said she would.

Rose went to the in-box and looked at the text messages. The last one she received had come on 29-09 17:35. Rose opened it.

New phone. Lost other. I no who killer is. Meet me 5.45 if you want to no. I won't wait. Lew

Rose read the message over several times. This was why Emma hadn't waited for her. She'd got a text from Lewis telling her to go early.

'Found something?'

'Yeah. A message changing the meeting time at the cemetery. It's from a mobile number that her phone doesn't recognise. It says it's from *Lewis*.'

'But it could be from anyone.'

Emma had read the message and believed it to be from Lewis. She'd gone early into the rose garden and somebody was waiting for her. That person killed her and then took the phone and buried it to hide the fact that they had texted her.

'No knife, though,' Skeggsie said.

She shook her head. She was glad in a way. A knife that had killed someone wasn't something she wanted to hold.

'Could the police find out who sent the text?'

'If the number is registered to someone, but if it's a pay as you go phone the only thing they could find out is which shop sold it.'

'So there's no point in handing the phone in to them.'

'They might be able to get fingerprints, but any of her friends could have handled the phone so that won't prove anything. What they need is a knife with some finger-prints on it. That would prove something.'

'Oh.'

'What you going to do with the mobile?'

'Try and find out who sent the message.'

'How?'

'I'm not sure. I need to think it through.'

'Shall we go?'

She nodded.

Skeggsie started the car up and she placed the mobile inside the plastic bag that he had brought and slid it into the front pocket of her rucksack.

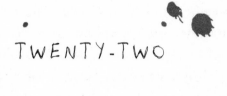

TWENTY-TWO

Joshua was waiting at the school entrance. It was 8.50 and Rose had a class at nine. He gave a tiny wave when he saw her and she wondered why he was there.

After getting dropped off by Skeggsie the previous evening she'd gone to her room and done some work on her laptop. Anna had been downstairs but she'd not faced her or spoken to her. She'd looked at her emails and kept her mobile by her side but there'd been no messages at all from Joshua. She'd considered calling him but had felt a little hurt by his behaviour.

She'd spent some time thinking about Emma Burke's mobile phone in the front pocket of her rucksack. She hadn't taken it out though, just remembered seeing Emma holding it when she was in the house on the day she died. She wondered who had sent the text that made Emma go to the cemetery early. It couldn't have been Lewis Proctor because Henry said he had gone in past the cemetery gate CCTV camera at six. It was very likely that Emma had already been stabbed by then. Could it have been Bee Bee? Could she have *actually* tested her boyfriend by sending him a note *as if* it came from Emma to tell him to meet her at the cemetery? Then sent one to Emma? She may well have seen some of the notes that Emma had sent Lewis over the summer and had used those as a template for her handwriting. Likewise it would be simple to copy Lewis's handwriting.

Was it possible that Bee Bee stabbed Emma and ran away, pausing only for a moment to bury Emma's phone in a newly dug grave?

She thought and thought about this until she was dog-tired. She slept fitfully and got up especially early, hoping she would not see Anna. She checked her emails before leaving home. There was nothing from Joshua.

So she was surprised to see him standing sheepishly at the school entrance.

'Hey, Rosie, dug up any dead people lately?' he said.

'Very funny.'

'Sorry about last night. I was just down. I couldn't summon up enthusiasm for anything.'

She shrugged.

'This morning I feel better. I've had a text message from Amanda at the B and B.'

'Really?' she said half-heartedly.

'She says the owner got back in the middle of the night.

So I'm going over there now to see if I can access the records.'

'Good,' she said, moving aside to let other students past.

'Come with me,' he said.

'I can't, I've got a class.'

'Please. Things have been a bit awkward between you and me. It would be good to just relax and talk.'

But not about Brendan and Mum, she wanted to say.

'I would but I've got this essay to give in,' she lied. 'Why not go with Skeggsie?'

'He's at uni.'

'Oh, right, so I was second choice anyway. If he hadn't been at uni then you wouldn't even be here.'

The words came out before she thought them through. Joshua was visibly taken aback by what she said. He began to shake his head.

'You know what, Rosie? I'll go on my own.'

He walked off and she watched him go with mounting panic. It was exactly as she'd thought the previous evening. They were going to fall out and then they'd stop seeing each other and that would be unbearable.

Rose, Rose, she said to herself, *why are you pushing him away?*

She went after him, her steps quickening to catch up as he turned a corner.

'Josh!' she called.

He looked round.

"Course I'll come. I can give my essay in later.'

He looked for a moment as if he wasn't going to accept her words, as if he'd been too hurt and was going to walk off anyway. Then his face broke into a grin and he put one arm around her neck and pulled her head roughly towards him and gave her a loud smacking kiss on her hair.

'All right!' she said, embarrassed to see some kids that she knew from her form group pass by. 'Let's go before any of my tutors see me.'

They got a tube and a train.

During the journey they talked. Joshua explained why his search was so important. *I understand*, she said. *Of course I do*. Even though she was uncomfortable about it she wasn't going to let it become a barrier between the two of them. Then she told him why she was so embroiled in the murders at the school. He nodded and said, *Sure, sure, I get it*, when she explained. After a while they talked about other stuff. Books, films, bridges and buildings in New York. The journey took an hour and twenty minutes. When they got off at Twickenham station it was bright and sunny. Rose unzipped her jacket. Joshua pointed which direction they were heading. The B and B was only minutes away.

'Hang on,' she said, as they came close to the entrance. 'You go in and talk to Amanda yourself. I'll stay out here. If you find out anything come and get me.'

'Why?'

'She's the sort of girl who irritates me. I'd only start huffing and puffing.'

'You're prejudging her, Rosie. Just because she's all done up it doesn't mean she's an airhead.'

'I'll wait over there, on that bench. Give you two time to get acquainted,' she said with a knowing smile.

Joshua grinned and went on over to the B and B. Rose walked towards the bench. She sat down and looked around. The Pay and Display car bays were all full up and a couple of cars were treading water on the yellow lines at either side. She felt the heat of the sun on her face. After the previous night's wind and rain it felt good. The streets were busy with shoppers. She looked across the road and remembered seeing Frank Palmer, the technician, going into a house the previous Saturday. She stood up and walked along the pavement until she was opposite the house. She looked at it through the traffic. The front door was dark green with no window or door number, just a slim brass letter box. His bag came into her head. A bright red holdall with a chequered flag across it. She wondered idly, as she was walking back to the bench, if he was a fan of motor racing. She had only just sat down again when she heard Joshua's voice.

'Rosie.'

She turned and saw him walking towards her. He'd been quicker than she'd thought he'd be. His shoulders were slumped and she wondered if he hadn't been able to see the records.

'No go,' he said as he reached her.

'What do you mean?'

He slumped down on the bench beside her.

'Amanda got the keys from the owner and found the records from five years ago. They were on floppy discs but she made a list of the names. There's also a signing-in book. One for every year. Fourteen people stayed at the B and B that night, three couples, a family of five and three singles. Dad and Kathy's names are not on the list. Dead end. Waste of time. Maybe Valeriya Malashenko's memory wasn't so good after all. Or it was a different B and B.'

Rose was quiet. She'd been right and yet it didn't make her feel good.

'I just thought if they'd been here it would lead somewhere else. You know, like a stepping stone?'

Joshua was leaning forward, his hands between his thighs. Rose struggled to find something to say.

'Looks like you were right,' he said, staring at the ground.

She looked sadly at him. She put her hand out and pulled at his arm. Using both her hands she clasped his. To anyone else they would have seemed like a couple of young lovers making up after a quarrel.

'Wait a minute,' she said.

Something was nagging at her. Some fact in her brain was pushing its way out. Her mum, Kathy, had changed her name from Christie to Smith. To start a new life away from her own mother. She'd shrugged off her identity by changing just one word.

'What?'

'What if they signed in under new names?'

'Not possible. Remember they check the passports, Amanda said.'

'But what if they got new passports? They were police officers. They were working on difficult and unresolved cases. Maybe they went undercover! Maybe that is what they are still doing.'

Joshua's face lit up for a moment. Then he groaned.

'Undercover for five years?'

'I don't know. Maybe . . .'

'Wouldn't the police have said something?'

'Unless it was something else. Not *undercover* but something to do with the state?'

'What?'

'The government? The cold cases they were working on might have been to do with terrorism?'

'Like, spies?' he said, standing up.

Rose didn't answer. It had only been a suggestion to cheer Joshua up but it had mushroomed into a theory and she didn't know where to go with it. Joshua was moving about. He was agitated, his face deep in thought.

'But wait,' she said. 'Possibly they were not meant to go undercover for five years. Maybe something bad happened.'

'They were discovered?'

She shrugged.

'It would explain a lot. Maybe they went undercover for a short while. Days perhaps and something went wrong . . .' Joshua said.

'Let's just check the records. Look at the names. They might have chosen something that was familiar to them.'

Joshua walked off towards the B and B. Rose felt a moment's trepidation. She went quickly after him.

'Wait . . .' she said, holding him back, making him stop.

'What?'

'What if it just adds up to the same thing? They're undercover, they're spies, whatever. If they're dead anyway? What's the point if at the end of all this we're still in the same position? Still on our own . . .'

'But we would know the truth. Even if that truth is really hard we should know it. That's the point. Come on, let's look at the names again.'

She let him go on ahead and walked behind him feeling cross with herself. Why hadn't she just kept her mouth shut? They'd be on the tube by now, on their way back to Camden.

Amanda was standing at the hallway table as if she'd been waiting for Joshua to come back. She had false eyelashes on that weighed down her lids. She looked as if she was about to drop off to sleep. She had a vivid pink top on that showed the shape of her bra. The previous week Amanda had been dressed for work, today she was dressed to kill.

'Hi, Rose. How are you?' she said, a lilt in her words as if Rose was Joshua's *seven*-year-old sister.

Rose made an *um* noise.

'Can we see the actual records?' Joshua said, 'Just to confirm something? Is that OK?'

'Mrs Harrison might be back soon.'

'We'll be five minutes, no more.'

Amanda looked at her watch in an exaggerated way.

'Please. I wouldn't ask but you've been so great . . .'

'Come on. This way. You might as well see them in the office.'

They followed her into a small room at the back of the house. There was a desk and a new laptop in the middle, its lid up. To the side was an old computer, its monitor taking up most of the space. Beside it was an ancient printer. Amanda pulled a drawer open and took out a box of floppy discs. Rose wondered what Skeggsie would make of such equipment. It took a few minutes to load one of them into the old computer. Then Amanda opened up a file and there it was. *November 2007*. It was a spreadsheet with dates running down the side and room numbers at the top. Josh pointed to 4 November.

'Here are the names, look.'

Rose's eyes moved along the page. Three couples, a family of five and three singles. Her eye focused on the three couples; Robinson, Brewster, Spicer. Amanda kept walking towards the window and back. She seemed ill at ease.

'Look at this one,' Rose said, pointing to the forenames. She read them out; *Kate Brewster, Dan Brewster*.

'So?' Joshua said.

'Brewster. We lived in *Brewster* Road. My mum's name was Kathy. And Brendan. *Dan*.'

'What do you mean *your* mum?' Amanda said suddenly, 'I thought you were brother and sister?'

'Stepbrother and sister,' Joshua said.

Amanda's face broke into a smile. 'Right.'

'Have you got the book? The one the guests sign?' Joshua said.

Amanda nodded and went to another drawer. She pulled out a black leather Visitors' Book and opened it flat on the desk.

'You'll have to be quick,' she said. 'Mrs Harrison said she'd be back at lunchtime and it's ten to twelve.'

'A couple more minutes and we'll be done,' Joshua said flicking through the pages until he got to 4 November. 'Here, this is it. Look.'

Rose looked at the signatures on the page. Dan Brewster was in a slanting backhand that she didn't know. Kathy

Brewster's was all too familiar. The K was elaborate with a curlicue at the bottom and each letter was carefully enunciated right down to the final 'r' of Brewster. She looked at it for a long time, her eyes eating in the signature.

'It's my mum's,' she said. 'It's my mum's Ks and Rs. It's her. She signed this!'

Joshua had a look of wonder on his face. Amanda looked at him and then at Rose. She had her hands together and looked like she might do a little dance. Rose, in spite of her gloomy predictions, was affected by the sight of her mother's handwriting.

'What are these?' Joshua said, pointing to some symbols after the names. 'What does *TH* stand for?'

'Let me see,' Amanda said, sticking her chest out, pointing one long tangerine nail down at the page. 'These are old symbols. We don't use them any more but I do know . . . Let me think . . .'

The bell went from out in the hall.

'Customers, I'll have to go. Will you take out the disc and put this stuff away.'

Rose picked up the Visitors' Book. She held it across her chest, cradling it.

'But the symbol, Amanda. What does it mean?'

The bell went again, more insistent this time.

'I'll think about it. No! Wait. I know. T is for taxi. That's it. They ordered a morning taxi.'

'What about H?'

'Heathrow,' Amanda said. 'Sorry, didn't I make that clear? They were going to Heathrow airport. They ordered a taxi the night before. That's what that symbol means.'

The bell went again. It shrilled out and Amanda made a *tsk*ing sound and went out of the room.

Joshua looked at Rose. Neither of them spoke. He turned away from her and pressed the print button so that an old printer made whirring sounds and produced a copy of the spreadsheet. He pulled the floppy disc out of the computer and replaced it in the drawer. He turned round and stared at her, his expression strange. She was aware that she was holding the book with a kind of bear hug.

'Look, on top of the filing cabinet.'

There was a photocopier. It was flat and small and looked basic.

'I'll do it,' Joshua said, taking the book from her.

He lay the book face down on the photocopier and pulled the lid over.

'Fingers crossed,' he said.

He pressed a button and the machine lit up. Moments later a sheet of A4 paper appeared. A copy of the page where the signatures were. Rose looked at it with a smile.

'Put these away.'

He handed her the copies and she folded them up and put them in the front pocket of her rucksack. The sight of Emma Burke's pink mobile phone startled her but she slid the photocopies in alongside it. Joshua held the door open and the two of them went out into the hall, where Amanda was standing in the middle of a family and their suitcases.

'Thanks, Amanda. I'll give you a call?'

'All right,' she said, smiling widely.

'Thanks,' Rose said under her breath.

They stepped outside on to the street and Josh looked at her with pure delight. She grabbed his hand and squeezed it and he ruffled her hair.

After five years they'd found something.

TWENTY-THREE

The euphoria lasted the length of the tube journey. They sat alongside each other, Rose's rucksack on the seat next to her. Josh was leaning forward, his hands moving when he spoke. The carriage was mostly empty, just a woman with a pushchair down the far end.

'Where were Dad and Kathy going? Which country?'

'I don't know. *Why* were they going? On a work assignment? Undercover?'

'And they changed their names? Why?'

'They needed a new identity. For whatever job they were on.'

'Or were they running away?' Josh said, his forehead tensing.

'The main thing is that we know that they just didn't vanish,' Rose said.

'They weren't abducted. That's really good news.'

'It is.'

'It's great news. It's the first new clue that we've had,' Joshua said.

'And it was your website that did it.'

'Skeggsie helped.'

'But you had the idea.'

'Right! I'm going to send an email to Valeriya. Let her know how important her information has been.'

'Good idea.'

'We've found out where they went. We have evidence. We know they went on to Heathrow.'

'And then on to somewhere else.'

'You know what's really exciting? We have the names that were in their passports so if we give them to the police they could go to the authorities at Heathrow and find out exactly where they flew off to.'

'The police?' Rose wasn't sure.

'I'm not saying we *will* give them to the police, I'm not saying that. Not yet. There may be some other way we could find out which carrier they went with and where they went to.'

'Maybe the police already know. If this is something undercover. If we go to them they might just hush it all up again,' Rose said.

They were at a stop. The doors opened and a young couple got in. They sat on the seats opposite, a little way along. The boy had circles of metal in his ear lobes. It was disconcerting and Rose tried not to look. Her eyes dropped down to the floor. The girl had leopard-skin boots with high stiletto heels and pointed toes; they positively growled at her. A picture came into her head of Bee Bee's silver boots with their kitten heels. She looked down at her own feet, black DMs; flat, sturdy, needing a polish, the laces only partially threaded through. Anna hated these boots. Maybe that was why Rose wore them.

'It could have been some sort of national security thing,' Joshua said. 'Like you said, terrorism or maybe anarchists.'

'Yeah,' Rose said, a little distracted.

'Since 9/11 there's been loads of that kind of work.'

'I know.'

But where are they now? The words went through Rose's head as if someone had just whispered them into her ear.

'Or they were running away from something. Some organised crime case they were involved in.'

'And using the street name. *Brewster Road,*' Rose said, making herself concentrate on what they'd found out.

'And your mum's signature! She didn't change it. You know what? It's almost as though they were leaving clues for us. The glasses case. The card for the B and B. The new surname, the forenames and then the signature. It's like a paperchase. They were dropping paper so that we could follow.'

Rose smiled. It was just like that.

After a while they stopped talking. Rose was lost in her thoughts and Joshua was staring down at his lap. When they got to their station they got up and Rose gave Joshua an encouraging smile. She stepped across the leopard-print boots and avoided looking at the perforated ear lobes.

'I might put an update on the website,' Joshua said. 'I won't give all the details away but I could mention Heathrow and the date and the new names. Something might come up.'

'It might.'

'Maybe there's another piece of the paperchase there, at Heathrow.'

'Maybe,' she said.

But where are they now? Rose thought, stepping on to the escalator.

They bought sandwiches and took them back to the flat in Camden. Skeggsie was at university so they had the place to themselves. Joshua was quiet. He went into the kitchen and put the sandwiches on plates. In silence he made hot drinks and together they carried them through to the room with the television. They sat on the sofa, the sandwiches in front of them, mugs of tea and coffee on the floor. Joshua had put the twenty-four-hour news station on. The sound was low and Rose stared at the screen, feeling disgruntled.

The mood had changed.

Where had her mum and Brendan gone? Why? Why hadn't they tried to contact them? To let Rose and Joshua know that they were all right?

These were the questions that needed answering five years before and now, even after finding out about the B and B and the taxi to Heathrow, they still didn't know.

The news reports went on and Rose watched in a detached way. Half of Joshua's sandwich sat uneaten. She had left her crusts and some of the filling that she hadn't liked.

'You know what I don't get?' Joshua said suddenly.

Rose took a gulp of her tea. It had cooled too much and she put it back down again. She noticed then that Joshua was sitting apart from her. There was room for at least one other person to sit between them. It made her feel cold.

'How it was all planned in advance! They had new passports. That must have taken a long time to arrange. They must have known they were going for days or even weeks.'

Rose sank back into the seat. She felt weary and stretched her arms out straight, trying to shake herself up.

'Let's say they only knew for sure for a few days. So, during those last days, when I was going to school or talking to dad about football or handing him a packet of Hobnobs, he knew what they were planning. He answered me. He chatted. He gave me some pocket money and all the time he knew, *they* knew that they were leaving us.'

Rose stared ahead. There was the tiniest of lumps forming in her throat.

'How could they do that?'

Joshua folded his arms. His coffee was on the floor, half drunk as usual. No doubt there would be a skin on it later. Maybe Skeggsie would pick it up and wash it for him.

'When they went missing it was bad. It was really *bad.* You remember those days?'

She bit her lip. He went on.

'But it was always as if it had been out of their control. Something had happened *to them*. But now it looks as though *they* organised this.'

He stood up suddenly, the seat creaking as he left it.

'I don't like this. I don't like it at all. At first I thought it was good news but now . . .'

'But we needed to know the truth. You said . . .'

'Not this truth.'

She took his hand and pulled him down so that he was sitting on the seat again. He kept talking, his words speeding up.

'So say there was this plan, maybe instigated by the police or maybe they did it themselves. They sat in our kitchen one day, while we were out at school, and they planned to leave us behind. They worked out new names and a place to go to. They *meant* to leave us.'

She looked at him. He was rigid, his neck and shoulders stiff. He seemed taller, bigger, puffed up with anger.

'We don't know that they chose to do this . . .' Rose said.

'Yes, we do! Yes, we know now that they went for a meal and then left the car there. They got a taxi to Twickenham and showed their new passports! Maybe they were having a laugh as they did it . . .'

'No, they wouldn't . . .'

'They planned a taxi the next morning to Heathrow. To fly off somewhere even though they must have known that we would be demented, worried, on our own. Two kids knocking round the house in Brewster Road, wondering if there'd been a car accident . . .'

'They wouldn't have gone without a good reason . . .'

'How can you say that?' Joshua said, looking round at her. His eyes were shining. 'They dumped us.'

'No, no. This is something they had to do . . .' Rose was desperate.

'Everyone said they were dead. The police said it, my uncle said it, my teachers said it. Even you said it. Well, now I hope they are dead. That's what I hope,' Joshua said, standing up, walking out of the room, slamming the door behind him.

Rose looked at the half-eaten sandwiches and the news programme and felt her neck tightening. She had told him not to do this but how could she say that? How could she say *I told you so*? The hot hurt of the disappearance had cooled and they had moved on with their lives. Of course, it had never been the same for either of them. They'd lost each other in the process but now they'd found each other again. Why couldn't Joshua have been happy with that? Why drag this all up again?

There was a noise from the other room. It was a moaning sound and she stood up quickly and went towards it. She opened Joshua's door lightly and saw him lying on his side on the bed, his face buried in his pillow.

'Oh, don't,' she said, feeling herself welling up.

She went across to the bed and sat beside him. Even without touching him she could feel how hot he was.

'I always thought that they'd come back. Just walk in one day and say, *You won't believe this . . .*'

She looked sadly at him. Underneath his misery there was anger, she could hear it in his voice. She edged further up the bed.

'Josh, don't get upset.'

'How can I not? He left me. He always said to me, *It's you and me against the world*, and then he left.'

He was crying. She put her hand on his chest and it felt tight like a spring. She remembered his tattoo then, there on his side. A butterfly on the point of flight. She let her fingers trace the shape.

'We're a team, you and me,' she said, pushing her sleeve up to expose her Blue Morpho.

His face barely flickered and he seemed to be staring somewhere far away. She wasn't reaching him and it gave her a fearful feeling. This boy had been her rock over the last six months. Ever since she got his first email it had changed her. Getting over the awful stuff at Mary Linton, the rows with Anna, her insistence at going to a new school – these things had only come about because she had gained strength from knowing that Joshua was in her life again.

If he fell apart what would she have left?

She began to cry, tears slipping down her face. He looked at her and softened. He put his arms out and pulled her face down on to his shoulder.

'Oh, Rosie,' he said, hugging her.

So what if they didn't have Mum and Brendan? They had each other.

She felt a wave of emotion. Nothing mattered now except the two of them. She lifted her face and looked up at him. His eyes were closed and he looked peaceful. She had an urge to kiss him on the cheek, to make a joke of it all, to laugh it off. To go back to the way they were before the email from the Russian girl. He turned his head, though, and she looked at his lips.

She felt a pull. A powerful urge to place her mouth there, lightly, hardly touching. His eyes were shut and he looked so peaceful and he was everything she had. She moved closer. She felt herself drawn towards him.

Then abruptly she stopped and pulled back.

What was she thinking of? Had she gone mad? She stood up and forced herself to step away. He noticed immediately because he opened his eyes. He looked sleepy and gave her a weak smile.

'What's up?' he said.

'I have to go.'

She walked away from the bed, looking around as though there was something of hers there. Her arms hung hopelessly at her side. What had she been thinking? What was wrong with her? Joshua was her stepbrother.

'I have to give that essay in,' she said, her voice croaky.

She went out of the room. In the living room she picked up her coat and bag and realised that he was behind her.

'Rosie,' he said, his hand out to stop her going. 'Have I upset you? Don't take any notice of the things I said about Dad and Kathy. I was just mad. I didn't mean . . .'

'It's OK. It's been an emotional afternoon. I have to go now. To get to school.'

She talked as she walked past him into the hallway and down the stairs. She could hear him following her. She wished he wouldn't. Just for now she wanted to be on her own, away from him.

'I just had a lot of anger to let out,' he said.

'It's all been too much,' she said, avoiding eye contact.

She reached out to open the door. At the same moment he put his hand on her shoulder and she felt it there, heavy and warm. She turned back to face him and his fingers moved on to the top of her arm. Her throat was tight as if it had been pulled by a drawstring.

'You're not annoyed at me? For losing my cool?'

She shook her head.

'Good.'

'I'll . . . I'll contact you at the weekend,' she stuttered the words out. 'I've . . . I've got stuff to do at school and it's Emma's memorial tomorrow so I'll be busy. So, if you don't hear from me you'll know why . . .'

'I'm busy too. I'll call you at the weekend.'

She went out of the door and stood on Camden High Street. She put her palm on to her arm where Joshua's hand had been and held it there for a few moments. There were people walking past, but she hardly noticed.

The weekend was three days away.

Three days to forget how stupid she had almost been.

Rose, Rose, she said to herself, *what were you thinking?*

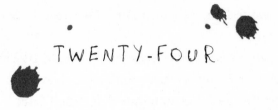

TWENTY-FOUR

Rose passed the tube station and kept going in the direction of school. It was a couple of tube stops but still she needed the walk. It was just past two o'clock and feelings of shame and confusion were flooding through her. She walked with her head down, staring at the pavement, sidestepping people coming towards her. She, who had never kissed a boy, who had never really known a boy in any real sense.

What had come over her?

The day had heated up. The October sunshine was heavy and unexpected and Rose took her jacket off. She folded it up tightly and forced it into her rucksack. Her white T-shirt had short sleeves and her Blue Morpho tattoo was clearly visible. The scabbing had finally gone and against her pale skin and black and white clothes it seemed vibrant and alive.

Instead of being pleased, however, the sight of it made her cringe. Since the day that Joshua had shown her his tattoo, her butterfly seemed somehow linked to his and now she had been on the brink of spoiling that relationship with some inexplicable urge to kiss him.

She walked on, her head down, her face creased up in irritation.

She didn't have any classes but she could give her essay in. It was better to go there than back to Anna's. She did not want to face her grandmother. They hadn't spoken since the row and she did not want to be in her company after arriving at another dead end regarding the disappearance of her mum and Brendan. Not for one second did she need to be reminded of Anna's version of events, her horrible accusation about Brendan.

She left the shops and cut through some backstreets.

She pictured the B and B and remembered the moments when they thought they'd found out something important. Joshua had been ecstatic and they'd both talked about it as though it had been a great discovery. *It was almost as though they were leaving clues for us. Like a paperchase*, Joshua had said.

But finding out that bit of truth had taken them nowhere. In fact, it had made things worse. Now it seemed as though her mum and Brendan had *planned* their own disappearance, thereby abandoning their children. And yet they had left clues. The glasses case, the false name, the handwritten signature?

A paperchase.

Rose could see the school entrance further up. She slowed down. She felt heavily weighted all of a sudden and pulled her rucksack off her shoulder and let it hang in one hand. There was a brick wall alongside her and she sat on it hoping that the householder wouldn't come out and shoo her away.

Her mum and Brendan had left a paperchase. Or had they?

According to Valeriya Malashenko it was her *mum* who had been upset at the meal, her mum who had stopped walking along the pavement outside. It was her mum's glasses cases that had been left behind and of the signatures it was her mum's that had been the same as normal.

Her mum was leaving the trail of clues, not Brendan. Had she been drawn into something that she hadn't wanted to be part of? Was that the explanation? Or was it something more sinister? Was Brendan *forcing* her mum and so the clues were her cries for help?

Rose sat very still and thought of what Anna had said. *You choose to befriend the son of the person who most likely murdered your mother!* She gripped the handles of her rucksack. Then she stood up and headed for the school. She would not think about that. She would not. Brendan would never have hurt her mum. He loved her. Didn't he?

For a second she thought of Joshua lying on the bed, her face inches away from his. Would she be as close to him

259

in the future? Or would their relationship stall because of her awkwardness about what nearly happened? Maybe they would lose contact again and then when Anna talked about it all being Brendan's fault, Rose would have no strength to disagree.

No, that couldn't happen. She had to hold on to Joshua.

There were a few students milling around the corridors but no one took any notice of her. Afternoon classes had started and she headed for the staffroom. She made herself think through her timetable for the next day and the pieces of work that were due in. Then there was the plot of the book they were reading and the characters and the themes. She made herself picture all these things as though they were written as a list on a piece of paper in her head.

Anything to stop unpleasant ideas creeping into her thoughts.

Brendan loved her mum. He did.

Then there was Emma's memorial the next day. It was due to take place at four o'clock in the George Bernard Shaw Studio. She was definitely going and was bracing herself for Sherry Baxter's sharp tongue. Emma's family were due to be there she'd heard, her mother and a younger sister. Rose wondered if Bee Bee would go and Lewis Proctor. The atmosphere was going to be tense.

And still, as far as she knew, no one had been charged with Emma's murder or that of Ricky Harris.

She passed by the library and headed towards the heart of the building where the staff area was. She came up to the IT suite and had to stop as the corridor was blocked by a group of students waiting to go into a class. Just then the swing doors opened and Henry Thompson came out.

'Hi!' she said.

The policeman was wearing regular clothes; trousers and a windcheater.

'Hi.'

'What are you doing here? Is it about Emma? Have you arrested someone?' she said, touching the pouch of her rucksack where Emma's phone sat.

'That's three questions, Rose. Which shall I answer first?'

Rose shrugged. Why wasn't he in uniform?

'I'm not here about Emma. The case is progressing but there have been no arrests. I am here on other police business. A number of computers and laptops have gone missing.'

'Why are you dressed like that?'

'Fourth question. Because I'm not really on duty. It's my afternoon off. I was on my way home and I was passing the school so I thought I'd come in and talk to a couple of the technicians. It's actually easier to come into a place like this not looking like a policeman.'

She studied him. He looked better than he did in the uniform. She remembered him asking her to help him out at his club. She'd forgotten the name of it but he'd asked her to go *twice*.

'I saw you this lunchtime. I was just finishing my shift and you were coming out of Camden tube with a lad.'

She nodded. How long ago that seemed. Joshua and her, elated by finding information at the B and B.

'Your boyfriend, was it?'

'No!' she said indignantly.

'I just thought . . .'

'He isn't my boyfriend. He's my stepbrother!'

Maybe it was obvious to other people how she felt about Joshua. Possibly it was written all over her face, in her body language. Maybe other people could see it.

'Calm down. I just presumed . . .'

'Well, *don't* presume. He is not my boyfriend.'

'Sorry.'

'Do you want to get a coffee?' she suddenly said.

She should spend time with people other than just Joshua. Maybe she shouldn't be so dependent on his company. She looked down at her rucksack and remembered Emma's phone in the front pocket. She patted the flap as though she was afraid it might spring open.

'We could go to the cafeteria?'

He looked surprised. 'OK. If you're still speaking to me.'

'Just about,' she said, her face managing a smile.

'I've just got to see the Deputy Principal.'

'And I've got to give my essay in.'

'Meet you in the cafeteria in twenty minutes?'

'All right,' she said, heading off for the staff area.

The cafeteria was busy. She bought a peppermint tea and found a table in a quiet corner. She put her rucksack on the chair beside her so that no one else came close. When Henry came in she waved to him. He went up to the counter, got a drink and then sat opposite her. They were alongside one of the windows that showed the High Street outside.

'Over there? That building next to the carpet shop?' he said, pointing. 'That's where the Sundown Club is. Every Wednesday, six to eight.'

She stared straight ahead, deciding not to answer him.

'Interesting tattoo,' he said eventually.

She wasn't sure what he meant by *interesting*.

'It's a Blue Morpho. My favourite butterfly.'

'Is it symbolic?'

'Not really. I just like it.'

'Something beautiful that dies young? Transformation?'

'No . . .'

'People used to capture butterflies and keep them in jars until they died. And of course they were collected and mounted in glass cases. I personally don't like that. Creatures, insects, animals kept in cages.'

'It's none of that,' she said sharply. 'It's just that I love the look of them. That's all. It's not symbolic or metaphorical or whatever. It's a great shade of blue.'

'Yet you wear black and white?'

'God. You sound like my grandmother now.'

'Point taken.'

'It's Emma's memorial tomorrow,' she said, changing the subject.

'I know. I've been liaising with her family. They're really looking forward to it.'

'Looking *forward* to it!' she said.

'These things are important for people who are grieving. It keeps them close to the people they've lost. This and then the funeral. When the funeral is over it's usually a really bad time for the parents or husband or wife, whatever. 'Course, in this case there won't be a funeral for a while because of the investigation.'

'What exactly is happening?'

'I can't really talk about it.'

'You mean nothing.'

'We're moving slowly forward.'

'No new suspects, then,' she said.

'We're doing our best.'

'I'll bet, if Emma had been a celebrity or the daughter of Prince Charles, then you would have found the murderer.'

'Prince Charles hasn't got a daughter.'

'You know what I mean.'

Rose huffed. Skeggsie was right about the police not making an effort.

She looked around. There were empty tables on each side of them. An exclusion zone. It was as though students *knew* that Henry was a policeman. Maybe they did, even out of uniform. The atmosphere was stiff and Rose didn't know whether she could be bothered to make any more conversation.

'We found the knife,' Henry finally said, lowering his voice.

'Really?'

'It was alongside the railway line. Someone had tossed it over from Cuttings Lane.'

'The person who was running across the bridge at 6.20,' she said, thinking of Bee Bee.

'Maybe.'

'Was it Lewis Proctor's knife?'

'It didn't have his name on it, if that's what you mean.'

'But were there fingerprints, stuff like that?'

'Rose, the only thing on the knife was blood.'

Rose felt herself wilting. Emma's blood caked along the blade of a knife that had lain on the gravel by the side of the train tracks. She had been on trains back and forward to school. She had sat at the window and looked out and perhaps passed right over the very spot.

'It's with forensics so they may be able to lift a print from it. So you see we are getting somewhere.'

Rose looked at the pocket on the front of her rucksack. If she thought they were really taking it seriously she might give them Emma's mobile phone.

'However, something new *has* opened up in the Ricky Harris case. I mentioned to you that I was here today because of some thefts in the IT suite? Well, it turns out that our friend Ricky may have had a hand in taking laptops from the suite after hours. We think he may have been let in by someone on the inside. One of the technicians has stopped coming into work over the last few days and we're looking into his background.'

'But Ricky was killed two weeks ago. What has this got to do with that?'

'It's been going on since the beginning of term. We think he might have been taking them and selling them down at King's Cross. There is some organised crime down there and we think that Ricky might have been trying to earn his stripes so to speak.'

'He was killed for a laptop?'

'Ten to twelve laptops. Maybe he was due to give money to someone else and a row happened. Remember I told you that he was killed with his own knife.'

'So he wasn't killed for love?' she said, thinking of Lewis Proctor.

'Not ruling it out completely. The Proctor boy still has no alibi but . . .'

She sat quietly, looking at her empty mug.

'Well?' he said.

'What?'

'You asked me about the cases and I told you even though, strictly speaking, I'm not supposed to talk to anyone about them. You accused us of not making progress and I've told you about two new lines of enquiry that we are pursuing. What have you got to say about that?'

She said nothing. Was he expecting a gold star?

'Are you this awkward with everyone, Rose?' he said.

She quite liked him in a grudging way. Not as a friend or anything but he was a nice man and she always seemed to be arguing with him. She thought of Joshua, his hand on her shoulder, patting her arm, unaware that she had been a second away from kissing him. Maybe Henry was right in his own way. She did need some other friends. A new scene, even if it was *cool*.

'Do you still want me to help you in your club?' she said. 'Whatever it's called.'

'The Sundown Club. Yes! But I thought you said . . .'

'Just to help mind. I'm not one of the teenagers you've got to save. I'd just come to help make the tea or whatever.'

'It's not an old people's home, Rose. I doubt anyone will be drinking tea!'

'That's exactly what's wrong with adults! You have a certain image of teenagers! We're not all eating McDonald's and swilling Coke. I like tea. No sugar, a touch of milk.'

'OK, OK. Come tomorrow. Six to eight.'

'I'll be here at Emma's memorial. I could do a bit of work in the library and come afterwards. Thing is, though, I wouldn't want to come on my own. Can I meet you?'

'Sure. I get there early, about 5.30. To set up.'

'Call me, when you get there. Here, take my mobile,' she said, pulling her phone out of her coat pocket. 'Put your number into it. Let me have yours and I'll give you my number.'

Henry handed his mobile over to her.

'God! You need a new one of these. How old is it?'

'Point taken.'

'Why do you *always* say that?'

'Don't know. You make me nervous.'

She took her mobile back from him, 'Ring me tomorrow and I'll come across to your Sun Club.'

'Sundown Club.'

'Who thought of the name, by the way?'

'I did.'

'I thought so.'

TWENTY-FIVE

Rose was late for the memorial. Her last class had run over and afterwards the teacher wanted to speak to her about her work. With one eye on the classroom clock she listened to complaints about her last essay, which wasn't long enough or detailed enough. She hurriedly agreed with the teacher's comments, promising to do better in the future. By the time she got away the corridors were packed with students milling around after the end of classes. She had to weave her way through and then walk across the site to the George Bernard Shaw Studio. When she got there the memorial was about to start so the main entrance was closed. She stood in one spot, perplexed. It had not been a good day. A teacher came by and directed her up the stairs to the rear doors. When she got in she was surprised to see the auditorium virtually full. She sat on an aisle seat on the last but one row.

She felt hot and shrugged her jacket off. She dumped her rucksack on the next seat and looked at the front pouch. Emma's mobile phone was still where she'd put it a couple of nights before and she didn't know what to do about it.

The tiered seats meant that she could see everyone, at least the backs of their heads. It was five or six times the number of people who had come to Ricky Harris's memorial. She looked along the rows and saw Sara and Maggie. Sara turned at that minute and gave her a wave. On the edge of a row about halfway down was Bee Bee Marshall, and Lewis Proctor was a few seats away from her.

Along the very front row was Emma's family. A number of adults and a small girl. Among them was Sherry Baxter, one side of her red hair pulled back with a black comb. They were talking to each other and a couple were looking round, waving to people they knew who were behind them. Sherry stared ahead, though, her back solid, her head very still. Rose remembered her weeping a few nights before in the rose garden. The sound had been heartfelt.

Rose didn't recall any of Ricky Harris's family being at his memorial. He had a mother and an older brother, Emma had told her, but he hadn't got on with either of them.

The principal entered then. She stood centre stage as classical music started to play. It went on for some time and the hall quietened. Rose listened to the sound of the orchestra, the strings giving the piece a melancholy feel.

She was reminded of the lessons she had given up, of the violin that sat in its case in her room. She'd started learning to play when she was eight and carried on all the way through her time at Mary Linton. Now she didn't do it any more. Everything in her life seemed like that at the moment. Things she'd started and not finished. The essay was no good. Her relationship with Joshua was muddled. She'd given up the violin. She'd got involved in Emma's murder and had half-heartedly tried to find the knife that killed her; instead she'd found her mobile phone. The hunt for her mum and Brendan had stalled.

Nothing was going right.

The music played on while the principal stood with her head bowed as if in deep thought. When it stopped she looked up at the audience, her eyes sweeping across those seated, allowing a moment's complete silence before she started to talk.

'May I remind students to have their mobile phones on *silent* during this service.'

There was a shuffling of movement as students reached into bags to check that their phones were off. Rose didn't need to check hers. She'd been looking at it on and off all morning to see if she had a text from Joshua. There hadn't been any. Neither had there been any emails. He'd said he was busy but still she thought he might contact her. It made her feel anxious. Had he perhaps sensed something on Tuesday afternoon? Was he avoiding her? No, that was ridiculous. She was imagining a slight where there was none.

On top of it all she had agreed to go and help Henry Thompson in the Sundown Club. She sighed.

The principal started to speak.

'It is the fear of all heads and principals of educational establishments that during their career they may have to convene an event like this. A service to mark the death of a student. In the last week I have had the unenviable role of presiding over two such events. It's a very sad time for the school and its students. Today we are meeting to remember and honour Emma Jane Burke, a student of this school, a daughter, sister and a friend to many people here. It is with great regret that I must . . .'

Rose listened for a while but felt her thoughts pull her away.

When she saw Henry Thompson again she would give him Emma's mobile. It would be difficult to explain because she could not tell him about the CCTV photographs. She would have to say that she had gone into the cemetery that very morning and had found the mobile by chance. It was a tall story but if she stuck to it, who could say whether it was true or not? The police would most probably be so pleased to have it along with the murder weapon that they wouldn't worry how they got it.

Or she could post it to them anonymously.

She sighed again. Why had she kept the phone at all? She'd intended to try and find out who had made the call. But that, like everything else in her life at the moment, hadn't been done.

What was wrong with her?

Someone from Emma's family had got up to speak. It was a woman of about thirty dressed in dark trousers and a denim jacket. She had flat hair that hung in strings down the side of her face. She was Emma's aunt, she said, and went on to read a statement from the family. Rose watched her. It was a painful sight. The woman was in tears and her voice kept breaking with every sentence. She was holding up the notepaper in front of her and her arms were trembling. Rose found herself tensing her breath, willing the woman to get through her statement and go back and sit down. Eventually she did and the person next to her put an arm around her shoulder and pulled her close.

Two female students got up and had statements to read. The music changed and a familiar song came on. It had been one of Emma's favourite's, one of the girls said, and everyone sat and listened while the girls waited for it to finish before reading their pieces.

Bee Bee looked round. Rose caught her eye. She'd never spoken to Bee Bee face to face and yet it seemed as though she knew her. *I saw you run across that bridge,* she thought, staring straight at her. Bee Bee turned back to face the stage. Lewis Proctor glanced round at her but made no sign that he saw her there.

Was it Bee Bee who made that call to Emma?

One of the girls started to read from a piece of paper. She read slowly but quietly so it was hard to hear every word she said. Rose stopped trying and pulled her rucksack on to her lap and opened the pouch at the front. In it she saw the pink mobile, still in the plastic bag where Skeggsie had placed it. She pulled it out and slid it out of the bag. She flipped the lid and turned it on, making sure it was on *silent*.

There was a way to try and find out the identity of the caller.

Make a call on Emma's phone.

Reply to the text that was sent to Emma.

Just about everyone who had any link to Emma was in the auditorium at that moment.

The principal was standing up. Her voice rang clear and loud after the nervous girls and the tearful aunt.

'I would like you all to take part in a minute's silence.'

The silence was solid. Everyone in the auditorium went very still. Rose looked down at the tiny screen and typed out a text.

Who are you?

She waited until the end of the silence. The principal thanked everyone and the classical music started again. A low buzz of conversation began and she pressed *Send*. She kept her eyes on Bee Bee and was disappointed when no sound came. Then she remembered that all phones were on *silent*. She waited as bit by bit people took their phones out of bags and pockets and began to look at them. The conversation got louder and she was worried that she wouldn't hear a tone as the text arrived. Her eyes stayed on Bee Bee, who had taken her phone out of her pocket and was staring at it.

Rose got up and walked a couple of steps down towards the stage. Now she was close enough to Bee Bee to hear a ring tone.

She sent the text a second time. *Who are you?*

She waited.

Bee Bee's ring tone sounded. Bee Bee looked at the screen and she heard her swear softly. Rose stood very still. She'd been *right*. She'd seen Bee Bee's silver boots and bangles on the bridge and now she had proof that it was Bee Bee's phone that made the call.

A sound came from the other side of the auditorium. A wailing sound. A loud cry. She turned round and saw Emma's family huddling around Sherry Baxter. Sherry was sobbing loudly and trying to shrug off her relatives. Rose looked at her with pity. Sherry had felt the loss badly. She had been crying at Ricky Harris's memorial, then at the rose garden and now here.

'Leave it, please, leave it,' Sherry shouted out through her tears, backing away from her relatives towards the doors of the auditorium.

She went out and was followed by some of the adults. Looking round Rose saw that Bee Bee was heading down the stairs towards the exit. She went after her, sidestepping students who were dawdling. Emma's family had congregated in the foyer but Sherry had gone outside into a small courtyard. She had a lit cigarette in one hand and her mobile phone in the other. She was walking up and down, her body language warding sympathisers off. Her face was blotched and she kept wiping her nose with the hand that held the cigarette.

Bee Bee was heading for the toilets. Rose followed her, one hand in her pocket holding on to Emma's phone. There was a short queue inside and Bee Bee was at the front. Rose was two girls behind her. She wished she could see Bee Bee's face, to see if there was any sign of upset. She would make the call one more time to make sure she was right. She'd wait until Bee Bee went into the cubicle and then send the text for a third time.

'Hey, Rose,' a voice said.

A girl from one of her classes were standing behind her in the queue. Rose gave a half-smile. Her name was Zoe something. She really couldn't get involved in a conversation with her now. She wanted to keep her concentration on the phone text and Bee Bee.

'Did you see that scene from Sherry!' Zoe said. 'Talk about drama! I call it hypocritical.'

Rose frowned. One of the toilets flushed and a door opened. Bee Bee went into the cubicle. Rose took the phone out of her pocket. Turning her back on the girls she accessed the text she'd composed earlier.

'All those tears and she was sneaking off behind Emma's back. Cow. How could she do that her stepsister?'

Rose turned round to face Zoe. She had half an ear to the cubicle and was going to press the *Send* button any second.

'What are you talking about?'

'Sherry and all her blubbering. I saw her snogging Ricky Harris a couple of weeks before he was stabbed. Behind her stepsister's back! She was all over him. It was up Canary Wharf. I didn't have any classes so I went there with my mum to look at the shops.'

'Sherry and Ricky?'

'On the escalator. We were going up. And they were coming down.'

The sound of a toilet flushing distracted Rose. The other cubicle door opened and the queue moved forward.

Sherry and Ricky Harris? Together? Behind Emma's back?

Moments later Bee Bee emerged, the door banging behind her. Rose found herself staring at her. She'd still not sent the text. She'd been thrown by a mental picture of Sherry's red hair and Ricky Harris's face. Together. She was astonished.

'What's your problem, girl?' Bee Bee demanded.

Rose couldn't say anything. In her hand was Emma's mobile. Bee Bee's eyes were boring into her. She looked down at the phone and pressed the *Send* button. Bee Bee made a loud *tsk*ing sound and shoved past her. She went out of the toilets.

Rose followed her. She pressed the *Send* button and watched Bee Bee walk back up to Lewis Proctor. She waited for her to get her phone out and receive the text for the fourth time.

But she didn't reach for her phone. She didn't pat her pocket to feel it vibrating. She smiled up at Lewis, her phone of no interest to her. Rose felt her shoulders slump. She'd been wrong. It had just been a coincidence. Bee Bee's phone had rung at the very moment she had sent the text.

Someone else had received it.

Another phone had got the message *Who are you?* Four times.

She swivelled round and looked through the glass window at Sherry Baxter, who was standing in the middle of the courtyard staring at her mobile phone.

Rose pulled out the pink handset. Instead of sending a text she rang the number at the top of the screen. She waited, hardly breathing, and moments later Sherry's face creased up as she looked at her own phone. She pressed a button and lifted the phone to her ear.

Rose put Emma's phone to her ear.

There was silence for a moment, then a voice.

'Who is this? You have the wrong number. You have to stop calling me.'

As she listened she looked out at Sherry, whose lips were synching the words.

'Stop calling me,' she said and the call was ended.

Sherry Baxter threw her cigarette to the ground and then walked off out of the courtyard. Rose waited a few moments, her chest puffed up with indignation. Emma's stepsister. How could she?

Then she followed her.

TWENTY-SIX

Rose kept her distance. She let Sherry Baxter walk ahead and stopped a couple of times to look in shop windows in case she caught up with her. Sherry went past the train station and headed for the bus stop. The High Street was crowded with students from the school but Sherry just walked ahead, not acknowledging any of them. She stopped when she got to the bus shelter and Rose turned into a shop. The window was full of sari fabric, dazzling colours, swathes of it hanging side by side, jewellery stacked along the lower portion. Rose saw rows of bangles, hundreds of them. She thought of Bee Bee.

Why was she running across the bridge on the night that Emma was murdered?

Rose looked round. Sherry was in the shelter waiting for a bus. She had her mobile in her hand. Rose registered then that Sherry was dressed from head to toe in black, in mourning for her stepsister. The colour of her hair seemed to contradict the emotion. It sat glossy and bright, one side held stylishly back by a black comb.

She and Ricky Harris had been seen together.

How could that be? How could Sherry deceive her stepsister so?

A bus was coming. It edged forward through the traffic and Rose could see that Sherry was standing forward, intending to get on it. She walked a few metres, keeping herself to the inside of the pavement, hoping that Sherry didn't turn suddenly and see her there. The bus stopped and Sherry moved forward. The doors took a while to open and when they did she stepped up on to the platform, followed by some other students and a couple of men in workmen's clothes. Rose moved closer to the stop as Sherry walked further into the bus. Then Sherry went upstairs. Rose stepped quickly across to the bus stop and on to the bus. She showed her travel card and then headed along the bus to the very back. She sat in the corner opposite a big woman and a toddler. From where she was she could see the foot of the stairs.

It was about six stops to Parkway East.

Sherry would get off there and head down Cuttings Lane towards the Chalk Farm Estate.

The bus moved off and she sat back. It stuttered forward and then stopped, waiting for a car to pull out from a parking place.

Why was she doing this? It would be enough to simply tell the police what she had found out. They knew where Sherry lived. They would go and see her, question her about the call to Emma. But Rose didn't feel happy about that. Sherry had made this personal by shouting Rose down at Ricky Harris's memorial. She had shamed her in front of all the other students by saying that she hadn't got to the cemetery in time to help Emma, that she hadn't bothered, when all the time she had sent the message that had made Emma go in earlier than she had planned.

There was another reason. Rose had seen Sherry answer the call and she didn't want to let her out of her sight. The events of the last couple of weeks had been fragmented and blurred. It had been impossible to get a clear picture of what had happened either on Parkway East station or in St Michael's Cemetery. Rose had found something out now and she wasn't going to let it go until she understood what had happened on those two occasions when she had stood over someone's dead body.

She was staying with Sherry.

As the bus stopped and started she remembered Sherry's tears at Ricky's memorial. Then she had thought they were for her stepsister but she had been wrong. Sherry was crying for Ricky Harris. Maybe she had been the only person in school who had cried for Ricky. Possibly she had loved him.

How long had she been seeing him?

Was it just during the summer when Emma had broken up with him? Did she fall for Ricky and convince herself that Ricky felt the same way? Then when Emma broke up with Lewis and went back to Ricky did that mean that she was out of the picture? Or did Ricky keep on seeing Sherry at the same time as he was seeing her stepsister.

Either way Sherry must have felt spurned.

Rose remembered the call Ricky had got on the platform that night he was killed. *Change of plans. Got to meet someone*, he'd said. Had that call been from Sherry? Was it possible that Sherry had been so broken-hearted that she had followed Ricky to the station and watched him talking to Rose from the footbridge? Had that made her even more jealous? Perhaps it was bad enough that he'd dumped her and gone back to his old girlfriend, Emma, but here he was looking as though he was chatting up someone else. Most certainly Sherry would have known where Ricky kept his knife. She'd argued with him on the footbridge. Had she slid her hand into his pocket, taken his knife and stabbed him with it?

Rose thought about this dispassionately. Ricky's death meant nothing to her. Emma was different, though. She didn't want to think about that night at the cemetery.

The bus was finally coming into Parkway East. Rose moved herself and slid down the seat a touch as she saw Sherry's feet appear at the bottom of the stairs. She picked up a newspaper that was on the seat beside her. She held it up in front of her face.

The bus stopped and the doors opened. A crowd of people were queuing to get on and off and Rose waited until Sherry stepped off the bus before she got up, dropped the newspaper, and followed her.

She waited a moment and let Sherry to walk ahead, across the road towards Cuttings Lane. A couple of other teenage girls were walking behind her and Rose let a gap open up. She allowed Sherry to get out of sight because Cuttings Lane only led to one place. When she got to the footbridge she glanced down at the railway. The knife that had killed Emma had been found down there along-side the track. She looked ahead and saw, in the distance, the red hair of Sherry in front of the other teenage girls.

She went across the footbridge and down the stairs and on to a pathway that had murals on each side. She moved quickly, worrying that Sherry would disappear off in the streets and cul-de-sacs of the estate. She kept to the side of the pavement and saw Sherry turn right up ahead. She quickened her step, passing the other two girls, and got to the corner just as a door shut.

She didn't know which door it was. She stood perplexed and looked at a row of four houses in front of her. There were other houses further along but Sherry couldn't have walked that quickly.

'You lost?' one of the girls said, walking up to her.

'I was trying to catch up with Sherry,' she said.

'Number twenty-two. The end house. You from her school?'

Rose nodded.

'I was going to go to college,' the other girl said.

'You was going to do childcare.'

'I didn't get the grades.'

'Oh,' Rose said, backing away, afraid that Sherry would look out of the window of her house and see her there. 'You should retake your GCSEs.'

'Can't, I'm suspended.'

'Thought you wanted to see Sherry?' the other girl said.

'Just remembered she told me to pick up some drinks and crisps at the shop.'

'See you then . . .'

They both called out and waved to her until she turned into the alley again. She waited, hoping they would walk on. She counted to twenty and then crept out along the pavement, pausing at the corner. When she peeked round she could see their backs right along the street. In seconds they turned a corner and were gone.

She stood looking at the fourth house along. She wasn't sure what to do. Should she go up to the front door? Show Sherry Emma's phone? See what she had to say?

Her confidence crumbled. Was she right about this?

There were other people on the street. Two mums wheeling buggies side by side, a group of young boys with a football, a man cycling past. She didn't know what to do. She heard a beep from her own mobile. She pulled it out and saw that she had a text from Henry Thompson. She opened it.

I'm here at the school. Meet me outside in five minutes.

Henry was waiting for her. She'd forgotten all about the arrangement she had made with him.

She thought hard for a moment. The thing she really wanted to do was to ring Joshua. To tell him what had happened. Ask him to come here, to the Chalk Farm Estate, then and there. That way they could talk it through and plan what to do together. She didn't feel she could, though. She didn't feel easy texting him out of the blue.

Why had she spoilt things between them?

The front door of number twenty-two opened. Startled, Rose moved back along the street. Sherry emerged from the doorway. Rose backed round the corner. The boys playing football were there and the ball hit her on the leg.

'Do you mind?' she hissed.

They all parroted her. *Do you mind! Do you mind! Do you mind!*

She ignored them and peeked round the corner. Sherry was carrying a black plastic rubbish bag in one hand. She was striding away from her house.

Rose followed Sherry, keeping back, pausing at corners, sticking to the hedgerows. Schoolchildren passed but didn't seem to notice her stopping and starting, so intent

were they on their own conversations. Shrieks of laughter rang out but she ignored them. Sherry did not stop or
look round. She was walking in a stiff but purposeful way,
holding the bag in one hand. She went quickly, making
it difficult for Rose to keep up without getting too close.
Eventually, moving out of the estate and into streets of
older houses, she turned into a small recycling bay. It
had giant green and brown bells sitting on the tarmac
for bottles. At the side was a blue square metal bin for
clothes and shoes. Rose stayed where she was, peep-
ing out from behind a high hedge. Sherry glanced round
the street. Her face was pale and she seemed unhappy.
She then lifted her black plastic bag and tried to force it
into the rectangular opening of the blue clothes bin. She
couldn't, though, because it was full up and Rose could
see that there were several plastic bags around the base
that had been dumped there by people previously. She
watched as Sherry stood uncertainly for a second. Then
she bent over and seemed to move the bags. When she
stood up again her hands were free and she moved to the
edge of the recycling bay and pulled a packet of cigarettes
from a pocket and lit one. She inhaled deeply and looked
round again.

Rose stepped back along a front drive and crouched by
a van.

Sherry walked off back in the direction of her house.

Rose let her go before she stood up. She waited a few

minutes and then went across to the recycling bay and looked at the plastic bags sitting around the clothes bank. There were about eight. All but one of them was covered in droplets of rain. She picked up the dry black bag, stepped outside the bay and sat on a garden wall, then undid the knot at the top and looked inside. She could see clothes but there was something heavy there as well. She pulled out some black jogging trousers and draped them over the wall. The next thing was a hooded sweatshirt, black. She laid it on top of the trousers. Then she reached in and felt shoes or boots. There was something else as well. Wires, or rings or something light and yet metallic. She grabbed a handful.

Silver and gold bangles.

She paused, thinking hard.

Then she upended the bag and they fell out over the tarmac. The boots came out at the same time; ankle-length, silver.

Sherry had thrown it all away.

The outfit she had worn to go to the cemetery on the night Emma was stabbed. The clothes she had had on when running back over the bridge. Skeggsie had enlarged the photographs and Rose had been sure it was Bee Bee Marshall.

And all the time it had been Sherry Baxter.

TWENTY-SEVEN

Rose gathered up the hooded top and jogging bottoms and pushed them back into the black plastic bag. The boots went in next and then she squatted down and picked up the bangles from the pavement. She counted twenty-seven metal circles. Some had fallen together, some were lying singly and were difficult to get hold of. She threaded them on to her arm for ease of carrying.

Her phone beeped.

Where are you?

It was from Henry Thompson. She should answer it but she was too stunned. Sherry Baxter, Emma's stepsister. She was the one who dressed up, who sent the text to Emma to tell her to get to the cemetery early. She *killed* her own stepsister. Rose felt the weight of it. She couldn't deal with this on her own. She needed help. She looked at the street name opposite and decided to reply to Henry's text.

At a recycling bay in Drummer Road. Come and get me. It's about Emma. I know who killed her.

She waited, sitting back on the wall, and began to think it through. On the day she was killed Emma had received a note from Lewis to meet him at the cemetery. He later said he hadn't sent it. He had received one, though, in Emma's handwriting, he said.

Sherry Baxter must have written those notes. She lived in the same house as her stepsister so she had access to Emma's things. She had most likely seen the notes Emma had received from Lewis in the summer and possibly even seen the ones that Emma was sending to him. Had she copied the handwriting? And drawn the signature smiley face and heart so that the notes looked authentic?

Why had Sherry tried to get Lewis and Emma together?

Sherry cared for Ricky Harris but he went back to Emma. Did Sherry kill Ricky because she was angry that he went back to Emma? Had this sent her off balance so that she ended up killing her own stepsister?

Or had Emma found out that Sherry had been seeing Ricky?

Rose dismissed this idea. When Emma came to see her that Saturday afternoon she seemed in harmony with her stepsister. She said Sherry was in Brentwood with her dad. She didn't know that Sherry was on the Chalk Farm Estate dressed up like Bee Bee, planning to ambush her in the cemetery.

A car came round the corner and pulled up in front of her.

Rose stood up. Henry got out and looked puzzled. His eyes dropped to the black plastic bag.

'What's going on?' he said.

She walked towards the car.

'We need to go to Emma Burke's house.'

'I've got to open the club up. There are kids waiting there already.'

'I've got evidence about Emma's killer. I'll tell you in the car.'

Henry's face darkened. He looked disapprovingly at her. He got into the car and so did she and they headed off. He was completely silent as she told him about Emma's mobile phone, making up the part where she'd found it that morning in the cemetery. She then explained about finding the last phone call that Emma had received. Without giving Henry a chance to speak, she described how she had sent texts to that mystery number and then made a final call, which Sherry had answered.

She expected some comment from him. A question or some response but he was mute. There was tension in the car and she filled it with nervous talk, sensing that he was not at all pleased with what she was saying. She pointed to the black plastic bag and the clothes and then, as they parked a few houses up from Emma's, she showed him the bangles on her arm and suggested that perhaps Sherry was throwing these out because she may have worn them to the cemetery in order to throw suspicion on Bee Bee. She did not mention the CCTV photograph.

'Well?' she finally said. 'What do you think?'

Henry blew through his teeth. He spoke quietly.

'Rose, you cannot go round the streets trying to solve a crime yourself. As soon as you have any evidence you need to ring the police. You've had Emma's phone all day?'

She took it out of her pocket. It lay on the palm of her hand, pink and cute. The metal bangles were still on her arm and hung gaudily. Against them her black jacket, T-shirt and trousers looked funereal.

'Rose,' Henry said, his voice hard with anger. 'These things are *evidence*. There's a procedure for evidence. You pick it up with gloves. You put it in a plastic bag. It's marked, filed, documented. Then it's examined in minute detail by a forensic scientist. After that any person who comes into contact with it has to sign it in, sign it out, so that when it comes to a trial it's admissible. It proves something. It hasn't been contaminated with another person's fingerprints or fibres. Or someone else hasn't added to the data base and confused the whole order of events.'

'I just . . .'

'You just mucked it up, Rose. You've ruined these things as evidence.'

'But I found out . . .'

'Any solicitor in his right mind will have them dismissed out of court.'

'But Sherry killed . . .'

'If what you say is true then she won't be charged because you've contaminated the very things that will make it possible to convict her!'

Rose closed her eyes to shut him out. She felt her throat tighten up. She had done what she thought was right.

'You have to leave these things to the police.'

Henry's voice sounded like that of a teacher and it made her angry.

'But the police haven't found out who killed Ricky or Emma. Ricky's been dead for two weeks, Emma for twelve days. What's happened? Who's been questioned? Arrested? What's going on with the investigation? You don't know *anything*.'

'We found the knife. We've interviewed suspects, we've looked after the families . . .'

'But you haven't found out who did it and I *have*. Doesn't that count for something? All you can talk about is procedure, filling in forms, contamination. I'll tell you what contamination is. It's Sherry Baxter. She killed her stepsister and all you're doing is sitting talking about plastic bags and how I shouldn't have bothered. But if I hadn't bothered no one would know. So . . .'

'So what, Rose? The evidence is ruined. What are you going to do now?'

'I'm going to go in there before she gets rid of her mobile phone and I'm going to get her to confess.'

'No, no . . .' Henry shook his head.

'This is the *moment*. She's upset. She's already thrown this lot out,' she said, holding up the corner of the black plastic bag. 'You and I can go in, together. You can tell her that I said I saw her at the cemetery and you've come round to ask her face to face. While you're doing that I'll send a text from Emma's phone and see if that sends her over the edge.'

'Rose, don't you get it? It's inadmissible.'

'Henry, don't you get it? She's upset. This is the *moment*. Take her to the police station and she'll have calmed down. I'm going in. You can come or you can stay here.'

'She'll withdraw the confession.'

'She won't be able to because I'll have heard it. You'll have heard it. We can be witnesses.'

He shook his head.

'You can't go in with that phone.'

'Yes, I can and I'm going to.'

Rose threw the door open and got out. She still had the bangles on so she pulled her T-shirt sleeve down and covered them. She headed for Sherry's house and then strode up to the door. There was no movement from the car but she went ahead. She rang the bell.

Sherry answered almost immediately. Her face was pink as if she'd been crying.

'What?' she said, staring at Rose.

'I have something to say to you.'

'Like what?'

Just then a car door shut and Rose heard Henry walking up behind her.

'Hello, Sherry,' came Henry's calm voice. 'I hope you don't mind. There's just a small thing I want to ask you. Something that Rose Smith, here, brought to my attention. It's a difficult time with the memorial I know . . .'

'Come in,' Sherry said, turning her back and walking into the house.

They followed her into the living room. The place smelled of cigarettes and air freshener, and the television was blaring out. Next to an armchair was a coffee table. An overflowing ashtray sat beside a packet of cigarettes and a mobile phone.

'Sit down.'

Sherry gestured to a sofa and picked up the TV remote and muted the sound. The picture stayed there – people looking at houses in the country.

Henry sat down but Rose stayed standing. In her pocket she had the pink phone. She had her finger ready on the text button.

'What?' Sherry said.

'Rose here said she thought she might have seen you in the cemetery the evening that Emma was killed. Do you have anything to say to that?'

Sherry's face screwed up.

'How come you're not in uniform?' she said.

'Were you there, Sherry? When Emma was killed?' he said.

'No!'

Rose pressed the *Send* button. A few seconds later there was a beep from Sherry's phone. She glanced down at it and then looked straight ahead. Her lips seemed to tremble and her hand went up to her head, fiddling with the comb that was holding one side of her hair back.

'Answer your phone, Sherry,' Rose said, then pressed the *Send* button again.

Sherry shook her head. She seemed unable to speak and when the phone beeped for a second time she burst into tears. She grabbed the packet of cigarettes. Her hand was shaking.

'This is Emma's mobile,' Rose said, taking it out of her pocket.

Sherry's face was pale against her hair, her eyes fixed on the pink mobile, staring at it as if it were a ghost.

'I dug it up from a grave, Sherry, where you buried it.'

'You dug it up from where?' Henry said.

Sherry continued to cry.

'You killed her,' Rose said. 'She was your stepsister. How could you?'

'I didn't mean to kill her.'

'Tell us what happened, Sherry,' Henry said, his voice measured.

'I wanted to confront Lewis. I know he killed my Ricky. I went to the cemetery to have it out with him. I wanted

Lewis to admit what he'd done. I wasn't intending to kill anyone. I texted Emma to come early to the cemetery. I wanted to get her on my side but she went mad at me. She told me to mind my own business. She said it was nothing to do with me so I told her about me and Ricky.'

'And you stabbed her?'

'She hit me. She kept hitting me and I just lost control.'

'So it was self-defence?' Henry said. 'You need to come down to the station so we can talk about this officially. If it was self-defence, then there's a good chance that you will be treated leniently.'

'It wasn't self-defence! She texted Emma on a mystery phone. She had a knife on her. Who goes to meet people with a knife in their pocket?' Rose said.

Sherry wiped her nose with the back of her hand.

'That's what you'll never get, people like you. You come from a posh house and a boarding school. You don't know what it's like living here all your life. I carry a knife. Loads of kids carry knives. While you're carrying your violin or your laptop, some of us are carrying knives.'

Rose didn't know what to say.

'Let's go to the station. It'll be good to get this stuff off your chest.'

Henry was standing up.

'She's lying, 'Rose said, incredulous. 'She planned it. That's why she called Emma there early. She killed her and wanted it to seem as if Lewis or Bee Bee had done it.'

Henry led Rose out of the living-room door. He was holding her arm too tightly and she tried to break free.

'Give me Emma's mobile.'

She gave it to him.

'I want you to go away now, Rose. I'll be speaking to you later tonight or tomorrow. You leave the bangles and you go home.'

'She planned it!' Rose said, tearing the bangles off her wrist and dropping them on to the hall table. 'Why would she dress up in black clothes and a hoodie and wear boots and bangles like Bee Bee's if she wasn't planning it in advance! Trying to put the blame on someone else . . .' Rose demanded.

'We'll never know, Rose,' Henry said, pushing her backwards up the hall, his voice dropping to a whisper. 'Because you have contaminated the evidence.'

'But what about Ricky! She could have killed Ricky too!'

'Leave it to the police, Rose.'

Rose stopped at the door. Henry opened it and she went out. He closed it behind her. Tears came into her eyes and she let them. This week everything seemed to have gone wrong.

Even this.

But at least now Emma's family would know the truth.

Much good it would do them.

TWENTY-EIGHT

It was Saturday morning and Rose was sitting on her own in the Dark Brew. In front of her was a cup of black coffee. It was stronger than she liked it but she sipped it anyway. Joshua was due to meet her at eleven. She had her coat on the seat opposite, saving it for him. The cafe was busy, though, and a couple of people had asked for the chair and she had said it was taken.

She was still reeling from her appointment with Detective Inspector Schillings at the police station. She stared straight ahead at the other people in the cafe and remembered the interview and the way she had been spoken to.

'Are you aware, Miss Rose Smith, that you could be charged with perverting the course of justice? What were you thinking of? I understood you were an intelligent girl. This is not intelligent. This smacks of complete and utter stupidity.'

Her cheeks burned thinking about it. When a woman quietly asked if the seat opposite was taken, she snapped at her.

'Yes! My friend is in the toilet!'

Where was Joshua? She'd said eleven and now it was ten past. She had virtually run all the way from the police station to get here on time and there was no sign of him. She'd not actually spoken to him when making the arrangement. The truth was she hadn't spoken to him at all since Tuesday afternoon when they got back from the B and B.

She'd hoped that today they could get back to normal.

Her interview with Inspector Schillings had upset her, though.

Henry Thompson had been to see her on Friday and informed her about the appointment with the Detective Inspector. After the commotion about Sherry Baxter's arrest had died down, he had called at her grandmother's and told her that she had to see DI Schillings at Parkway police station at ten on Saturday morning. He'd been cold and distant and said that there were issues to discuss and told her to be polite and conciliatory. He did not warn her about the ticking-off she was going to get. No doubt that had been on purpose. If she'd known she might not have gone.

Neither did he mention her coming to his club again.

Maybe he'd washed his hands of her.

Arriving at the station she'd smiled at Detective Inspector Schillings, a little nervous, aware that she was in trouble because of the contamination of the evidence.

He had shown her into a small interview room in the police station. He had not asked her to sit down. He had not offered her a drink. He'd hardly made eye contact with her at all. His annoyance was clear from the slow inhalation of breath he took before blasting her with his words.

'We are dealing with the investigation of a girl's murder here. A heinous crime. This is no time for a jumped-up Nancy Drew to go around trying to solve the crime herself. What were you thinking of, young lady? Are you aware that we could charge you? That you may have compromised the whole investigation?'

Her throat tensed at the memory. *Jumped-up Nancy Drew*.

How dare he speak to her like that?

She'd gone there expecting grief but among it all she'd thought that there might have been a single comment *congratulating* her for working out the identity of the person who sent the text to Emma. Instead she'd been shamed. When he had finished Detective Inspector Schillings stood up and turned his back to her.

'You may leave now, Miss Smith and I do not wish to see you in this establishment again.'

Leaving the interview room she'd almost bumped into Henry. He was standing talking to another police officer, looking at some papers. She didn't want to face him though, not after being humiliated by Schillings. She walked quietly along the corridor back the way she came, pausing at the locked door for someone to let her out. She didn't want to see any police officer ever again. Walking out on to the street she found herself taking a deep breath, her shoulders and arms tight with tension.

How dare he speak to her as if she was ten years old?

The cafe was filling up and it was becoming more difficult to save the seat for Joshua. She was on the brink of plucking her coat off it when the street door opened and he walked in, followed by Skeggsie. Her mood dipped even more. He hadn't come alone. Just then the people from the next table got up to leave and Skeggsie grabbed one of their chairs and pulled it over to Rose's table, oblivious to the leaden stares he was getting from other people in the cafe.

'Coffee? Skeggsie? Bun? Rose?'

Rose looked straight at Joshua. She searched his face to see if there was any change there, as if somehow on Tuesday, even though his eyes had been closed, he had known that something odd was happening between them.

'Rose? Do you want anything?' he said.

She shook her head as he went up to the counter. She eyed him standing in the queue. He didn't look round at her. It gave her a heaviness in her chest.

They'd been in touch via emails. On Wednesday she'd emailed him (adding Skeggsie's name) and told him all about the events at the memorial and how she had worked out what Sherry Baxter had done. A number of emails followed where she explained what she thought had happened, leaving out the problems with the evidence and Henry's annoyance with her. He'd been amazed with her and even Skeggsie had sent his congratulations.

If either of them had seen her with Inspector Schillings they might not have been so happy about it.

Joshua sat down with the drinks.

'Well done, Rose,' Joshua said. 'You persevered. You stuck with it and you got a good result. It's made me think about Dad and Kathy. I admit I was upset on Tuesday . . .'

Rose looked down at the table, using her finger to rub at a mark on the surface.

'I've decided to continue with the search. Skeggsie and I are going to Twickenham today. We're meeting Amanda and the owner of the B and B. She's agreed to talk to us.'

She looked at him with dismay. He was still continuing the search? After what they'd found out? After how upset he'd been?

'It would be mad not to follow it up,' he said, as if reading her thoughts.

She nodded in a forced genial way. Joshua and Skeggsie were going to Twickenham. There didn't even seem to be an invite for her. She drank some of her bitter coffee. It was almost cold but she didn't care. Joshua was not including her.

Her phone beeped and she looked down to see that she had a text from Henry.

'I'll just get this,' she said.

Joshua and Skeggsie carried on talking as she accessed the message.

Where are you? I'm on the High Street near Parkway East.

Henry was looking for her. Across the table she saw Joshua and Skeggsie making their plans for the day, their chairs turned in towards each other, excluding her.

Another beep came.

I need to talk to you!

Henry was bothered about her. It touched her. She sent a text back to him.

In the Dark Brew opp station.

He replied immediately. *Meet me outside.*

'Sorry,' she said, interrupting Joshua and Skeggsie. 'That was my policeman friend. He wants to see me. I won't be a minute.'

He was outside the cafe. He looked tired but he smiled at her. There was a police car across the road, the window open, another officer in the driving seat. It was parked beside a tall lamp post on top of which was a camera. She frowned at it, remembering the CCTV photos. She had almost revealed their existence to Henry when she told Sherry that she'd dug up Emma's phone. Henry had quizzed her on that when he came round to Anna's and she explained to him, in desperation, that she hadn't actually 'dug up' the phone, but that she'd been speaking metaphorically. Thank goodness he believed her and no one knew about the images. Detective Inspector Schillings' face came into her head. It was hard to imagine it but the interview could have been worse, much worse.

There were people milling past and Henry took her arm and led her to a small alley between two shops.

'The DI gave you a bad time, I heard,' he said.

She shrugged.

'I had to tell him, Rose. It all had to come out.'

'I know.'

'You angry?'

She shrugged.

'These things always come out.'

'I was trying to help. No one else seemed to be doing anything.'

'I can't go through this whole argument with you again. I know you did it for the right reasons but it was the wrong thing to do. You do understand that.'

'I understand,' she said grudgingly.

'This makes a first then. You agreeing with me.'

'Don't push your luck.'

'Unofficially I thought you should know that Sherry Baxter has been charged with the manslaughter of Emma Burke. She's due in court Monday morning. She'll plead guilty, she says, and argue that the whole thing was an accident, a row that went wrong.'

'And the clothes? And the notes she sent? And the text asking Emma to come early to the cemetery? All these things were accidents too?'

'We don't know what will happen in court. '

Rose let out a dramatic sigh.

'What about Ricky?'

'Sherry had nothing to do with Ricky's death. She was at her dad's house in Brentwood. We checked it out. Her dad's new partner agreed and there were neighbours that came in while she was there. I told you we are looking into a new line of enquiry. Ricky Harris was working with someone inside the school, nicking hardware and software. We've been investigating one of the IT technicians for a while. Turns out he was using a false name, false papers, false address.'

'Who was it?' Rose said.

'A man called Frank Palmer. We wanted to question him but he hasn't been seen around for a few days.'

'I know him. He helped me in the IT suite,' Rose said.

It was the technician who had come to Ricky Harris's memorial. He had been the victim of Ricky's cruel taunts and once he had told Ricky off for harassing Rose. Could *he* have been stealing stuff from the school? Could he have links with Ricky Harris? Surely not. He seemed too nice. He'd spoken to her in the cafe one day and she'd seen him going into his house in Twickenham.

'Well, he's not what he seemed.'

'I thought all employees had to have a CRB check?'

'He did. The check was done. His papers were passed. It looks like someone has made a big mistake.'

'So his name's not Frank Palmer?'

Henry shook his head.

'And he might have stabbed Ricky?'

'We don't know that. It's just something we're looking into. At the moment we're doing door to door in King's Cross. Asking his neighbours about him. That's what I'm doing today so I should be off.'

'King's Cross?'

He nodded. 'That's where he lived.'

'But . . .'

'I just wanted to be sure that you were OK after DI Schillings spoke to you.'

Rose looked away, her forehead scrunched up. King's Cross?

'Are you OK? You've been through a lot.'

She nodded in a distracted way.

'Now I've really got to get off.'

She watched him go. He walked swiftly away and headed towards the squad car. He gave a half-wave as he got in. Did Frank Palmer live in King's Cross? Surely she had seen him opening the front door of a house in

Twickenham? The squad car drove off and she headed for the cafe.

A jumped-up Nancy Drew.

Let the police do their own investigations.

Once inside the cafe she saw that her seat had been taken and that Joshua and Skeggsie were on their feet, putting their coats on.

'You were a long time,' Joshua said.

'Something's come up,' she said, looking distracted.

'Are we going?' Skeggsie said pointedly to Joshua.

'Yep.'

'Can I come?' Rose said.

'To Twickenham? I didn't think you would be bothered again.'

'And I've got some stuff in the back seat of my car so there's not really room,' Skeggsie said, giving her a frown.

'Please?' Rose said, trying a pleading look.

She didn't want to be on her own again, knocking round the house, avoiding the rooms that Anna was using, thinking over the messiness of all that had happened that week.

'There's not really room,' Skeggsie said.

'I don't take up much space.'

Joshua looked puzzled. 'Why do you want to come?'

'I don't know. I just do.'

'Come on, then.'

Skeggsie scowled at her as she went after Joshua.

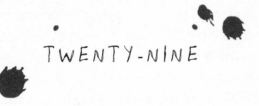

TWENTY-NINE

The journey to Twickenham was quick. Rose was sitting on less than half the back seat, her legs squashed up against the rear of Joshua. Beside her sat the box of a brand-new printer. On the side were the words *Laser Jet CP36525dn Colour Laser Printer*. She wondered where this would fit in among Skeggsie's vast array of IT equipment.

She half listened as Joshua explained the reasoning behind going back to the B and B for a third time. She nodded and ummed but really she didn't care about any of it. On the previous Tuesday they'd found out more than they ever thought they would. Her mum and Brendan had planned their own disappearance. What was the point of returning to the B and B? What would they find out? Information that would simply rub away at the hurt and grief they already felt.

And in the end what did it all mean?

Her mum and Brendan were still dead.

So what if the first days of their disappearance were something they organised themselves. Perhaps, like the inspector who came to see her said, they had been targeted by career criminals and killed to stop them uncovering evidence of organised crime. Maybe this had happened after they'd flown off from Heathrow. Nothing had been heard for five years. Now she wished, more than anything, that Joshua would leave it alone.

In Twickenham the Pay and Display parking bays near the B and B were full up and Skeggsie had to go further up the road. He parked the car almost opposite to where Rose had seen the technician, Frank Palmer, going into a house the week before. The front door was green with no glass and looked unwelcoming. Next door's was completely different – solid wood with frosted panes and a brass knocker and letter box.

'I'm going to stay here,' she said.

'How come?'

She shrugged. Skeggsie closed his door and walked off.

'You all right, Rosie?' Joshua said.

'Just got some stuff to think about.'

He nodded and then followed Skeggsie. She watched them approach the B and B, Skeggsie stopping and waiting for Joshua. When they went inside she found herself relaxing, stretching her legs along the side of the printer box.

She looked at the house across the road again. If she could *confirm* that the technician, Frank Palmer, really did live there then she could make an anonymous call to the police to inform them. She would not want Henry or anyone else knowing that she had been the source of the tip. She remembered Detective Inspector Schillings' reprimand. She never ever wanted to see that man again.

She might see Frank Palmer going by; perhaps coming out of his house or returning to it after shopping. She'd seen him the previous Saturday – why shouldn't she see him today? After a few moments she sighed, leaning her head against the corner of the printer box. It was a stupid plan. Frank Palmer may be staying in all day or going out all day. Either way she could sit there in the back of Skeggsie's car for hours and not see him. In any case they wouldn't be parked there for hours. Joshua was going to talk to the owner of the B and B. How long would it take for her to say that she didn't remember anything from five years ago?

It might be that Frank Palmer didn't live in the house at all. She'd seen him use a key on the front door but it may be that it was a key for a *friend's* house.

She could get out of the car, go across the road and knock on the door of the house and see if he answered. If so, then it would prove that he lived there. If he didn't, she could ask for him by name. Whoever answered the front door would know who lived in the house. But that plan wasn't good either. If Frank Palmer did answer, then he would recognise her. If he really was on the run from the police, then her presence would alert him to the fact that someone knew his real address. He would just run away again.

She looked across at the house. Part of the front of it was obscured by an old tree on the pavement. Its leaves were going yellow and its branches looked heavy as though it was weary. The building was two storeys high and had two bells by the front door; two flats. She looked at the large bay window on the ground floor. The lower half of the window was covered with a net curtain and drapes hung at the sides.

The net curtain moved and she saw a face at the side of the window. It was only there for a second before the curtain dropped back into place. Had it been Frank Palmer? She didn't know. It had only been a glimpse.

She sat back in her tiny space in the back of the Mini.

Why did she care who killed Ricky Harris? Henry said he had been killed with his own knife, that possibly *he* had been the aggressor. That tied up with everything she knew or thought about Ricky. As well as being a bully he had deceived his girlfriend by seeing her stepsister. Then he was stealing stuff and getting involved with dangerous people.

Why should she give a hoot about that obnoxious boy?

She didn't. But Ricky's death had started a chain of events. Sherry had blamed Ricky's death on Lewis Proctor. She was almost certainly wrong about that but, still, that's what she thought when she went to the cemetery to meet Emma and Lewis and have it out with them. Had it been in a fit of rage or had she planned it in some way to get back at Lewis? *You took away the person I loved, why shouldn't I take away the person you love?*

It was complicated but Rose couldn't help feeling that if Ricky hadn't been killed then Emma would be alive today. The Sherry/Ricky/Emma/Lewis/Bee mix would have sorted itself out in the way that romances did. People would move on, hearts would get broken, new couples would emerge from the debris.

But Ricky Harris had been stabbed.

If Frank Palmer killed him then he should be arrested. She was still resentful that by pleading manslaughter Sherry Baxter wouldn't get the punishment Rose thought she deserved. If Frank Palmer was involved in Ricky's death, then it was suddenly important to her that he paid the price for it.

The passenger car door opened and Joshua's face was there. He was smiling. The driver's door opened and Skeggsie got in. Joshua started to speak breathlessly as he sat down and both doors closed at the same moment.

'What?' she said.

'Mrs Harrison has this system where she keeps every bit of paper that passes through her business!'

'And?'

'She had an arrangement with the taxi firm. She displayed their cards and every ride they picked up from the B and B they gave her a percentage. So, every three months she got a printout from them of the rides from the B and B and the destinations.'

'We already know the destination,' Rose said, feeling a need to dampen down Joshua's enthusiasm. She had seen on the previous Tuesday how that had turned to despair.

'But when the taxi is booked for Heathrow they always ask upfront which terminal, which flight and the time of the flight. Just so that they can gauge the time it takes to get there and so on.'

Rose glanced out of the window at the house across the street. She could hear Joshua talking but she refused to join in with his excitement.

'So, on the printout, it tells us that on the morning of the fifth of November Kate and Dan Brewster picked up a taxi at 7.30 for Heathrow Terminal Two for a flight to Warsaw at 11.30. The cost of the taxi was thirty-two pounds of which Mrs Harrison got three pounds twenty-two, five per cent.'

'Warsaw?' Rose said.

'I don't think this is to do with organised crime at all. I think it's about security. I think they were working undercover for something to do with national security.'

Rose couldn't trust herself to speak. *So what? So what? So what, they're dead anyway. Does it matter why or how?*

'That's good, isn't it, Rose? That we're beginning to piece it together?'

What about the other night? she wanted to say. *When you said 'I hope they are dead.'*

'National security, I think. Skeggsie and me, we can continue the search.'

'But once they stepped off that plane in Warsaw? Doesn't the trail end there?' she said.

'No!' Joshua said. 'We can set up websites in Polish. Maybe we'll be lucky and find someone who knew them, saw them. We have pictures we can put on the web. Remember how we got lucky with Valeriya Malashenko?'

Skeggsie started the car.

'Wait!' Rose said, dismayed at Joshua's plans. 'There's something I need you to help me with before we go.'

Joshua looked round, puzzled. Skeggsie put the handbrake back on but kept the engine running.

'I want you to go across to that house with the green door and ring the bell for the downstairs flat. If no one answers, ring the other bell. You can make up some excuse like you're looking for a room to let or something.'

'Why?'

'It's a long story but I think it might be the technician from my school. You remember I said I saw him round here? He's gone missing and Henry, my policeman friend, thinks he might know something about the murder at

Parkway East. I don't want to say that he is here unless I'm completely sure.'

'How will I know if it's him? I've never seen him.'

'I'll know. I'll be nearby. I'll stand behind that tree over there on the pavement. If it's him I won't move. If it's not him I'll come forward and ask if he knows Frank Palmer. Maybe he's a friend or something.'

'Sounds a bit dodgy,' Skeggsie said, turning the engine off.

'It will only take a minute.'

'Why don't you just tell the policeman what you saw?'

'I don't want to. I can't explain why. It's just a small favour. Please?'

Joshua opened the passenger door. Rose got out of the back seat and followed him across the road and stood by the tree. He gave her a look of pained forbearance and for a second she wanted to punch him in the face. Then he got back in the car without a word. Rose pushed her annoyance down and followed Joshua across the road and stood by the tree. Joshua went up to the front door. He looked round at her once before he rang the bell. Rose stood back. The green door stayed shut.

Josh rang the bell again. Rose could hear it, loud and insistent.

Was no one in?

The door opened a moment later and Rose heard a man's voice. She peeked out. It was Frank Palmer. She pulled her head back, not wanting to be seen. She could hear Joshua talking to him.

'Excuse me, there was this advert. Down at the newsagent's? On a card? In the window? It gave this number and said that you had rooms to rent?'

'No, mate. No rooms for rent here.'

'That's odd, maybe I read it wrong.'

'Yeah, you read it wrong.'

'Do you know any other houses round here that have rooms to rent?'

'Sorry, mate. Look in the local paper.'

'Will do. Sorry to have bothered you.'

Joshua's voice was moving closer to Rose as if he was backing away from the door. He passed the tree and continued on across the traffic until he got to the car. Rose was waiting to hear the front door shut before she moved off. There was no sound of it closing, though, and she stood impatiently as Joshua got back to the Mini. He opened the passenger door and pulled the seat forward and climbed into the back of the car.

The door of the house finally closed. She heard it bang and she quickly walked out from behind the tree and headed across the road towards the car. She got into the passenger seat and looked over at the house again. She'd been right. Frank Palmer did live there. As soon as they got back to Camden she would make the anonymous phone call. She looked round at Joshua to thank him.

He had a funny look on his face, though.

'What's up?' she said.

'You all right?' Skeggsie said.

'What's the matter?' she said when Joshua didn't reply.

'I know him.'

'Who?'

'Him, in that house.'

She looked at Skeggsie as if he had some answer.

'You know *him*? The technician from my school?'

'He was a friend of my dad's. He was a policeman who worked with my dad. His name was Frank. I know him.'

Rose sat very still, stupefied. Skeggsie caught her eye, holding it for a moment. Then she looked across at the house and saw the curtain at the bay window pulled back. There was a face there watching them. This time it didn't duck away.

It was Frank Palmer.

THIRTY

Frank Palmer was a friend of Brendan Johnson.

The car was getting hot and Skeggsie opened the windows. Cool air came in but so did the noise of the passing traffic.

'Yes,' Joshua said, leaning forward, more in control of himself. 'He used to come round when we lived in Brewster Road. I saw him a load of times and I saw Dad out with him as well. I know it was him. His name was Frank. I don't remember his surname. I don't think I ever heard it.'

'He was a policeman?'

Joshua nodded.

'Why's he working as an IT technician at a school?'

'I don't know.'

Rose looked across at the house. The face at the window had gone.

'How come he didn't say something? When you rang his bell. How come he didn't recognise you?'

'It's been five or more years. I've grown up. He hasn't changed, though. He looks just the same.'

'Don't you think it's significant,' Skeggsie said, 'that he lives there and your parents came to this B and B?'

'What's that got to do with anything?' Rose said sharply, the mention of the B and B, yet again, irritating her.

'If they were arranging their own disappearance and they had a friend who knew where there was somewhere safe that they could stay . . .'

'He might know something about Dad and Kathy?' Joshua said.

'Maybe . . .'

'Shush! Look!' Rose hissed.

The green front door opened and Frank Palmer came out of the house. He was in his shirt sleeves, holding some keys in one hand. He closed the front door behind him and walked towards them.

'He's coming over here,' Skeggsie said.

Frank Palmer walked briskly, glancing sideways at the traffic as he crossed the road. When he got to the Mini he bent over.

'Hi,' he said, leaning into the car. 'Joshua and Rose. And friend. How about you two come across to my flat so that we can talk about a few things.'

'Who are you?' Joshua said.

'You know who I am, Joshua. You remembered me.'

'But you work at my school. You gave a false name . . .'
Rose said.

'Come over to my house. There's a lot to talk about.'

Nobody moved. Frank Palmer leant down to the window again.

'Your dad and your mum would want you to talk to me.'

He turned and walked away. There was an electric silence.

'*What* did he say?'

'He said that Mum and Brendan . . .'

'He *knows* something. Skeggsie is right. This is not just a coincidence. Don't you see, Rosie? Dad and Kathy came here, to the B and B. Across the road from Dad's old friend. I'm going over there . . .'

'But he might have *killed* a boy from my school!'

'Skeggsie, open the door. Let me get out. I've got to talk to this guy.'

Skeggsie opened the door and got out, flipping his seat forward as he did.

'Come on. We have got to find out what he knows.'

'He might be a murderer . . .'

'Skeggsie, if we're not back in fifteen minutes ring the police. Just make up some story to get them here. Now, Rosie. Let's go.'

She got out of the car.

'I'll wait for fifteen minutes,' Skeggsie said.

Joshua took Rosie's hand and led her across the road.

They walked towards the green door. Frank Palmer was standing waiting, holding the door open for them to walk inside. When they got closer Rose examined him, her eyes travelling over his face, down his chest, along the arm that was holding the door open.

Her breath caught in her throat as she focused on Frank Palmer's wrist. His shirt had fallen back and she could see the tattoo there as vivid as the real thing.

A butterfly.

The three of them stood in a room with kitchen units. There was a small table by a wall with a single chair by it. Round the back of the chair was the leather biker jacket that Rose had seen Frank Palmer wearing. There was nothing on the work surfaces; no toaster, no kettle, no breadbin, plates or cups. The room felt cold and had no smell at all, as if nothing had ever been cooked there. On the floor was a small black suitcase and on the work surface was the red holdall that Rose had seen Frank Palmer carrying a couple of times. The black and white chequered flag looked a little worn close up, the fabric peeling at the corners.

Joshua was asking question after question. Frank Palmer wasn't giving any answers. Rose looked at some things on the work surface. There were folders, papers and a book; a wallet, a glasses case, a camera and a toiletries bag. They were in neat piles as if waiting to be packed in some methodical order. Rose looked curiously at the book. It was an old hardback. On it was the title *The Butterfly Project* and illustrations of several well-known butterflies overlapping each other.

'Are you going to say *anything*?' Joshua said, irate now.

'Who *are* you?' Rose said.

'Do you know where my dad is?' Joshua said.

Rose looked sharply at him. *My dad*? What about her mum?

Frank sighed.

'One thing at a time,' he said, 'I can't tell you much and I shouldn't be telling you this. But your dad and your mum are all right. I've not seen them myself for a while but I know, from speaking to other people, that they are all right.'

'They're alive?' Rose said. 'But why haven't they contacted us?'

'Where are they?' Joshua said.

'There are things I can't tell you. Things I don't know.'

'Where have they been for five years?' Rose said, her mind whirling.

'I can't tell you.'

Joshua stepped forward. 'You can't tell us that our parents are all right and tell us nothing else!'

Frank closed his eyes as if he was trying very hard to control himself. Joshua stared at him, fired up. Frank finally managed a shaky smile.

'Joshua, don't get upset, lad. I can only tell you that your dad is well. And, Rose, your mum is well. But I can't tell you any more than that.'

'Why not? What are they doing?' Joshua banged the table in frustration. Are they imprisoned somewhere?'

'No, no . . .'

'Are they working undercover? Is it a police thing?'

'No . . .'

'Government? National security?'

'No. That I cannot talk about. I will tell you one thing. They think about you a lot. I know that for a fact. An absolute fact.'

There was silence. Joshua was puffed up, moving from one foot to another. Rose was leaning against the work surface, her fingers touching the corner of the red holdall.

They think about you a lot.

Her mum and Brendan were alive; flesh and blood, walking, talking, breathing, laughing, crying. Rose was full of confusion.

'Are they in this country?' Joshua said.

Frank shook his head.

'In Europe? Warsaw?'

'I don't know.'

'I don't believe you!' Joshua said, furious now. 'You're making this up. You don't know where Dad and Kathy are – this is just a lie!'

'It's true.'

'You haven't a clue what happened to them. You've made up this story for some weird reason of your own.'

Rose frowned. 'Josh said you're Brendan's friend but I don't remember seeing you. I know you worked at my school. The police think you know what happened to Ricky Harris . . .'

'Wait a minute. I do remember something about you,' Joshua said, cutting across her. 'Didn't you get kicked out of the force? I remember Dad talking about it. *Poor Frank got sacked for doing his job. Poor Frank.* That's what he said.'

Frank stiffened. 'I did lose my job.'

'So now you're working as an IT technician in a school and nicking stuff from there. You've got *no idea* what happened to them. You're just living some kind of fantasy.'

'I'm not nicking stuff from anywhere. My job in the school was a cover,' Frank said.

'A cover? For what? What about Ricky Harris?' Rose said. 'What do you know about him and the way he died? Did you kill him?'

'I'm not allowed to . . .'

'You're not denying it? You mean you *did* kill him?' Rose's voice was loud. She couldn't believe what she was hearing.

'Rose, don't waste time. This is not what we should be talking about. It's Dad and Kathy . . .'

'He killed someone, Josh,' she said, interrupting him.

'I don't believe that either. I think he's making this all up,' Joshua said, walking past him. 'Come on, let's get out of here.'

'I did not make it up. I'm not lying.' Frank Palmer moved to block Joshua's way out.

'Did you kill Ricky Harris?' Rose demanded.

'I did.'

Rose felt limp. The station walkway came back into her head; the flickering light and the black sky; the smell of autumn, of fireworks and damp leaves; a boy's blood on the ground.

'But he can't tell us anything about Dad and Kathy. He doesn't know anything. He's making all this up. Don't believe him, Rose.'

'I am not lying!' Frank said, his face taut, his lips stretched across his teeth.

'Tell us something, then. Tell us one thing that might make us believe you!' Joshua shouted.

'All right, all right. I killed the boy because I was protecting you, Rose. That's what I do. I look after you. I keep my eye on what's happening to you. I don't know where Kathy and Brendan are *now* but five years ago they told me it was my job to make sure you were safe.'

'Oh my –' Rose said weakly. 'You killed Ricky Harris because of me?'

Joshua made a dismissive sound and turned away.

'What happened to that boy, on that footbridge, was part of my role in protecting you, Rose.'

'How can you . . .'

'Wait. You need to understand what I've been doing. Best to say that I've been around you when changes came into your life. When you went to the Norfolk school, I was there, for a while, to make sure you were OK and that there was no sign of anyone watching you or taking any undue notice of you. I'm not there every day, I'm not following you. But when there are changes to the routine, I'm there, for a while. So I worked in the school to watch you. To make sure no one else is watching you.'

'But *who* would be watching *me*?'

Frank shook his head. 'I cannot tell you any more.'

Joshua was at the work surface where Frank's things were waiting to be packed. Rose could see him looking at the items there. He picked up the book that she'd already seen, *The Butterfly Project*. He frowned, turning it over, looking at the back.

'I'm not allowed to explain. I just want you to know that your mother's main priority was making sure that you are safe.'

'What about me? Am I not supposed to be safe as well?' Joshua said, tossing the hardback book back on the work surface.

'That's for someone else. My role was to look after Rose and when that young man began to harass and bully her then I stepped in. I told him in school to leave her alone. I was more vigilant about her. That particular unfortunate night I followed her to the station and saw her go down on to the platform. My plan was to just see her get on to the train but then I saw him, the boy from school, and I saw him bother her, following her up and down. I was about to go down on to the platform and have it out with him but he came back up the stairs . . .'

'You killed him because he was harassing me? How could you? What sort of person are you?' Rose said, her throat caked and dry.

'It was never my intention to kill him. I spoke to him. I told him that if he didn't change his attitude to you, then I would see that he was suspended from school.'

No one spoke.

'He pulled a knife out. I wasn't expecting it. The stupid boy was going to use it. He didn't know who he was dealing with, though. I had no choice. It was a terrible thing but I did it in the course of my job, doing what Kathy wanted me to do.'

Rose felt herself on the brink of tears. Ricky Harris had been killed because of her. Not by Lewis or Sherry or by some crook who wanted IT equipment.

'He brought it on himself, Rose. It is in the past.'

A bell rang. Twice, three times. The noise split the air and Frank looked alert.

'Who have you told that you are here?' he said.

He opened the kitchen door as the bell kept ringing. He walked out into the hallway and went into the room at the front of the house. Rose thought that he was probably looking out of the bay window. When he came into the hallway seconds later he looked different, businesslike.

'It's the police,' he said. 'Who called them? Your friend?

Rose and Joshua looked at each other.

Skeggsie had done as he was told.

THIRTY-ONE

Frank opened the front door.

Rose and Joshua stayed in the kitchen. Rose's heart was racing.

'We could tell the police,' she said. 'They could arrest him for Ricky Harris's murder.'

'No, it's too soon,' Joshua whispered. 'There's more stuff we need to ask him.'

She could hear a loud confident voice from the porch.

'Good morning, sir. We've had reports of a domestic disturbance coming from this address.'

'That's ridiculous. There's no disturbance here.'

'We take these things very seriously, sir. May I ask your name and whether you are the owner of the property?'

Joshua pulled Rose away from the kitchen door.

'He killed someone, Josh.'

'Not *now*, Rosie. If they arrest him now we'll never find out anything else about Dad and Kathy.

'He deserves to go to prison.'

'It was self-defence . . . he was looking after you . . .'

'You're sticking up for him now?'

'No, I'm just saying if you tell the police we'll never see him again and we won't find out anything else about Kathy and Dad.'

Rose was confused. Joshua was right but there was justice to think of. Frank Whatever-his-real-name-was deserved to be charged, to stand trial. He had said he was protecting her but how could he kill someone like that and not seem to care? Hadn't she thought, when she saw him walk back across the bridge, that he had been *smiling*? Something in the way he held his shoulders, his gait? As though he'd been pleased with what he'd done?

She could hear voices from the hallway.

'It's some prank call, officer. I'm here with some of my family. They're seeing me off on a short holiday, actually.'

'Very nice. sir.'

He was describing them as his *family*. It made Rose mad.

'I've had enough of this. I'm going to tell them,' she said.

Then Joshua was beside her. He put his arm round her shoulder and pulled her towards him. He felt hot and his arm was tight, gripping her. There was more talk out in the hallway and it sounded as if it was moving closer, as if the policeman was coming into the flat. Joshua's voice dropped to a whisper. He spoke into her ear, his breath burning her face.

'Rosie, this is our one chance. Don't give him up.'

'We *have* to.'

'I'm not saying never go to the police. I'm just saying not now.'

She didn't answer.

'Let's find out as much as we can now, then we can go to the police later.'

She was leaning on him, her whole body feeling heavy. What was the right thing to do? For Ricky Harris? For Emma Burke? For Joshua and Rose? The noise in the hallway wasn't coming any closer. Instead there was the sound of footsteps going into the front room. Joshua was pulling her away from the door. No doubt he thought her silence meant she had agreed not to tell the police. Maybe he was right.

'Come over here and look at this stuff.'

He drew her across the room, holding her hand, grasping it tightly, towards the things on the work surface.

'I've seen the butterfly book,' she said, her voice croaky.

'No, these notebooks. Look at them.'

There was a pile of books. They were small, like exercise books. There were six in all and each one had a label. Joshua picked one up. Rose took one with *Notebook Six* written on the front. She opened it. Inside was a photo of Ricky Harris. It was taken from a newspaper cutting. She flicked a page. There was a map of Camden and then a plan of Parkway East station.

There was laughter coming from out in the hall. The sound of footsteps coming towards the kitchen.

'He's coming in here,' Joshua said. 'Remember, we need to keep this Frank guy free. We need to find out what else he knows.'

Rose nodded. She was resigned to it. She did not have the strength to go against Joshua. She could hear footsteps along the hallway but she kept looking at the pages of the notebook in front of her. There was a key down the side of the map like a piece of homework. Numbers were written in red and each number had some writing by it but she couldn't decipher the words because they were just jumbles of random numbers and letters.

She replaced the book on the side as the kitchen door opened and Frank came back in, followed by a policeman.

'Good afternoon,' he said.

Frank was looking tentative as if he didn't quite know what was going to happen. He looked from Rose to Joshua and then back again.

'I was telling Mr Richards,' the policeman said, 'that we had an anonymous phone call about a possible domestic incident at this address. I fear we've been misled but we did need to check the premises. You are?'

'This is Rose and I'm Joshua.'

'My niece and her boyfriend,' Frank said. 'They've come to see me off. As you can see I'm just going on a trip. I'm a bit pushed for time, actually.'

'That's fine, sir. And I guess, from the way the flat looks, that you are also relocating?'

'I'm selling it. Moving to the coast.'

'Very nice. I'm very sorry to have troubled you. May I ask where you're going?'

'A short break in Spain,' Frank said.

'Lovely. A bit of sunshine at this time of year is always welcome. Now I'll leave you folks alone. Good day to you.'

The policeman walked towards the front door. Frank followed him. Rose looked round at Joshua. He had picked up two of the notebooks and was putting them into his inside pocket. The sound of the front door closing made him move away and stand against the worktop next to Rose.

Frank came back in.

'I appreciate that,' he said, looking serious.

He walked across and picked up the holdall and began to put things into it. Joshua eyed Rose. Then he started to speak.

'We understand about what happened to the boy on the footbridge. We know it was self-defence.'

Frank looked away from his packing, nodded and gathered his papers and the book together, and placed them into the holdall.

Joshua persevered. 'I'm sorry if I was a bit off. You know it's been a long time for us. We've not seen or heard of our parents for five years and I was sceptical about your story.'

Frank nodded.

'So, if I was rude I'm sorry.'

'It's all right. I have to go. You'll have to leave.'

The atmosphere had changed. The police visit had made Frank sober and busy.

'Is there nothing you could tell us? Just one thing that would make us feel happier?'

'I've already said too much.'

He zipped up the bag and began to roll up the sleeves of his shirt. Rose saw the tattoo again. She saw Joshua look at it, his forehead wrinkled.

'Aren't you going to look after me any more?' Rose said.

'Yes. I will. I'll be around sometimes. But you won't know it.'

'But, Frank, what if Rose was in trouble and you weren't around? What then? What if someone else began to follow her and you didn't know about it. What would she do? How would she get in touch with you?'

'She can't get in touch with me.' Frank began to shake his head. 'I've already given too much information away.'

'Just a phone number for emergencies. Please.'

Frank picked his jacket up from the side. He put it on, staring at Rose all the time.

'I'm sorry. I need to go now. You'll have to walk out with me. I need to pick up a taxi.'

They walked behind him. At the front door he stood to the side so that they could pass. He looked unhappy. When they were out of the house, standing on the path, he pulled the front door shut and then slipped a set of keys through the letter box. He pulled his case on wheels and had the red holdall over his shoulder.

'Just a phone number, Frank. Only ever to be used in an emergency. Just something that Rose will have in case something happens. You'd hate that, Frank, if something awful happened to Rose?'

'Don't say that. It's my job to look after Rose whenever it's necessary.'

Frank stood on the pavement. He had his hand half up in the air for a taxi. The road was clear, though, no sign of a black cab in either direction. He put his bags down, took an envelope out of his pocket, then reached down into the zip compartment of his case and pulled out a pen. On the back of the envelope he wrote something and gave it to Rose. A taxi was coming towards them. Frank waved at it.

On the envelope was a mobile number.

'I'll never answer this number,' Frank said. 'No one will answer it. But you can leave a message for me and I will get it. But one thing . . .' He looked pained, as if everything had not gone the way he wanted it to. 'If you tell anyone about this, then you will put Brendan and Kathy in extreme danger. I've told you too much but I have to trust you. They love you and they've done this to protect you. Trust me. But if you tell anyone it could end badly for them.'

A taxi pulled up and Frank put his bags into it and leant into the window. Rose heard him say *Heathrow*. He got in and did not look back as the taxi drove off.

Rose and Josh watched it go.

A beeping sound made them look round. They saw Skeggsie across the road, sitting in the Mini. They walked towards him.

THIRTY-TWO

Rose stood on the footbridge at Parkway East station. It was dark. The sky was clear, deep blue and the moon was sharp and intense. Her eyes dropped to the tracks that went off into the distance – St Michael's Cemetery on one side, inky black; Chalk Farm Estate on the other, a hue of light seeping into the night sky.

There were people standing on each platform awaiting trains. Some people passed behind her. They must have wondered what a seventeen-year-old girl was doing standing on the walkway at 7.30 on a Tuesday night, holding a single white rose.

Above her the bulb that had once flickered now shone brightly.

It was three weeks since the night that Ricky Harris was stabbed. In that time Rose had had no sympathy for him, no grief for him, not a single moment's sadness. Now it was different. He had been killed because of her. She had not meant it to happen. Frank Palmer had not meant it to happen. But it had.

She laid the white rose on the ledge of the walkway.

Too little too late.

She looked round to see Joshua coming from the ticket office end. He smiled at her. She felt this tiny leap in her chest at the sight of him. He was wearing a jacket she hadn't seen before and his hair looked shorter, as if he'd had a trim. She hadn't seen him or been in touch since the previous Saturday. After Skeggsie had driven them home from Twickenham she'd needed time on her own, time to think. He'd needed time to think. It had been a couple of days of walking round dazed, taking in all the things they had found out.

That afternoon she'd decided to come to the station and pay her respects to Ricky Harris. She'd sent Joshua a text to let him know. He'd replied immediately and said he wanted to be there.

He came up to her and stood a few steps away. He didn't speak for a minute. She felt awkward, not sure how to greet him. It didn't matter, though. It wasn't as bad as it had been last week. The events since, the things they had found out about her mum and Brendan, had swept all that embarrassment away. It was unimportant now that they knew about Frank Palmer and what he'd done.

'This where it happened, Rosie?'

She nodded and pointed. 'He was laying there.'

'Horrible.'

'I didn't care about him. I didn't like him but . . .'

'I know,' he said, reaching out and rubbing the back of her arm.

Some people went behind them, half running, half walking, looking over the edge of the walkway to see if a train was coming.

'Hey, a rose from a Rose,' Joshua said, pointing at the white flower.

She gave a weak smile.

'What have you been doing since Saturday?' she said.

'This and that,' he said, moving closer to her. 'Skeggsie and me have been trying to decipher the notebooks we took from Frank Palmer or *Richards*, whatever his name is.'

'And?'

'Nothing. Skeggsie says there doesn't seem to be much logic. He's tried using some software but nothing's coming up. He thinks the codes might come from a book. You know, where two people have the same copy of a book and the code is page number, line number, letter number.'

'*The Butterfly Project*. That old book he had. Maybe that was it.'

'Maybe.'

In the distance she could see a small square of light. It was a westbound train heading for Hampstead Heath and Finchley. She could just about hear the sound or maybe she was imagining it.

Joshua reached across and pulled up the sleeve of her jacket until her butterfly tattoo showed.

'Why did you have this done?' he said.

'My mum had one. You?'

'My dad had one, on his ankle.'

'What is it? What does it mean? Is it some kind of club membership?'

'Seems pretty juvenile if that's what it is.'

She thought of the significance of the butterfly. Henry Thompson had asked her if her tattoo was symbolic – was it about something beautiful that dies young? He'd also told her that people used to catch butterflies and keep them in jars until they died. And mounted in glass cases. She'd told him that none of those things had anything to do with her tattoo. *It's a great shade of blue*, she'd said.

Even Frank Palmer had one on his arm.

It must mean something, she thought, *it must*.

'I don't understand what Frank Palmer meant when he said he was watching you. Protecting you. From what?' Joshua said.

She shook her head. She didn't know. She didn't know what to make of any of it.

'Maybe we're right about Dad and Kathy being involved in national security? Terrorism? Maybe that's why you were in danger?'

'What about you? Why isn't there someone watching over you?'

Joshua shrugged. 'We can't know. Not until we find out some more.'

It was all a mystery. Did she really know any more now than she had three weeks earlier? That very first night when she virtually danced down to the station with her violin case on her back. Changing her clothes in the public toilet, putting make-up on like a schoolgirl on a first date. She'd been so excited, so thrilled to see Joshua again. What had it brought but anguish and uncertainty?

'We have the notebooks, Rosie.'

The notebooks that Joshua had stolen from Frank Palmer. They had maps and pictures in them and page after page of coded writing.

'The one I looked at had Ricky's picture in it. It was as if it was some kind of report on his death.'

'A notebook about a murder.'

'Do you think the others are the same?'

Joshua sighed. 'It's hard to say, not knowing *who* the people are. We might be able to find out. The information might be there if we can just find the code.'

'Not very likely.'

'*The Butterfly Project* is out of print but we may be able to find a copy on the web or in a second-hand bookshop.'

'Is there any point!' Rose said, frustrated.

''Course there is. You thought that we wouldn't find anything at all! Look what we've achieved. The B and B. The signatures. The notebooks, the address in

Twickenham, Frank Palmer, the phone number. These are doors which we are going to push open. Skeggsie's going to help.'

The westbound train arrived in the station. At the same time Rose could hear one coming from behind, eastbound heading for Canonbury and Dalston. It trundled into the station under the walkway. She could feel the movement of it slowing down. It was the train she should have got on three weeks before. She'd stood uncertainly waiting for the doors to open. Then she'd looked up to see Ricky on the walkway, in an argument with someone. Finally she'd left the train, run up the stairs and found a dead body. How sudden it had been. To hear him arguing and then find him lifeless.

'Frank Palmer is free, though. He'll never pay for killing Ricky,' she said.

'Yes, he will. I told you we would turn him into the police when we've found out more about Dad and Kathy.'

'We've lost our chance. We'll never see him again.'

'We will. We have his phone number. When the time is right we can find a way to get to him again. It's not over.'

Rose wondered what it would be like to see Frank Palmer again. The man was a killer and she should hate him for that. At the same time, though, he was connected to her mother and Brendan. Her mother had given him a job to look after her. It had ended in tragedy but still Frank Palmer or Richards, whatever his real name was, had told them the truth about their parents. In her mind he was somehow responsible for bringing her mother and Joshua's father back to life. And for that she had to be grateful to him.

Rose turned and looked at Joshua. What were his feelings about this man? She wanted to ask him but felt that enough had been said. His eyes were dark and his face had a heaviness to it. He seemed terribly alone and she stepped closer and leant against him, pushing her head on to his chest. He put his arm around her and held her tightly as one of the trains moved off, under the walkway, its wheels creaking on the tracks.

'The best thing of all is that we know that they are alive,' he whispered.

She felt for his hand and held it tightly, too full with emotion to speak.

Her mum and Brendan were alive.